Praise for Michael Okon and Monsterland

"The adventure ramps up to an enjoyably gore-soaked finale ... full of both mayhem and heart."

—*Kirkus Reviews*

"... Monsterland [is] an intriguing read, one that provides a solid narrative, intriguing characters capable of growth and change, an ideal setting as a backdrop, and an underpinning of fervent social consciousness trans-formed into a story."

—Michael Collings, *Collingnotes*

"Loved it! I'll be seeking out more from this author!! My customers will love it too!"

—Bonnie Scherr (Bookseller), *NetGalley Reviewer*

"... a gripping story with a Jurassic Park *vibe ... he manages to explore social and political structures that make the unbelievable story of a theme park where one can walk among the zombies and be chased by were-wolves, feel fairly believable."*

—Bianca Schulze, *Book Reviewer*

"... belongs right up there with the modern great of horror writing, Stephen King. Anyone who enjoys well written, fast paced, complex horror stories with authentic detail should read this book."

—*Lemon Bee Book and Blog*

"Monsterland is an interesting and intriguing book that starts to build characters at an even pace with a rich understanding towards the younger

characters. The plot is interesting, and he [handles] action and description very well which gets you to the meat of the story in this rapid page turner."

—Anjuli Clayden (Bookseller), *NetGalley Reviewer*

"... peppers the narrative with real-life significance ... a talented and clever enough writer to imbue his characters with real emotion ... It is this deepening of the plot that elevates Monsterland *above standard monster fare. The novel will prove an entertaining and thought-provoking read for both teenagers and adults."*

—Scott Neuffer, *Foreword Reviews*

MICHAEL OKON

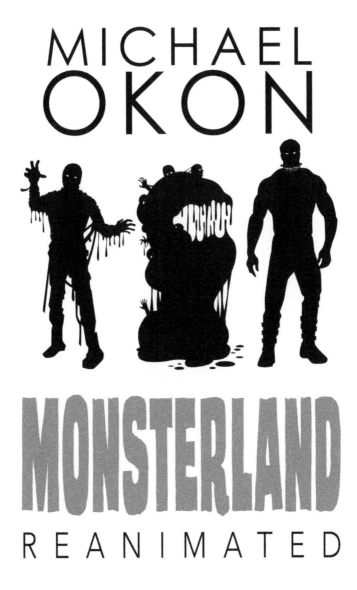

MONSTERLAND

REANIMATED

ISBN: 978-1-61475-672-9

Cover design by Michael Mastermaker

Cover artwork images by Michael Mastermaker

Edited by Kevin J. Anderson

Kevin J. Anderson, Art Director

Published by WordFire Press, an imprint of WordFire, LLC PO Box 1840 Monument CO 80132

Kevin J. Anderson & Rebecca Moesta, Publishers

WordFire Press Trade Paperback Edition April 2018 Printed in the USA

Join our WordFire Press Readers Group and get free books, sneak previews, updates on new projects, and other giveaways. Sign up for free at wordfirepress.com

❀ Created with Vellum

For my rose of Sharon

"Plan B. You've always got to have a Plan B."

—Sylvester Stallone

Front page of the *Copper Valley Sun*

President of the US, World Leaders, and Thousands Dead

Many still missing as the world reels from the impact of the Monsterland disaster

Multitudes are still unaccounted for and presumed dead. Escaping werewolves, vampires, and zombies of Dr. Vincent Konrad's theme parks inexplicably escaped en masse and massacred unwitting parkgoers ... Massive government shutdowns as the world teeters on the brink of chaos.

Chapter 1

The Night After the Monsterland Catastrophe

A bright moon painted the desert's surface pewter. Here and there, dark spots soiled the landscape like oil spills. Most of the bodies had been taken before the troops were ordered to leave. They carted away the corpses, bulldozing the zombies into mass graves, until radios chirped with urgent orders deploying the soldiers to the bigger threats that erupted in the main cities like a chain of angry volcanos.

Monsterland was extinguished, its carcass left for the vultures to pick, the exhibits silent as a tomb.

The dead president and his equally dead entourage were whisked away on Air Force One, along with the dark-clad special operatives that came and left like the brisk desert wind that now howled through the empty streets.

A gate screamed in the silence, slamming with a reverberating smash. The uneven gait of someone with a physical challenge filled the void. The scrape and plod of his limp echoed against the wall of mountains framing the theme park. His labored breathing huffed as he made his way down the streets.

A door creaked loudly as it was blown by the wind. He stopped, his distorted figure silhouetted in the pale moonlight, his body turning silver. He looked at the broken glass littering the pavement like diamonds, then up to the still, pre-dawn sky. He considered the sun peeking over the jagged horizon in the east, its golden light painting the dips and hollows of the hills. Soon the coming day would chase the darkness away.

Time was the enemy now. He had to move faster, or it would be too late. He picked up his pace, lurching along the winding road. A keening howl ricocheted through the streets, bouncing off the walls. It sounded like a … *no*, he thought, *it couldn't be.* The werewolves were all dead, destroyed by Vincent Konrad when he made their heads explode.

The old man paused, listening for it again, and was not disappointed when the animal whimpered. He gauged it to be inside the defunct vampire exhibit. He moved toward the entrance. The storefronts had been destroyed. A few body parts lay on the pavement, as if people had discarded them in a rush. He heard the scraping of paws on the street and a shiver went down his crooked spine.

He knew the werewolves were dead; he had seen it with his own eyes. A figure detached from the shadows. Igor flattened himself against the wall. He watched it move stealthily down the street, stopping when it scavenged a morsel of rotting flesh. It looked up to stare at Igor, its eyes glowing in the darkness.

A coyote? He waved a hand, dismissing it. It had to be a coyote; it was too small to be a wolf, too big to be a dog. The beast twitched its ears, then resumed its meal.

Igor knew the coyote was not a threat, and he continued his mission. His lame foot hit a can, sending a cacophony of sound like an explosion in the deserted park. The beast dropped the bone it was gnawing on, sniffing the area. Its iridescent eyes searched the streets.

It could be a baby wolf, Igor thought, keeping himself as still as possible. He felt it watching him, even from this distance. It was not a threat, yet.

Igor skittered away, hugging the walls of Monsterland, putting as much distance as he could between them. Not an easy feat, considering his distorted hips. He muttered to himself about carrion and the wind. His eyes darted nervously, scouring the hills, not exactly sure what he was looking for. Adrenaline coursed through his veins. His heart pounded so loudly he was certain that the creature watching him could hear it too.

His feet stumbling to a halt, he bent over, gasping for air, cursing Vincent and those meddlesome teenagers, as well as the rest of the world.

The beast gave another mournful howl that went right through him. Igor glanced at his empty hands, berating himself for not bringing a weapon. He searched his surroundings for anything to protect himself.

Then he saw it, one of the axes they had on almost every corner. All of them had been pulled from their protective cases. One was lying in a pool of coagulating blood, the blade long gone. He picked up the broken axe handle, turning in a semicircle. He was ready for an attacker.

A new, larger outline made his heart quiver with fear. It crouched in a corner, its snout covered with blood. This one was bigger, not a coyote, a wild wolf. *Wait,* he thought. *Weren't the gray wolves of California all but extinct?*

Igor narrowed his eyes. The beast was a light reddish brown and not the silver gray of a wolf's pelt. A chain hung from its neck, the pendant of a werewolf's head dangling, emerald eyes flashing. What was it? Was it a mutant coyote? A wolf? *Some weird hybrid,* he wondered for a minute, his breath harsh in his ears. They watched each other soundlessly.

A hybrid then. He'd heard about them, a rare mixture of wolf and coyote. *What did they call them? Coywolves ...? or was it Woyotes?* He shrugged indifferently. Perhaps someone's pet, he decided. Igor's mirthless laugh came out like a snort.

The coywolf stood still, its ears alert, its head cocked as if it was observing him.

Igor dropped the makeshift weapon, calling out, "Eat the rest of your meal, you dumb beast."

The animal continued to watch him, its two front paws on the remains of a zombie's chest.

Igor wiped his forehead, waiting, his eyes coming back to search the village, confirming it was empty, except for the carrion eaters like the coyotes and vultures. He looked up, noting the circling predators waiting for him to move on.

"Interrupted your meal," he chuckled. *Just the local scavengers looking for food.* That was all; the shadows revealed nothing else. Satisfied he was alone, he moved on. He had work to do.

A paper flew past him, hitting a kiosk as the wind plastered it against its surface. It flapped like a dying bird. Igor reached over, taking the fluttering paper, peering at the map of the park, the one they gave people as they entered Monsterland. A bark of laughter escaped his mouth.

He looked up at the giant monolith that was once the Werewolf River Run, its hulking shape obscuring the horizon. "You are here," he giggled, pointing a grimy finger on the paper's surface. He dragged his deformed body further down the pavement. The storefronts that used to be Monsterland's Main Street yawned vacantly, the wind whistling through the narrow alleyways. "Now, you are here," he laughed. Shouting, he listened to the sound of his voice bouncing off the blood-splattered walls.

He made his way to the back end of the zombie village, feeling like the last man on earth. He glanced around at the desolate landscape. His home, the beautiful theme park, was little more than ruins destroyed by the army.

His nose twitched from the fetid smell of rot. The US Army had massacred the zombies. The troops came like a force of nature wiping out everything in its path, every last one of them blown away by the troops.

They were black ops, special forces, he knew from their uniforms. He wondered if things were indeed going as planned. He shrugged, knowing right now nothing mattered except for what he had to do. The irony that he was just about the most important man on earth brought more amusement to his smile.

The local police force was gone, as were the leaders of most countries in the world. He knew all was chaos outside, perhaps even war, each nation blaming the next for the loss of their leadership. *Not to worry,* he thought. Vincent left America in capable hands.

Dreams do come true, he snickered. *Nightmares too,* he finished the thought. A long line of drool pulled at his lower lip. He paused at a pothole in the road, decomposing body parts glistening, the disappearing moon turning the bits of bone and brains pearly.

Anxiety bloomed in his chest as he passed the opaque windows of Vincent's derelict Monsterland hotel, the Copper

Valley Inn. He hated that place. Abandoned construction vehicles were frozen in their spots, testimony to the hotel's unfinished business.

Despite the pastel colors of its exterior, it sat like an ominous crypt to the part of the theme park that Vincent could never control. *Told Vincent it was a money pit.* Crews couldn't work because … well, it didn't matter anymore. The help was all dead. He thought he saw a light flicker in the window, but when he turned, he realized it was nothing more than a sputtering gas lamp that had never been disconnected.

He stood for a while, staring for more activity, and then jerked with the realization that he waited too long and wasted precious time. Surely no one expected him to go searching during the heat of battle.

Vincent said it was enough time to set up the timetable. Vincent knew everything, and Igor felt his panic ebb. It had been barely twenty-four hours since the attack. For all he knew, he could be on a fool's errand.

He pressed his hand on his hip, his back screaming with resentment at so much movement. He was not used to any exercise. He sighed, wiping his brow with the ragged end of his costume, the lace scratching his skin. He caught the cuff, snagging the material with his teeth, tugging it free from his velvet jacket. He loathed the show and was glad he'd never have to endure the humiliation of performing again, especially with the vamps. *Those condescending, blood-sucking parasites.* He wouldn't have to worry about them anymore, he thought with satisfaction. Vincent had promised he'd not have to endure them for long, living up to his part of the bargain quite nicely. They were gone, torn apart by the werewolves or transformed into a tasty dinner by the zombies. Either way, they wouldn't be bullying him with their nasty insults. Something buzzed around him, and he swiped at it.

It felt as though he walked to the other side of the earth. Why Vincent had to pick Zombieville to make his last stand, he'd never know. The Werewolf River Run would have been much more convenient. It was getting lighter now, and he could easily make out the smoking devastation.

He searched the horizon, his eyes resting on the burnt

wreckage of a golf cart, the torched skeleton listing at an odd angle.

Pulling his lame foot, he pushed himself as fast as his body could travel, his breath hitching with the effort.

The corpse was gone. He knew they would have taken that for DNA testing, proof that the enemy was vanquished. The only things left were the putrid carcasses from Monsterland, the decaying zombies, massacred vampires, and what was left of the werewolves after Vincent had exterminated them.

He climbed a small hill, his bad leg screaming with pain. Igor crowed with triumph when he saw it, the discarded lump of flesh, lying forgotten in a ditch, face down. He shivered as the desert wind stirred and eddied around him. *Damn, but it was desolate here.*

He hunkered down, forcing himself to skitter on the hard-packed earth. He wondered what his son, the vice president—no, he corrected himself, the new president of the United States, Mr. Nate Owens—would think of his father now, scrambling like a dung beetle in the dirt.

He cursed. The drool was back, dripping from his mouth like a sparkling spider web. Instead of rising—it was beyond him at this point—he shimmied over to the severed head, reaching forward, reverently, grabbing it by the matted hair, and grasping it to his chest.

The black eyes stared back dully, the dark depths reflecting the hunchback's twisted smile.

Vincent Konrad's lifeless face lay in his hands, the pale lips open in a soundless scream.

"I'm so happy I could kiss you, Vincent!" he told the decapitated head. He cradled the face of his friend. "We'll get you fixed up in no time."

The moon bathed the face a pale blue. The hunchback jiggled the dead weight, cackling with delight as the one papery eyelid drooped as if it were winking.

In the distance, that coywolf howled, making Igor suck in his breath with fear. He tucked the head under his arm as he struggled back up the small hill, mumbling something about Plan B.

Chapter 2

Copper Valley, California
Three Weeks Later

The sun had crested over the top of the houses across the street. Things appeared to have calmed down. Wyatt peered through the blinds. He missed Howard Drucker, Keisha, and Jade, and not necessarily in that order. Mostly, he missed Melvin. Their lives would never be the same.

His eyes were gritty from lack of sleep. A few empty boxes lay abandoned on the pavement. The army had airlifted MRE emergency rations to the town over a week ago. He wondered if there would be new supplies coming in.

Wyatt and his family had started dividing the food up into days. The stores were empty, but they had running water, so he guessed they were still all right.

It was quiet. The stray cat was finally gone from the yard. It had created quite a ruckus, yowling and growling last night. No matter which way he covered his head with his pillow, its screams penetrated his skull. The cat must have gotten into the trash can; the lid was off, and plastic bags were strewn across the grass. He'd better clean it up, he thought in disgust.

Crickets chirped. A formation of drones buzzed overhead making their way west across the milky sky. He watched an armored utility vehicle lumbering down his street. He opened the screen door as another passed by. The olive canvas parted, rows of battle-weary troops swaying as the truck made its way toward the interstate. He raised his hand tentatively with a self-conscious wave. The soldiers stared ahead, ignoring him. He quickly put his hand behind his back.

The soldiers looked as bad as the zombies, he thought, watching them diminish as the truck disappeared. These were not the same trucks as the ones that crammed the streets recently. Those vehicles had driven back and forth for the last three weeks, urging residents to stay home and report if they saw anything unusual. As if anything could be more bizarre than watching werewolves, vampires, and zombies duke it out in an epic battle. Nope, he laughed. Nothing was ever going to be the same in his world.

He had watched the news while he lay on the couch in the little porch they built outside the small bungalow where he lived. He couldn't sleep; maybe he dozed for a bit, but he'd swear on a stack of Bibles that he hadn't closed his eyes once.

He wanted to do something. It was crazy staying here, nice and safe at home, knowing what had happened. Wyatt was still reeling from the shock of learning that his father was a zombie and still alive. *Well, not anymore,* he swallowed past the lump in the back of his throat, his eyes burning. His father hadn't survived the final confrontation with Dr. Vincent Konrad.

He kept replaying the final minutes of his father's life. Wyatt's chest tightened, and he balled his hands into impotent fists. He had believed his estranged father died a year ago while working somewhere out of the country. He'd had no idea, no idea at all, that his father had the plague.

He covered his eyes with his forearm, blotting out the memories of his father's pocked skin, the way he shuffled, his missing fingers, the tortured sounds that came from his throat when he tried to speak. A tear slid down Wyatt's cheek, and he hastily wiped it away.

His parents had fought, they all did. Their divorce was as ugly as any implosion when a family broke apart.

Wyatt pulled at a loose thread from his sleeve, unraveling the seam and leaving a gaping hole in his shirt. He rolled the soft thread in his hand, feeling that his own life had unraveled too, leaving a rip in his midsection.

He wasn't sure of anything anymore, not his mom, his father, and not Carter White, his stepfather. He hadn't been able to discuss it with them either. Carter was stuck in the hospital, his bullet wound turning septic. He had almost died.

Carter had collapsed at Monsterland before he even had a chance to talk about anything with Wyatt.

Wyatt knew his stepfather had a private confrontation with Vincent Konrad, but never discussed it with him.

Wyatt's mother came home for a few hours to check on them each night and then returned to the hospital to stay by Carter's side. Half the nurses had perished in Monsterland; the remaining half were busy taking care of the survivors. There had been no time for talking.

Had they lied to him? His throat clogged with emotion. Just thinking about it made him want to throw up. What if his mother had known? Wyatt couldn't believe she would have kept that from him.

He cursed, banishing the thought. She would never let Wyatt's real dad, Frank Baldwin, suffer. No matter what a selfish, arrogant, self-centered person his father was, she could never let another person live like that, or had the divorce changed her?

And what was Carter's role in this? Did he know his father was sick with the plague? Did he want Frank's family so badly, he was willing to hold that information from them, making them turn to their stepfather rather than their father?

Just weeks ago, when they almost died at Monsterland, he had called Carter *Dad*, for Chrissake. He wasn't quite sure he felt comfortable doing that, even if that's what his mother wanted. The title Dad, his father's name, felt specific.

Wyatt pressed his fingers into his eyes, twin drops of tears leaking from the corners. He had called his stepfather *Dad* while his birth father was still alive. It was true his real father had dropped the ball regarding both him and his brother, but Wyatt's thoughts roiled with confusion. He was still their father.

His brain kept replaying the carnage of Monsterland; like a broken news loop, the images wouldn't stop. That day had started with such promise. He and his two best friends scored tickets to the grand opening of Monsterland from Dr. Vincent Konrad himself!

He couldn't believe how they had waited in the car before the colossal gates, breathless with excitement to get in. News reporters lined the red carpet like it was some big Hollywood movie premiere. It was the most exciting thing to ever happen to him. Thousands of people were there, more than half his town, world leaders from all over the globe, and now nothing was left. Not in any of the parks stationed strategically on six different continents.

Monsterland was finished, Vincent Konrad's dream of a chain of giant theme parks to contain the monsters of the world was destroyed by its inhabitants and finished off by the armed forces.

Wyatt and his friends were rescued after the massacre and brought home. His stepfather Carter was medevaced in a helicopter and had been in a medically induced coma for weeks.

Wyatt learned that all the parks worldwide were obliterated. All seven of them: two in Africa, one in Asia, Australia, Brazil, France, and of course, the one in Copper Valley. Each one was devastated: the vampires dead, zombies shot on sight, and the werewolves had their heads inexplicably blown off by a device around their necks.

Nothing made sense. Vincent's vision was altruistic. He was Wyatt's idol, and then somehow, it all went wrong. Wyatt couldn't figure out what Vincent's motivation would have been. He didn't understand why Vincent went through all the trouble of setting up these theme parks to protect the monster populations, reignite the world economies, and then have it all explode, destroying everything he built.

He did admit to himself though, on that fateful opening night of the park, the more he did see of Monsterland, the more disillusioned he was with Vincent.

Monsterland sucked. It was a glorified zoo that exploited the sick and encouraged mad consumerism. You had to feel sorry for the poor creatures living there. Maybe that's what caused the rebellion, Wyatt thought.

Yet, in his final confrontation, he saw a side of Vincent that scarred him. Vincent wanted to kill him and Carter, and if not for Melvin, would have succeeded. He just couldn't figure out why.

No matter how much Wyatt tried, he couldn't get rid of the images of all the blood.

Vincent's intention of uniting the world ended up leaving it shattered instead. The one news report that managed to broadcast speculated that Vincent had simply lost his mind.

Every world leader was murdered, and governments all over the globe scrambled to set up new regimes. The former vice president, now President Nate Owens, was on television when he declared the United States was in a state of emergency. Congress met to authorize martial law.

"Don't panic," President Owens urged.

Wyatt smirked. "Yeah sure, no reason to panic." Leadership across the globe was wiped out on opening day in the parks, as a result of Vincent's catastrophe. Wyatt had such faith in Vincent's vision, and couldn't believe his altruism ended in an epic disaster. Nothing made sense to him.

After Monsterland fell, Wall Street crashed. Economies all over the world were teetering; governments were collapsing. Trade was at a standstill. All airports were on lockdown. Nobody was allowed to go anywhere until they sorted the good guys from the bad.

It was going to take years to clean up this mess. And here he sat in Copper Valley while the world burned around him. Wyatt took a long gulp of the soda he'd abandoned earlier on the coffee table. It was flat, but the artificial sweetness warred with his fatigue, giving him a giddy rush of adrenaline.

He pulled out his cell phone from his back pocket, cursing when he saw it was still dead. The phones lost their signal in the early hours of the morning; the cell tower must have been compromised. It went down twice last week, but they managed to get it restored quickly. He wanted to call Howard Drucker to rehash what happened. Wyatt couldn't seem to stop talking about it to him. Howard was probably sleeping anyway. Any sane person would be getting as much rest as they could.

Wyatt rose and looked out the door of the screened porch, then walked outside into the morning. The reassuring chirp of the birds eased the tension in his shoulders. He looked down at the dead cell phone in his hand, wishing he could call Jade. His eyes prickled, and he swiped them, glad he was alone. He missed Jade with every fiber of his being. A shuddering breath rocked him, and he knew it would be better if Jade didn't see him like this.

He glanced back at the smoke rising from the remains of the giant theme park. There was nothing there anymore; he put his hand over his eyes to shield them from the morning rays. Squinting, he tried to make out the outline of the Werewolf River Run, but all that was left was a broken silhouette.

A screen slammed. Wyatt watched his neighbor walk down toward the street. The man turned, trying to catch Wyatt's attention with unblinking eyes. Wyatt hadn't meant to make eye contact, but it was too late. The only thing left to do was stare back with steely resolve, willing the other man not to talk.

Wyatt glowered again for a long minute, his gaze unwavering, his jaw tight with as much unsuppressed rage as he could manufacture. They seemed locked in some battle.

Please don't start a conversation, Wyatt silently begged. Hank Roberts was the most annoying man in Copper Valley. Once he opened his mouth, he had little control of what came out of it.

Wyatt saw Hank's Adam's apple move, heard him clear his throat noisily, and regretted his amateurish attempt at machismo. Hank broke the silence first. Well, at least Wyatt was the winner of the staring contest.

"Carter okay?" Hank asked. He was older than Wyatt's mother and Carter, probably nearing fifty, his thinning hair uncombed and sticking up in tufts around his head. He wore pajama bottoms, ratty old slippers and a sleeveless tee shirt that pulled against his bulging belly.

Wyatt cleared his throat, his voice rusty. "He's still at the hospital."

Hank took this as an invitation to conversation, moving across the lawn to Wyatt's house. Wyatt watched the grass envelop the other man's feet. It sparkled with early morning dew.

"Heard you kids kicked some serious monster butt at the theme park."

Wyatt's face reddened, and he shifted on his feet. He felt unaccountably shy and didn't want to talk about what happened in Monsterland yet. He hadn't even examined his actions, let alone his feelings. Wyatt and his friends had done things they never thought they were capable of doing. It still felt like an out-of-body experience.

"You guys developed some superhuman powers overnight, huh?"

"Superhuman powers? I don't know what you're talking about," replied Wyatt.

Wyatt put his hand on the door handle as if he was ready to go in. Hank shuffled his feet faster, his thin arms moving like pistons from an old locomotive. He called out breathlessly, cutting off Wyatt's escape.

"Crazy, just crazy … making a theme park with monsters. Werewolves, vampires, and zombies." Hank shook his head. "Was it bad?" He stood so close that if Wyatt opened the door, it would hit his neighbor in the chest.

Overhead, a trio of helicopters flew by, their rotors breaking the morning silence. They both watched them pass. Hank gruffly said, "News. They've been busy."

Wyatt watched the choppers make a hard right toward the small airport, realizing with a start that a soldier sat in the opening of one of them, a machine gun in his hands. *Why would the news have an armed soldier on their aircraft?*

Hank spit on the ground and said, "News ain't on. TV's gone dead."

Wyatt's eyes darted to the dim interior of his home. He didn't want to talk to Hank, his probing expression making Wyatt feel violated. He stared dumbly back at him. Hank wouldn't move. Wyatt knew he wasn't getting out of there without something.

Wyatt nodded to acknowledge the conversation, his throat clogged with emotion. He had seen ugly things. No matter how much he wanted to close his eyes, the horror filled his brain. He couldn't sleep, couldn't eat. He could smell the zombie decay, feel the vamp's creepiness. His stomach was tied into a hard ball of nerves. The thought of his father living in Zombieville like an animal made him nauseous. Sweat dotted his forehead. The street swam for a minute, but he focused on Hank's big nose, covered with blackheads.

A coyote howled nearby. It was so loud, it reverberated,

followed by another, and then another call. They both turned to look for the animals.

"Damn nuisances, those coyotes. Gonna get my gun," Hank informed him, then headed back to his own home.

Wyatt shivered, a cold sweat enveloping the rest of his body. It didn't sound like any coyotes he'd ever heard before. Wyatt moved down the walk to stare at the mountains. He must have been there a while. The sun traveled higher in the sky, but he hadn't felt the time pass. He was thinking about Melvin. He reminded himself all the werewolves were dead, well, almost all of them were. He stopped his galloping thoughts, wondering if his friend was okay.

Hank was back, seconds later, a rifle cradled in his arms like a baby. Wyatt came to awareness to look blankly at the neighbor who was saying something. "What? I wasn't listening," Wyatt murmured.

"Heard Nolan Steward got killed. You know, I work for his dad." Hank shook his head, a smirk on his face. He seemed lost in thought.

Wyatt cleared his throat to say goodbye; he wanted to leave, get away from his probing questions. The older man stopped him by tugging on his arm. Wyatt pulled away to a safer distance.

"Well, see ya," Wyatt said.

Hank ignored him. "Was it a werewolf? Can't believe the president is gone. Ripped to shreds, they said. Imagine that, ripped to shreds!" Hank went on, oblivious to Wyatt's impatience. "Knew that Steward boy was a problem, though. That kid was always bothering me at the shop. 'Fix my tire, wash my car.' Real nasty-like. You know, like he expected me to be his servant or something."

Wyatt made a move to leave, but Hank looked up at him again, still blabbering. "He got bit or something? That must've hurt." He chuckled to himself. "TV's out again. Internet too. On one minute then off, must be ... hey," he called as Wyatt escaped back to the house, his face bleached as white as the bones burning in the destruction of Monsterland.

Wyatt reached the haven of his front porch, ran in and closed the door behind him, hoping to drown out Hank's grating voice.

His back against the door, he closed his eyes, trying to blot out the image of Nolan Steward's zombie hands reaching for him. The disease got to him so quickly, his tanned face turning to sickly pale green, his eyes ... Wyatt thought, the dead, lifeless eyes zeroing in on living flesh, reaching, grabbing ... He squeezed his own eyes tightly shut as if it could block that image, but saw instead his father's body lying like a pile of empty clothes in the street.

Startled by noise, he turned to face the inside of the house where the light from the kitchen spilled over the floor. He didn't remember leaving it on. Heart pounding in his chest, he snatched a standing lamp to use as a weapon. The shade unbalanced it, making it wobble in his hand. "Sean?" he called out, a panicked look on his face.

"It's just me." Gracie, his mother, walked from the kitchen, pausing in the doorway to lean against the jamb, her palms wrapped around a steaming mug of coffee.

"When did you get back?" Wyatt asked, placing the flimsy chrome lamp next to the armchair. He frowned, wondering why he thought it might be useful. He needed to stash some of his and Sean's baseball bats around the house.

"A few minutes ago. Did you sleep?" Her face was so drained she looked like a ghost. Her dark hair was pulled off her face and tied in a sloppy ponytail. She looked exhausted. "Want?" She held out her cup of steaming coffee. She grimaced when she noticed the can of soda with the name Whisp sprawled across the red surface. "Whisp." She said the name of the product distastefully. "I thought we agreed you weren't going to drink that stuff anymore."

Wyatt glared, then picked up the can, taking a long swig. "How can anything this good be so bad?"

"Wyatt," his mother said tiredly. "It's got red dye 47 or something that will peel the paint off cars."

"I saw a video on the internet once where it turned gasoline into water. It's the end of the world, Mom. What's the difference?" He sighed. "It helps to keep me up. I don't want to sleep. Every time I close my eyes ..." He looked up. "How is Carter?" He wanted to ask her about his father but found when he focused on her hollow eyes, he couldn't start that conversation.

"He's up now. Fever broke last night. I tried to call, but the phones aren't working. They wanted him to stay, but they are stretched to the limit …"

"They let him leave?" Wyatt's eyebrows lifted to his hairline. "He's home?"

She held her finger in front of her mouth. "Sleeping. They loaded him up with antibiotics and painkillers." She sat down on the worn sofa, a puff of dust erupting as she settled back. "We need to talk."

"I know we need to talk, Mom. I …"

Gracie interrupted him, her voice soft and tender. "You'll feel better if we discuss it. I promise you."

Wyatt pressed his hands against his eyes, trying to blot out the image of his father as a zombie. He was haunted by the memory of his father shuffling into the street, his arms outstretched in supplication, his grunts the only communication he could muster. Frank couldn't talk, yet he still tried to protect both Wyatt and Carter from the ruthless megalomaniac Vincent Konrad. He learned on that fateful night his estranged father had worked for the billionaire as his lawyer, helping him to organize the parks until he supposedly died on the job, disappearing without a trace.

He sat down next to his mother, a groan escaping his lips. He kept his distance, needing the separation until he could sort the whole thing out. *Had she known?*

Gracie opened her arms, pulling him against her. Wyatt stopped fighting his reluctance, letting his exhausted body go limp. He felt five years old again. She smelled safe, like starched linens and cookies. Her familiar fragrance, the softness of her hands as they stroked his head, retook him to when he had the chicken pox. He leaned into her. It felt good, and for a minute, he wanted everything to change back to the way it was.

"Did you tell Sean?" Gracie asked, her hand combing back Wyatt's dark hair from his brow. The reassuring heat of his mother's body made him feel as though nothing had ever happened.

"No, I haven't told anybody," he said, needing to ask her, yet afraid. "I don't want to tell him. He thinks Dad died on his last business trip, Mom." He turned to look at her, his lips trembling, his chest tight with suppressed emotion. He stuttered for a minute, then said, "He was falling apart, his fingers were broken stubs, his voice …" Wyatt's voice cracked, and hot tears made a trail from the sides of his closed eyes. He felt his mother pull him to her. He shook with sobs, the image of the pus-covered, green-tinged skin of his father filling his thoughts.

"In the end," he heard his mother's muffled voice, "he tried to save you." Wyatt looked up at her. She continued, "Carter told me. After all that happened between us, I will always be grateful to your father. It's erased every bad thought, every time I've hated him. He proved that being a father was more important than money or his career." She paused. "Maybe Sean needs to know that Frank was there for you, after all."

Wyatt picked at the bandage on his hand, feeling it tug against the healing cut he got when he broke a glass pane in the theme park. No stitches, but the skin still pulled and felt tender. He had decapitated a werewolf with a silver axe—he shook his head in disbelief.

There was so much to tell his mother, but all he could think about was his long-lost father. Should he ask? Did she know? Did his father sacrificing himself to save Wyatt and Carter erase the years of enmity between his parents? He felt shy, not ready to ask the questions that plagued him.

Gracie placed her warm, dry hands over his. "I know Carter did everything he could for you and your friends."

"Yeah, Carter was there for us too," Wyatt admitted grudgingly.

"Um-hum." He could hear Gracie's smile when she replied. "But that's nothing new."

"It was for me," Wyatt admitted, almost under his breath.

"Are you hungry?" Gracie lifted his head. "Or would you rather just go to sleep?"

"I need to talk to you about something."

"It will keep," she assured him.

He wanted to tell her it wouldn't, but his eyes drifted shut. His breath deepened until everything faded. He lay there for a minute that might have been an hour when he stiffened, alert, coming out of his stupor. He was flat on his back; a soft afghan covered him from the morning chill. His head moved from the comfort of the cushions, his lips taut with concern, consciously aware of the silence.

He sat up abruptly, looking out of the oversized windows of the screened-in porch.

"What is it?" Gracie asked. She had been sitting silently on the couch, watching him sleep.

"It's so quiet," he said as he stood to look out the window. It was not just quiet; there seemed to be a complete absence of sound. What had his neighbor Hank said? His television was out. He stood looking out the screen porch, searching the skies. Not even a bird chirped. Where had they gone?

"What time is it?" he asked. "I fell asleep?"

Gracie nodded. "For a bit. It's almost on eight, why?"

"Where's KNAB's helicopter?" Wyatt glanced outside for the ever-present morning reporters that flew overhead in choppers. "It's usually circling about now."

Even if they were ordered to stay in, there were a host of other vehicles on the road: army, first responders, and the people who never listened.

"Everything was grounded," his mother replied.

"Even the reporters?" his brother Sean asked from where he entered the room. "There were a bunch of news helicopters going back and forth until about an hour ago." He was standing bleary-eyed in the doorway, yawning loudly. "The army finally locked up Monsterland last night. Man, they finished that place off."

"I know that," Wyatt said. "Did that cat keep you up?"

"What cat?" Sean laughed.

"The one that screamed all night."

"Didn't hear a thing," Sean replied.

Wyatt made a wry face, then paused. "Wait a second. Listen."

"I don't hear anything," Sean said.

"Yeah, I know. Not even a drone. Nothing's moving out there."

"The battle is over. The United States one, Vincent Konrad zero." Sean threw himself onto the couch, his long legs sprawling across the cushions.

"I know. They should have lifted all the orders already." Wyatt searched the streets, his green eyes looking in the direction of the small airport to the east of his town. What did his jerky neighbor say about the television? He ran from Hank so fast, he hadn't quite listened to what he was nattering on about.

"What planet are you on? Monsterland is finished. They don't have to stay here anymore. The threat is over," Sean told him as he spied the soda can. "You got Whisp? Any left in here?" He grabbed the can, chugging the last of the drink.

"Sean!" Gracie wailed. Both boys went on as if she hadn't spoken.

Wyatt made a noise, his teeth biting his bottom lip. "Okay. Where are they now?"

Sean shrugged then gestured to the television. "Check the news?"

Gracie picked up the remote, turning on the television that hung over the door, the secondhand set they bought when the old hospital closed. It was one of those old clunkers, bulky, like a square box. Wyatt was mildly ashamed to have his friends see they didn't own a flatscreen.

Gracie clicked the remote. Static filled the room; the screen was covered with snow. She pressed the remote repeatedly, her fingers turning white from the effort.

Wyatt snorted and said, "Mom, pressing it harder isn't going to make it work."

"What a time for the TV to die," she said.

Wyatt snatched the remote, clicking the channels. "It's not the television." He looked at his mother and brother. "There's no reception. Sean, go check the set in our room."

Sean left the enclosed porch just as Carter stepped into it.

"What's going on?" his stepfather asked, adjusting his arm in a white sling against his broad chest. He raked his dark hair with his other hand.

"Carter, you're supposed to be in bed," Gracie said, her face worried.

"Too much to do." Carter waved away her concern, but Wyatt noticed his stepfather seemed relieved to find a seat on the couch. Their eyes met over his mother's head.

"What's going on?" Carter repeated.

"Well to start with, they're drinking soda. You know how I feel about soda."

Wyatt turned to watch how Carter was going to handle this

one. Smirking, Wyatt picked up the empty can, crushing it in his fist.

"I think there are more important things to worry about other than what they're drinking, Gracie," Carter said.

Sean returned, a big grin on his face. Wyatt watched his step-father, fighting the smile tugging at his lips. So, it was the boys against the girl, he grinned. He could live with that.

"I don't know why the reception should be out. I'm sure everything is under control," Gracie said, changing the subject, knowing she lost a round.

Carter leaned forward and nodded, waiting for Wyatt to elaborate. Wyatt's chest puffed out just a bit. Carter seemed to be talking to him with a different attitude. Wyatt felt older.

"Television in our room is out too," Sean announced.

"Cell phones are dead," Wyatt added.

"They're not dead. You haven't recharged them." Sean pulled his phone from his back pocket.

"I charge it every night, dumbass," Wyatt shot back.

"Boys," Carter rumbled wearily. He retrieved his cell phone from his shirt pocket, confirmed it too was not working. "When did that happen?"

"Not sure. Hank said his internet has been acting up."

"Hank's a moron," Sean added, as if that summed up everything you needed to know about Hank.

"While that may be true," Wyatt answered, "his personality traits have nothing to do with television reception."

"What do you think is going on?" Gracie asked.

Carter rose to his feet. "I don't know, but it can't be good." He looked at Wyatt. "Have you seen anything come out from Washington?"

"Yeah," Wyatt said. "Owens is president. They destroyed Monsterland."

Carter shook his head. "It doesn't make sense." He looked up. "Owens was in cahoots with Vincent."

"President Owens and Vincent Konrad?" Wyatt asked.

"Wyatt, this is bigger than you think," Carter said. "I don't even know who to call. Sean, get my shoes."

"Wait … you're not thinking of going to town!" Gracie's voice was shrill. "You can't drive with one working arm."

"I have to see what's happening, Gracie. It's been over three weeks. Wyatt." He turned to his stepson. "Feel like giving me a lift?" He rose slowly to go back into the house.

"In your car, the police cruiser?"

"Has to be. Yours is still in the parking garage at Monsterland. The keys are on my night table."

"I'll get them." Wyatt turned to leave the room when he saw Carter move toward the kitchen.

"Carter, where are you going? The car's that way." Wyatt pointed out the screen door.

"My gun," he muttered. "Can't leave without my gun."

Chapter 3

Wyatt fiddled with the radio as soon as they jumped into the car. "I tried both AM and FM, nothing. You should have made the town invest in satellite radio."

Carter smiled. "In a police car? How much did you tell your mom?" he asked as they pulled out of the driveway.

"Not much. Just the basics." Wyatt wasn't satisfied with the conversation, yet he didn't feel like blabbing all this to Carter. Monsterland changed everything.

There was so much between them at this point.

Carter was observing him, his gray eyes heavy-lidded. He was leaning back, his bad arm cradled against his chest.

Wyatt sighed and said, "I don't know where to start." His voice cracked, making him sound twelve years old again.

"Want to talk about it?" Carter asked.

Wyatt shook his head. He didn't trust his voice.

Carter raised an eyebrow, adding, "You need to talk about it."

Wyatt struggled; his Adam's apple bobbed in his throat. He concentrated his burning eyes on the passing scenery, as if he could will his thoughts away.

"Vincent was insane, Wyatt," Carter began softly.

"I can't believe it."

"I'm sorry to tell you; he had a plan to take over the world.

Monsterland was going to be his prison to keep the population in line. He was going to use the zombies, like your dad, as a deterrent to make people obey his laws. Make no mistake; he wasn't the altruistic philanthropist you thought he was."

Wyatt nodded. "I'm having trouble wrapping my mind around this." He swallowed convulsively, then added, "Carter, I did see him try to kill us. I'm not stupid. But it's like my whole world has been turned upside down."

The air between them stilled, and they were both quiet, allowing some time to pass. Wyatt was wrestling with much more than Vincent Konrad's warped morality; he wanted to know about his father.

There was a strained silence, then Wyatt heard Carter's calm voice say, "We didn't know."

Wyatt's face reddened. "You don't even know what I am going to say! I wasn't even thinking that!" he lied. He felt manipulated; fury roiled through him. "I have to leave here. I can't stay in Copper Valley anymore. I'm …"

"You're what? School starts in the fall. You've been accepted to Copper U."

"I can't go. How can you even talk about school after what happened? You don't even know what's going on, you've been in the hospital, out of touch. It changed … I changed! I'm not the same person I was three weeks ago. That life is over."

"I realize you've had a shock."

Wyatt steamed, his eyes turning bright with unshed tears.

"Look, we're not even sure where the cards are going to fall with this whole Monsterland thing. Vincent told me that Nate Owens is on his payroll."

Wyatt slammed on the brakes, coming to an immediate halt. Carter groaned and said, "C'mon Wyatt, watch the brakes."

"I can't believe that, not for one second."

Carter nodded once. "I don't even know who to contact, or how far Vincent's tentacles reach into our own government. Who would even believe me at this point? President Owens bombed Monsterland. I can't tell which side everyone is on."

"What are we going to do?"

"Right now, my concern is Copper Valley." Carter paused for a minute and looked at Wyatt. "And my family."

"This is bigger than Copper Valley," Wyatt said to himself.

"I know, Wy," Carter said.

Wyatt bristled; he hated when Carter used that nickname. Wyatt pressed the gas, easily rounding a corner onto the main thoroughfare of the town.

Wyatt was silent for a minute, then said, "I feel like I have no control over any part of my life."

"Join the club, kid. We're all struggling with what happened. You're not unique here."

Wyatt shook his head and said, "Oh, I think I am unique. You know there is more to this story than you're willing to talk about."

"Running away from your problems isn't an answer."

"I'm not running away," Wyatt yelled.

"What do you want to do, join the army?" Carter asked.

Wyatt squirmed. How the hell did Carter know what was going on in his head? The car was thick with silence, then Wyatt said defensively, "You did."

"Yeah, it was different for me."

"How was it different? You told us you felt that you didn't belong, so you left."

"I didn't have a family—you do!" Carter's face was flushed.

"The point is, Carter, you did leave, and there was nothing your parents could do about it."

"That may be true, but I'm not like my parents."

Wyatt forced a laugh that came out filled with bitterness. "You're, like, not my parent either."

"It doesn't work like that, Wyatt."

"Just because I called you Dad at Monsterland, doesn't make you one." Wyatt watched Carter, knowing he'd struck a nerve. "I don't want to talk about it anymore." He set his face mulishly, his lips sealed shut.

"We'll address it later with your mother," Carter said, his face grim. He stared at the empty streets. "What did I miss?" He changed the subject, despite Wyatt's simmering anger.

Wyatt tempered his resentment, knowing the fight was not done. Wyatt's jumbled mind sifted the events. He was as unbalanced as if he were wobbling on a tightrope. He needed to find his feet. Carter repeated the question, asking what had transpired while he was sick. Wyatt answered reluctantly.

"Just what Sean said. The army came through and stayed for a couple of weeks. We were told to stay off the streets. Monsterland's a ghost town." His voice was sullen. The words were pulled from him. After a long silence, he heard Carter's voice.

"How are your friends?"

For the first time, Wyatt felt a smile tug his lips. "They all made it out okay. Well, except for Nolan."

"I never thought of Nolan as your friend."

Wyatt shrugged. "And Melvin. He's still missing."

"He'll turn up."

Wyatt opened his mouth, then decided not to share that he doubted he'd see Melvin ever again. One werewolf made it out of the theme park after it ripped off Vincent Konrad's head. A lone wolf with a dangling golden pendant attached to a thick chain around its neck. Melvin's golden pendant.

Carter grunted, clearly uncomfortable as Wyatt took a turn a little too fast. Wyatt mumbled an apology, slowing the car. They crossed over the interstate, the absence of vehicles making it look surreal. Copper Valley's main drag was one of the busiest roads in the country. It cut across the town and traveled through the entire state.

"Pull over," Carter said.

Wyatt watched Carter leave the car and observe the freeway. Wyatt followed him. "What are you looking for?"

Carter didn't answer for a minute and then said, "How long has it been like this?"

"Like what?" Wyatt asked.

"Deserted. How are they keeping the stores filled with food?"

"They're not. No trucks or trains. The stores ran out of food and stuff. It looked like it was going to get dicey, then a little more than a week ago the army airdropped food, so we had supplies," Wyatt responded.

"But trucking didn't resume?" Carter looked at Wyatt.

"Trucking will resume … or the army will airlift it in again."

Carter walked back to the car, shaking his head. Wyatt heard him say, "I don't like it."

Wyatt caught up with him and asked, "What don't you like?"

"The president. Now that Vincent's dead, who is he working with?"

"Well, we're never gonna find out staying in Copper Valley. Someone has to go to a bigger town and find out what's going on."

Carter didn't respond.

Wyatt considered his stepfather as he got into the car. It wasn't that he didn't like Carter. It felt hard having someone, almost a stranger, insist that they were a family. It was artificial.

His birth father had been indifferent to him—at times downright nasty—and missed important events, yet there was an invisible connection tethering them. A smile, a shared moment watching the Dodgers hit it out of the park, lit up their shared DNA as if it were electrified, and somehow Wyatt always forgave him. He could go months without speaking to him, but a single phone call healed the breach. Carter was all right, Wyatt thought, but he wasn't … he just wasn't Frank.

"How is Jade of the *Dairy Queen*?" Carter asked after a few moments, interrupting Wyatt's thoughts. The tension seemed to ease. Wyatt looked at Carter, seeing the grim lines around his mouth. His stepfather was in pain. He saw that Carter appeared to be struggling too, his jaw working with unsaid emotion. Wyatt softened his tone; Carter wasn't the enemy, he just wasn't his father.

"She's shaken up," Wyatt said. "She'll be okay."

"Have you seen her since Monsterland?"

Wyatt shook his head and said, "There's been a curfew, but we've spoken on the phone when you could get a signal."

Carter digested the information and said, "I wonder who is making these mandatory sanctions?"

Wyatt shrugged. "Look, we're never going to know if we're isolated here."

Carter changed the subject. "That Keisha was something else."

"Taekwondo," Wyatt replied with a smile. He thought for a minute, then said, "Carter, it's nothing against you. What you want, it doesn't feel right."

Carter glanced out the window, watching the passing scenery for a bit. Wyatt thought the subject was finished until Carter replied. "I never had a family. My father, he was, you know, I told you. He was a drunk. He and my mom, they had their problems. I hated foster care, but she had her addictions as well. I missed … I wanted a family, kids."

"Why didn't you get married and have children?"

"When I came back from Afghanistan, my mom was sick."

"But she abandoned you." Wyatt shook his head.

"You above anyone else should understand how I felt. I couldn't leave her; she needed help."

"You sacrificed your life for her."

"Not really, I met your mom and you guys. It was the greatest thing that ever happened to me."

"But you still gave up the best years of your life."

"Sometimes we have to sacrifice for the greater good of others."

Wyatt made a face. "You make me want to throw up!"

"Now that's the Wyatt I know." Carter grinned. "A man's gotta do what a man's gotta do."

Wyatt felt lightheaded with doubt. Maybe he was all wrong about his relationship with Carter. Right now, he felt closer to him than that fateful night at Monsterland when Carter shielded him from Vincent's guns. Guilt crushed his chest. He tightened his hands on the steering wheel, his feelings warring inside him.

"How will I know what to do when the time comes?" Wyatt asked, more to himself than Carter.

He felt Carter's warm hand on his shoulder. "You'll just know."

They passed the next few blocks, watching the quiet streets.

Carter adjusted his arm, nodding toward the road with his chin. "Nothing's moving from any other towns. It's not just here." He paused. Wyatt felt the air thicken between them again, but he refused to look at his stepfather. "Listen, Wyatt; I didn't say this before, there was no time. I'm sorry about your dad."

Wyatt shifted in his seat. He cleared his throat. "Carter, I'd like to know … will you be honest with me?"

"I always am. What?"

Wyatt stared at the ridge of the mountains, wrestling with the subject. He wasn't sure which made him feel more dread, the question or the answer.

"My dad. Did you know he had the plague?" Wyatt heard Carter sigh, and it filled him with dread.

"You mean infected by the virus?" Carter shook his head. "We knew he worked for Vincent Konrad. He was head of his legal department."

"Is that why you hated Vincent?"

"I thought the doctor was a bombastic megalomaniac. No, I never saw your father until that night. He was traveling all the time."

"I didn't know my dad worked for him. I mean, I knew he used to work for a big corporation and moved around a lot," Wyatt stated.

"He was never home. That's what ended your parents' marriage."

"I know what ended the marriage," Wyatt said. "He was cheating on mom." Wyatt shrugged as if he were indifferent, but his face tightened with anger. "I knew about that. All he cared about was his job. He left us for months at a time, and when they divorced, he cut us off without a penny. Okay, he was a bastard about the whole thing, but did you know …did you know he was a zombie?" Wyatt's voice broke on the last word.

"He may have been a bastard, but in the end, Frank proved what it means to be a father. He tried to protect you."

"That's not what I'm asking."

Carter began his response, but was interrupted by Wyatt.

"Fire." Wyatt noticed a trail of gray smoke winding its way toward the horizon. He pointed to the dark smudge against the bright sky.

"Something is burning," Carter agreed. "It's miles from here. It looks like it's happening in Henderson Springs."

Wyatt looked at Carter. "Should I head out there?"

Carter shook his head. "Someone else's jurisdiction. We have to find out who is in charge here and see what the hell is going on."

Wyatt swallowed, his throat thick. "Carter, I hate to keep bringing this up, but I have to know about my dad."

Carter looked at Wyatt, his jawline rigid.

"You still haven't answered my question." Wyatt pressed his eyes, glassy with fatigue and hurt.

"We heard he got sick and died. Period. We never knew it was the plague." Carter paused, his face weary. "I'm sorry. Maybe we should have asked. Are we guilty of ignoring the signs? Hindsight is always twenty-twenty." He sounded regretful.

"This is my father we are talking about."

"Yeah, Wyatt. I know. The same guy who repeatedly betrayed and hurt your mother." Carter looked out the window, his eyes bleak. "He abandoned his sons." He seemed almost to be talking to himself, then he turned and looked at Wyatt fiercely. "We never knew he was in a containment camp. Despite everything your father did to you, your mother would have never let him rot away in there. She ... we would have arranged to get him into one of the colonies offshore until the disease consumed him."

A minute passed where their gazes never wavered. Wyatt searched Carter's face, wanting to believe him. *What is he not saying?* Was Wyatt's need for this to be the truth going to make him blind to what happened? *Twenty-twenty hindsight? Or do we all see what we want to see?*

Slowly, in small degrees, Wyatt felt the tightness ease in his chest. He knew there were secret colonies of plague victims on islands where they were hidden away from the government and the containment camps. Places where they were allowed to die with dignity, not like the circus of the internment sites or the horror of Vincent Konrad's Monsterland.

Carter's voice cut through the silence. "I swear, we would have made him more comfortable, even if he didn't deserve it. Nobody deserves what Monsterland did to them. Vincent Konrad took away that choice."

"Vincent Konrad lost his battle," Wyatt said.

"Don't let him win, Wyatt."

Wyatt knew his stepfather was referring to the moment they had shared before he found out his father was alive.

Wyatt shrugged, then added, "Vincent Konrad is dead."

"Good, let his legacy of hatred and mistrust stay six feet under with the rest of him," Carter said, closing the subject. Wyatt nodded, agreeing to let the matter go, but deep in his soul, a part of him still wondered if the truth was more acceptable when it aligned with what was convenient in life.

They pulled down Red Diamond Road, making the right onto Western Boulevard, heading to the center of town. Loose paper blew down the deserted streets. All the stores were closed, no lights blinked. Even the traffic lights had stopped working.

"Power's gone out," Carter observed.

"It was on when we left the house."

"Well, it's not on now."

"If the power's out, we may as well go home. You won't be able to do anything at the station."

"I gotta see who's in charge."

Wyatt watched Carter assessing the streets as they cruised down the boulevard. "There's a backup generator. Strange about the power though. It's not sporadic—looks like it's out everywhere. That means it's out in Stocktonville. That's where the power plant is located."

They pulled into the police office parking lot. The door was open, the shades up. Two other cars were parked outside, a patrol car and the Cadillac Escalade belonging to the town's mayor.

Carter cursed under his breath; he disliked the mayor. Usually, Chief Jessup handled all the locals, but Jessup was dead now, killed in a battle with a pack of werewolves.

Wyatt followed Carter into the two-room police station. It was an old building, one of the originals from when the town was created in 1854 by prospectors searching for gold but found copper instead. They heard movement in the back office. Carter called out, "Wattles, is that you?"

They heard a woman's voice blurt out a response. "No!"

"Mrs. Wattles?" Carter walked toward the chief's old office.

"Carter White!" Renee Wattles exclaimed with relief. "I thought you were dead too." The mayor's wife stood in a rumpled white tracksuit. Her usually neat blonde hair was stuffed under a baseball cap.

"Where's Roger?"

She held her fisted hands to her red cheeks. "He's gone, Carter. He was up there with the President … and Jessup. They're all gone," she wailed. "Bernie's also dead." She pointed to an empty desk next to Carter's. "Marcus Holloway, Fred Tannen from the fire department, Melody from the bank …

they're all dead." She named several of the leading citizens of the town. "I don't know what to do. I'm so glad you're here." She ran into his arms, sobbing. "It was horrible. I don't even have a body to bury. They wouldn't let me go up there and get Roger." She sat down, slowly looking out the window. "Not that I could have done anything with his body, Stan Pearce from the funeral home is still on the missing list."

"There are no missing, Mrs. Wattles," Wyatt said. "Everybody is dead."

She burst into noisy tears.

Carter patted her back. He gestured for Wyatt to hand her a tissue from the box on the desk.

"What were you doing here?" he asked.

Mrs. Wattles sniffed. "There was no one in charge. Somebody has to do something. The army pulled out. Nothing is working. Nobody knows what's going on."

"Wyatt, get the generator out of the storeroom. There's a hookup by the back door. Let's get some light in here."

"You want *me* to turn on the generator?"

"You can figure it out," Carter said.

A fleeting memory of backwashing the swimming pool with his father in L.A. years ago filled Wyatt's tired brain. His fingers shook, remembering his father's shouts. "Turn the dial, you imbecile! Can't you do anything right? I raised an idiot who can't even clean a pool." His father had a way of stripping Wyatt's confidence.

Wyatt looked at Carter, bubbles of panic filling his chest. "I don't know how to do those kinds of things."

"Wyatt," Carter said calmly. "You killed a werewolf; you battled zombies. You can do anything."

Wyatt exhaled and ran back to a storeroom to get the generator on.

"Just plug it in," he heard Carter call. "There should be a full gas can next to it."

Wyatt rolled the generator over to the back door, feeling along the wall for an outlet. He filled the tank, plugged it into the wall and pulled the cord, feeling very independent. He didn't need to ask Carter once how to do it. It was like it all came naturally.

The generator sprang to life; all the lights flickered in the building. He could hear the television in the front room give a blast of static. Wyatt walked in to stare at the snowy screen. Carter looked at him, nodding his thanks.

"Anything on the news?" Carter asked. He took a remote from his drawer, pressing the button to see if he could find a station. When nothing worked, he tossed the remote to Wyatt. "Keep looking until you find something." Carter disappeared into Chief Jessup's office. "Try some of the local channels," he called from the back office.

Renee's shrill voice filled the room as she followed Carter, dogging his heels. It had a timbre that could drive nails into a skull better than an electric nail gun.

"I was looking for numbers, anything. I don't know … I have children, Carter. We have to get organized. If Roger is gone, who is the new mayor?"

Wyatt heard Carter's calm voice inquiring about townspeople, then Mrs. Wattles' tearful responses. It appeared that the bulk of the town had perished.

Wyatt clicked each station, watching for anything to materialize other than the static screen. He heard the voice before the grainy picture emerged. "Carter, I got something." He moved closer to the set as if he could hear it better. He turned to see Carter standing in the doorway, watching the television intently.

It was a street; Wyatt could tell it was in somewhere foreign. The gates to the Monsterland in that city were blown apart. There was nothing left but rubble. Army tanks lined the pavement; there were wavering images of people dashing through the streets, throwing rocks at the military vehicles.

"Widespread panic, but it appears to be under control in France. The new president of France, Gaston Fournier, has declared martial law. The acting prime minister in the UK has mobilized the army. Germany still has no radio contact with anyone. The European Union has fragmented into multiple pieces. There has been a military coup in Italy, as well as Spain and Portugal."

The fuzzy screen now showed an exhausted newscaster, his jacket off, his sleeves rolled to his elbows, his face haggard. "Relations with the Russians have been cut off since the start of the

Monsterland meltdown. There has been a report of a nuclear explosion in central Russia, but the authorities can neither confirm nor deny. Central and South America are in the throes of several revolutions sparked by the extermination of the leadership in the countries there."

The newscaster held his finger to his ear as if listening to better hear his newsfeed. The screen changed to the White House, now a burned out shell. "This just in. President Owens was supposed to address the country from his protective bunker sometime around eight tonight. At this moment, we are having trouble locating him. It has been confirmed that he was not, I repeat, was not among the dead at the battle for the White House."

Wyatt turned to Carter, and blurted, "Who attacked the White House?"

"Ssshh," Carter said, his face intent on the screen. He then murmured, "Right now, we don't know who is attacking whom."

The newscaster continued, "Secretary Bertrand and Speaker Farrell are counted among the casualties." Faces of the politicians flashed on the screen.

The ruins of the White House were surrounded by the flashing lights of military police vehicles. Wyatt heard sporadic gunfire on the television. The screen went back to the newscaster.

"Again, we urge people to stay indoors and wait until we know the dangers are past. As you saw in France, the remaining zombie population has escaped the confines of the theme park and are on the loose in the city of Paris. The same has happened at Ground Zero, or what used to be known as Copper Valley."

Renee screamed. Wyatt turned to stare at his stepfather. "Why is he saying that, Carter? It's not true. All the zombies are dead."

Carter shut off the set, his face pale. He reentered the chief's office.

Wyatt followed him in there. Papers were strewn all over the desk.

Renee's loud cries filled the room.

"Zombies?" she shrieked. "We don't have a police force; it's a

disaster. Everybody is … who will protect us?" Her voice esca-
lated with each sentence.

"That's enough," Carter ordered as he sat down slowly.
Wyatt and Mrs. Wattles surrounded him. Carter opened a
bottom drawer. "Wyatt. Pick this up for me."

Wyatt moved over to find an old two-way radio in the drawer.
He pulled it out, turned it on. The radio didn't work.

"Two-way radio?" Wyatt asked.

Carter shook his head. "Citizen's band radio. Private radio.
You can usually pick up chatter on these things. All the truckers
have them."

"But the zombies!" the mayor's wife wailed.

"They're all dead!" Carter snapped. "I saw it with my own
eyes, Renee. Did you see any zombies running around
the town?"

Her jaw worked and then she pointed to the television. "But
he said they were on the loose!"

"The newscaster was apparently misinformed. Trust me; they
are all dead, Renee," he spoke with deliberate calmness. "The
zombies … I don't know why they're saying that."

The mayor's wife's cries subsided to hiccupping sniffs.

"Look in the front office for batteries. There should be some
in my desk," Carter ordered.

Wyatt sprinted into the outer office, returning with a handful
of batteries. All his resentment was gone. He felt useful. They
worked well together. Carter rapped out commands, and Wyatt
knew what he needed before he finished what he was saying. It
felt kind of good.

He opened the bottom of the radio, loaded it up and turned
it over. The radio squawked loudly in the silence. Wyatt moved
the knob, trying to catch one of the bands. The radio whined like
an old science fiction movie.

"Move it slower," Carter told him. "Gently." The voices were
faint, and no matter how delicately Wyatt tried to rotate the knob
and lock on some of the garbled sounds, it wouldn't stay put.
The voices were indistinct, fading as he turned the dial.

"Let me show you." Carter held out his good hand. He
turned the knob slightly, and Wyatt swore they were collectively

holding their breaths. When the voice broke through, they all jerked back with surprise.

"This is Stocktonville. My name is Espinoza. Sebastian Espinoza. Is anyone out there? I need to know your status." This was followed by a high-pitched whine and a stretch of static.

"Captain Sebastian Espinoza from the Third Battalion, Fourteen Marines?" Carter asked.

There was a long pause, and Wyatt thought they lost the connection. When the voice came back on, it was wary.

"Who wants to know?"

"Carter White."

"Well, I'll be damned. Sergeant Carter White."

"Not anymore." Carter paused for a second, then added, "Provisional Chief of Police for Copper Valley. Can you tell us how are things in your neck of the woods, Sabby?"

The radio was quiet for a good long minute; then the gravelly voice came through. "Copper Valley ... you mean Ground Zero ..." There was a blast of interference. Wyatt winced at the noise. Espinoza continued, "... thought you were all dead."

Carter demanded, "Who said that? Repeat ... can you repeat?"

"All over the news. Zombies are on the loose and headed this way."

"All the zombies are dead. Repeat, all zombies are dead. Who is in charge of the government?"

Static filled the room again. They could hear Espinoza speaking but couldn't make out the grainy voice.

Carter sighed heavily and said, "We saw some smoke coming from Henderson Springs. Can you report their status? Repeat, can you report their status."

The radio hummed a bit before Espinoza answered. "Yeah, there's been ... fires. Roving looters, it's out of control. Everything's ... down, phones, radio. Social media, banking, trucking, gas ... name it ... all collapsed. President ... battle ... White House. News ... television's been on and off. It comes on for a bit, but it's like they don't got juice or ... went to hell after the massacre ... governments are scrambling ..."

Carter cursed. He depressed the button. "What exactly is the government doing?" He waited then repeated the question, his voice frustrated.

"Who knows?" Sebastian said with disgust. "… world financial markets crashed, money's worthless … left their jobs, police … the army … the government officials. There are massive shutdowns …"

"How can that be happening? It's only been three weeks."

"How should I know?" came the exasperated reply. "It's chaos … no utilities, airports, the trains … food deliveries … weird stuff going on in lots of towns … Bakerton."

"What's going on in Bakerton?" Carter demanded.

"Said the town is leveled. Husks of …" A long burst of static interrupted the comment.

"What are they saying?" Renee whispered. "How can a town be leveled?"

"They said the same thing about us," Wyatt told her. "Who knows what the truth is?"

"What's your condition in Stocktonville?" Carter asked.

"I'm holed up … a warehouse near the tracks. Things are bad."

"What have you heard?" Carter asked, then repeated the question.

"Something's happening out there … purple … I repeat … it's purple … they said … roving gangs … people are not … everyone's dead in Bakerton."

"They said we were all dead and I'm telling you we're not," Carter responded. "What's purple? What are you talking about?"

There was a loud whine followed by a long bout of silence.

"Something happened over … sheriff sent someone to … only … left."

"What? Where? Repeat, repeat what you just said."

"Look, I don't have time … got some supplies … to trade."

"Trade?" Carter asked.

"Yeah … new currency."

Wyatt moved closer to the radio. "What does that mean?"

"Sounds like the world's been sent back a thousand years and things are going to get really bad," Carter said grimly. He tapped his fingers on the desk.

"How could this be happening to us?" the mayor's wife

wailed in horror. Her mascara made two trails down her chubby cheeks.

Carter opened his mouth to ask about the purple reference again when the unmistakable sound of gunfire came through the speaker of the radio.

"Gotta go … got visitors. Espinoza out." The line went dead.

Chapter 4

"What the ..." Wyatt said. "You know him?"

"We served together." Carter turned to the weeping woman. "I need you to calm down, Renee."

"What happened in Bakerton?" Renee asked.

"I don't know. We are cut off right now," Carter said, his face taut.

The door opened, making them all turn to find an older man entering. He looked as though he hadn't slept in ages, rumpled clothes and a stained shirt a testimony to a series of long nights. Wyatt looked closer at the rusty droplets on his white shirt, realizing it had to be blood.

"Keith, you couldn't have come at a better time," Carter said to the older man. "Wyatt, get a chair for him."

Doctor Keith Morris looked at Carter with professional expertise. "How are you feeling, Carter?"

"I'll do," said Carter.

"You were pretty sick there for a while."

Carter shrugged and said, "I'm fine now. Work has to get done. Doc ... have you heard anything from anyone outside of Copper Valley?"

"No," Dr. Morris said. "Everything is down. Hopefully, they'll get it back up."

"Carter, don't you think it would be wise if I drove to …" Wyatt started.

"Nope." Carter cut him off. "Copper Valley first, Wyatt."

Wyatt grabbed one of the metal chairs and pulled it to the desk for the aging man to sit. His face was as gray as his hair, his glasses resting on the blood-flecked front of his shirt.

"Doctor Morris, I don't remember seeing you at Monsterland. Didn't you go?" Wyatt asked.

The pediatrician sat down slowly, shaking his head. "Gave my tickets to my son." He swallowed convulsively. "He loves …" He stopped for a minute, his eyes forlorn. "I mean … he loved werewolves. He was so … it doesn't matter."

"How are things at the hospital?" Carter asked.

"You saw I was understaffed. I've got a few nurses left. Most of the doctors went to the opening." He leaned forward. "Generators are acting up. They start, then they go down. I have to get some dry ice for refrigeration. You think we can consolidate what Amir Mansour has left in the hardware store?" He sighed. "Oh yeah, drugs are running low. I've got Old Jimmy Vilardo standing with a gun in front of the pharmacy. We have to get our ducks in a row."

"We should secure the water tower first," Carter said.

Wyatt watched his stepfather's jaw clench. "Why? What's happening?"

They heard shouts as a car raced down the street, making them all turn to face the window. The people were driving luxury cars.

"They've stolen cars!" Renee screamed.

"I don't know about that," Carter said. "They're not from around here."

"How do you know that?" asked Renee.

"I know everybody in Copper Valley."

They observed the large sedan, all four windows open, stuffed to the gills with men holding weapons. They were clean cut, like a car filled with regular guys going on a fishing trip. Only they weren't carrying fishing rods; they were loaded with automatic weapons.

"They don't look scary," Wyatt said.

"Let's reserve judgment until we find out why they feel the need to be driving around with all that hardware," Carter said.

The car slowed as it neared the police station. One man's face filled the car window. He seemed oddly familiar.

When Wyatt moved to get a closer look, Carter called out, "Stay away from the window."

"I know that guy," Wyatt said. "I can't remember where, but I've seen him before."

"Carter, what are we going to do?" Renee implored.

Wyatt watched his stepfather's eyes narrow with steely resolve.

"We are going to get organized." Carter reached into the desk and pulled out a heavy set of keys. He tossed them to Wyatt, who caught them.

"That's the gun locker. Pull out everything you can find and put it here. Let's take account of what we've got."

"Half the town is armed. You know everybody's got weapons."

"Son," the doctor said. "We don't know who is even left in this town."

"What can I do?" Renee asked in a trembling voice.

Carter pulled his lip, thinking for a minute. "We are going to have to go door-to-door and get everybody to meet at the VFW hall."

"Door-to-door, Carter, we'll never reach everyone. It'll take all day," Dr. Morris said.

"Got a better idea?" Carter raked his dark hair. Wyatt knew he was running close to empty.

"Where are the megaphones I borrowed from Chief Jessup?" Renee asked, her voice high. She moved back to the police chief's office. "I borrowed them for Kristin's Sweet Sixteen." They heard her muffled voice as if it were coming from inside a closet. There was a thump, followed by a curse, then, "Found them! I've got four of them."

Carter opened a drawer and pulled out an old creased map. He flattened it on the desk, smoothing it with a shaking hand.

Wyatt's eyes fell on Feldspar Drive, where Howard Drucker lived. He placed two shotguns to the right of the map. He pointed. "Feldspar is a couple of blocks from here. I'll go and get

Howard and his three brothers. I'm sure they can use their dad's car. Can I have mace?" he asked, holding up a can of the abrasive spray.

Carter nodded. "I know there are more guns back there."

"I've only got two hands," Wyatt called as he walked back to the gun cabinet.

"The Drucker boys didn't go to the opening?" Dr. Morris asked.

"Howard went with me." Wyatt paused, gulping, laying four automatics on the desk. The physician's sad eyes probed him. "He got out with us. His brothers didn't have an invitation." He turned to his stepfather, pulling a Glock out of his waistband. "I'm taking this."

"Carter, no!" Renee yelled. "You can't let him have a gun." She was standing in the doorway, a horrified look on her face.

Carter ignored her. "Know how to use it?"

His stepfather pulled a loaded magazine from inside the drawer. He held out his hand for the gun, then showed Wyatt how to eject the empty magazine. He slammed the loaded one into the grip of the gun and racked the slide back, chambering the round.

"Point and fire," Wyatt whispered.

"Carter! Is this necessary?" Renee stood, quivering with outrage.

"The world as you knew it is no longer here, Renee," Carter said. "Things have changed." He then showed Wyatt how to check the safety.

Wyatt tucked it into his back waistband. "I'm getting the Drucker boys. That will give us four more guys to comb the neighborhood."

Carter nodded. Doctor Morris stood. He reached over the desk grabbing a shotgun, then held it in his hands. "I'll take the blocks north of Gillespie. We'll meet at the VFW hall?"

Wyatt turned to look back at the older people in the office, their faces as colorless as the vampires. They were going to need everybody. "I'll swing by and pick up Jade and Keisha as well," he called as he ran down the steps. "I'll meet up with you in a couple hours." His heart took that moment to skip a beat at the thought of reuniting with Jade.

Chapter 5

Igor opened the refrigerated door and stared down at Vincent's face, submerged in purple fluid. He felt like he had waited for this moment forever. The last three weeks seemed endless. In reality, Igor had bided his time, hiding in a small cavern underneath Monsterland, while Vincent's head was bathed in a special container.

Reaching in, his gloved hands holding large tongs, he plucked Vincent's head from where it had rested for three weeks and plunged it into a chest he'd prepared filled with icy water.

Igor sang while he worked, the words of the old Rosemary Clooney classic tripping off his tongue. *"I ain't got nobody, and nobody cares for me!"* He chuckled at the irony of the lyrics. Igor couldn't wait to see Vincent. Vincent Konrad was his special friend, he thought with a broad smile on his face.

He'd been born Andrew, but Vincent had renamed him Igor, and that's who he became. He liked being Igor better. All the indignities he suffered as a child disappeared with his new identity. He was Igor, Vincent's respected right hand. Well, respected by everybody but those damn vampires. Not that it mattered anymore, they were all dead. Killed by the werewolves, never to humiliate him again, just as Vincent had promised.

"I'm so sad and lonely, won't somebody come and take a chance with me?"

He rolled the head round and round, letting the water clean away the muck. Once he was satisfied that the nose and mouth looked clear of the gelatinous substance, he raised the head and shook it, watching the clear droplets sprinkle the surrounding area. Vincent's sightless eyes rolled in his skull.

Igor laid it on a soft towel and tenderly patted it dry. He then carefully wrapped it and tucked it under his arm like a football. He felt Vincent's nose dig into his armpit.

Igor began his trip in the winding passageways of the chambers honeycombing the ground under the surface of Monsterland. His left foot dragged uselessly on the dusty floor. Every so often, he paused to check on the dead head, *tsk*ing at the bluish lips lying slack against Vincent's teeth. A few of them had been chipped from the abuse it took from the werewolf's mouth. Using his dirty finger, the hunchback pried open the mouth, examining the interior with sympathy.

He shuffled on until he reached the inner bowels of the tunnels. It was dark, but he didn't need light. He knew his way around, because he had helped design the place with Vincent. Using existing tunnels that looked as if carved by gigantic hands, they added new conduits and finished it with a control center.

He paused in the gloom, his free hand feeling the walls until his fingers found the panel. He pressed a few buttons and the lights went on, the room sprang to life to the sound of gears grinding and machines humming.

"It worked, my friend. It may have taken some time, but Plan B is alive and well. You see," he said, "nothing to worry about, Vincent," Igor assured him, and then he cursed under his breath.

Vincent's fancy scientist hadn't arrived in time, and Igor wondered what held the mad doctor up. Now everything was on Igor's crooked shoulders, and he would have to get the ball rolling.

He walked over to a passageway that diverted into a vast cavern of a laboratory. Here he picked up his pace to a central console in the middle of the room. It was on an elevated platform, as if it were the command center. Well, it would be, once Igor did what he was supposed to do. He shivered from the cold of the room and hugged Vincent's head to his chest.

The structure in front of the command center was a large

circular well separated from the room by a waist-high glass partition. Surrounding the pit was a wall of clear glass tubes. In the center of the pit was an enormous wheel-shaped object with glass spokes radiating from a central pillar. It looked astonishingly like a huge stagecoach wheel. Wires hung from the ceiling on either side of the column. Igor admired the contraption, marveling at the brilliance of Vincent's great mind. "Time's a wasting," he said, his voice filled with rising excitement.

Igor unwrapped the head then reached over the railing to place it on the center spoke. It was further than he thought. He overreached, losing his grip, cursing as the head slipped from his fingers to bounce and roll to the other side of the sloped wheel. He watched it tumble down the slight incline, wincing with each jolt. "Sorry, Vincent. That has to hurt." He looked around guiltily, glad no one was there to see his clumsy attempts to place Vincent's head on the central pillar.

"Not a chair in sight, I knew we forgot something," Igor said aloud as he searched the room for anything to stand on. "How am I supposed to get you in there?" He spied a stool and ran to get it.

He climbed the three-foot-high seat, trying to reach over the protective partition, but Vincent's head eluded his grasp. He stretched as far as he could, his fingers catching on a loose flap of the skin on the neck. His movements only made it roll further away.

Igor pushed himself as much as he dared, only his toe remaining on the base of the chair. His tongue poked out of the side of his mouth while he concentrated. A long line of drool dripped onto the wheel's pristine surface.

He wobbled precariously, falling onto the lab floor, unsuccessful in his effort to retrieve Vincent. He rose and moved the seat closer to the glass wall, attempting the climb again. He felt his back muscles scream with overuse, but stretched his hand until he hooked the head by the nostrils.

He inserted his fingers into Vincent's nose, like a bowling ball, but the nose twitched, clear liquid coming out, making it slippery.

He dropped it, the flesh of Vincent's cheeks slapping against the glass surface, thumping loudly as it rolled over to the far side of the wheel. "Oops," Igor said.

The head lay still, and Igor's brow wrinkled while he contemplated how he was supposed to retrieve it.

Igor muttered to himself as he looked at the wheel and the now-distant head ten feet away. He knew the wheel would not support his weight, and he grabbed the spoke, wanting to strangle something in his frustration. The wheel moved ever so slightly, sending Vincent's head further away.

A slow grin spread across Igor's face. Gritting his teeth, he spun the wheel, his hands eager to catch Vincent's head. The wheel picked up speed, and Igor's outstretched fingers looked like talons. Once again, Vincent's slippery skin glided past him, and out of his grasp.

This time Igor stomped his feet and cursed as he waited for the wheel to slow. "I'll take a vowel," he snickered to himself.

"Now for the money shot." He nudged with less force, so it spun lazily. Crouching, he waited for the head, grabbing it and cradling it safely against his chest.

He kissed Vincent on the forehead with a loud smack and said, "Let's try this one more time."

Chapter 6

Wyatt hopped into the front seat of Carter's car. Automatically, he reached for the radio button, turning it off as static burst from the speakers. He pulled out, tires squealing, knowing he was going to hear about that from Carter when he returned.

He slowed as he made the right turn down the center of the town. Just as Doc Morris said, Old Man Jimmy Vilardo stood in front of the drug store, a 12 gauge in his gnarled hands. Wyatt waved. Jimmy nodded with a slight shake of his head, his face impassive.

The donut shop was closed, as was the row of storefronts that serviced the best of Copper Valley. The dress shop, auto parts store, and Chinese takeout looked as normal as they could on an early Monday morning.

Sunlight sparkled on the floor in front of the hardware store, as though the sidewalk was covered with ice. It was broken glass, the storefront window smashed, an extension cord and blister packs of batteries strewn across the pavement.

Wyatt reached for his cell phone to tell Carter, then chucked it onto the passenger seat, remembering that nothing worked. He felt the comforting weight of the Glock nestled in his waistband.

He pressed the gas pedal, making a sharp turn on the next block. This was an older part of town, the mid-century ranches in pink or green shingles lining the road. Here and there, more contemporary khaki stucco houses were newly constructed. Wyatt searched for any activity, but the streets remained devoid of life.

He pulled into number thirty-nine, behind the Drucker family minivan. Wyatt looked up at the top of the driveway, spying two bikes thrown on the ground blocking the path to the front door. They belonged to Howard Drucker's younger twin brothers. They were about twelve, maybe thirteen ... Wyatt tried to remember. He paused to take out the gun from his pants, then placed it under the driver's seat.

Wyatt vaulted up the front stoop, knocking on the door. The brass knocker fell with a hollow clank. He saw the drapes part. Howard Drucker's pale face peered through the window. Their eyes met, and Howard smiled brightly.

A minute later the door opened, and he was pulled into the hallway, surrounded by all four brothers. They all looked like Howard at different ages in life. Each had a full head of black, springy hair, thick glasses, and that same concave chest with slouchy shoulders.

He wanted to talk to Howard, tell him what he was thinking of doing, but the crowd of brothers stilled his tongue. Besides, he couldn't get a word in with them all talking at once.

Twins Barry and Garry and Howard's older brother Sheldon peppered him with questions. Mrs. Drucker came in, wiping her hands on a dishrag, interrupting them with a shrill whistle.

"Stop talking all at once. He can't get a word out." She eyed him critically, then reached out to give him a tight hug. "Thank God you made it out alive. Howard told me all about your battle with the zombies."

Her brown hair was tied up in a kerchief, and the sleeves of her dress were rolled up as well. She reminded Wyatt of the old World War II poster, Rosie the Riveter. She was tough, had to be. Howard Drucker's father worked at some base out west. Mrs. Drucker refused to leave the town where she grew up, choosing to bring up her brood of four boys in quiet Copper Valley. Colonel Drucker used to commute but had recently retired.

"Where's the Colonel?" Wyatt asked. They all still referred to Howard's father by his army rank, even though he was no longer serving.

"Boarding up the windows." She looked at the twins and finished, "Alone." Her hands on her hips, she motioned with her head, and the two younger boys ran to the back of the house to help their father. "What are you waiting for?" She asked the older boy. Howard went to leave, but she pulled him back. "You can stay, Howard." She turned to Wyatt. "How is Carter doing?"

"He's out of the hospital now and went to the police station. Everybody is ... well. He's running the place now. He ... I mean we ... we need help. We have to find as many people as we can and get them down to the VFW hall. Carter's going to ..." Wyatt felt ten years old. Mrs. Drucker listened intently. "He asked if the boys can help round up everybody with me."

"I don't know, Wyatt. We have to prepare ..."

"Yes." Colonel Drucker walked into the room. He was wearing his T-shirt, and Wyatt felt his face color up. He had never seen Howard's father in anything but a uniform. His retirement was relatively new. His fish-belly white skin reminded him of a zombie, and for a minute, words failed him.

"Arnie, you need help here," Mrs. Drucker barked. "They told us not to leave the house. We should all stay together."

Colonial Drucker looked at Wyatt and said, "I would have met Carter at the police station, but they ordered everyone off the streets." He turned to his wife and said firmly, "Ellen, town's more important. I'm glad someone's finally taken control."

"Doc Morris said something about securing a food supply," Wyatt added.

"Food supply! Surely that's not a problem?" Mrs. Drucker twisted the dishtowel in her hands.

"Could be, honey," he told her. "Barry, Garry, Howard, and what's the last one's name?" It was an old family joke, but somehow no one was in the mood for humor. "They need help gathering volunteers in the neighborhood. Go with Wyatt. I'll finish up here. Leave me this block; I'll handle it and meet you at the hall. You think Carter might like a hand?"

"I'm sure he'd be happy if you helped out."

Colonel Drucker nodded. "Let's get these windows finished, and I'll head up to the Hall. Boys, let's get cracking."

Barry, or maybe it was Garry, grabbed the keys to the minivan from a hook on the wall.

"Shotgun," the other twin called.

Sheldon was tall and rangy, just over twenty. He brushed back his long dark hair and stood silently in front of the door, holding out his hand. Barry tried to duck around him, but Howard pulled him by the back of his tee. "There's no time for that. Give Shel the keys." He exchanged a long-suffering look with his older brother. "You take one twin; I'll take the other. There will be fewer problems that way."

Sheldon nodded.

Wyatt was already out the door and down by his car. He saw the four brothers standing together on the small stoop, as if they were taking a family picture.

A chill of dread traveled up his spine, making him shudder uncontrollably. A thought that this may be the last time they were together as a group flittered through his mind. He shook it off.

"I'll take the east end of Silverado Boulevard. You take the other side of town. C'mon, Howard Drucker. Carter's waiting!"

The brothers split apart. Howard and either Barry or Garry —Wyatt wasn't sure which one of the devil twins he got— bounded toward the car like puppies. He made a quick U-turn, heading towards the north side of town.

Chapter 7

The machinery buzzed and hummed, filling the underground chamber with heat, as well as noise. Igor could barely hear himself think. His skin felt clammy; the room smelled ... funny, as if something awful was cooking. The old man resisted the urge to gag.

Vincent's head was propped against a pole, its jaw sagging open. Igor looked from different angles, knowing he hadn't centered the head correctly. He was doing something wrong, but what?

It's no good like this, he thought. *It was missing the connection; it will never work.*

He wasn't even supposed to be doing this without Vincent's doctor.

When they had practiced, the wax head slid into the spot, electrodes locking it in place. *Where was that damn doctor?* Vincent's head was centered in the middle of the wheel on the elevated pillar.

Well, there was no help for it. Igor curled his lips with resentment. He sat on the floor, kicking off his shoes, then peeled the socks from his sweaty body. He grunted from the effort, cursing at Vincent and the missing staff.

The hunchback climbed over the glass wall, gingerly testing the spokes to see if they would bear his weight. His long toes gripped the spokes. Satisfied it was strong enough, he lowered himself to crawl on his hands and knees to retrieve the head. He slipped it under his arm, then balanced himself on his knees, trying to center it on the stand. The contraption was killing him; he could hear his joints pop, his knees ached from the effort. Vincent's head listed sideways then slid off. He plopped it on again.

Nothing happened. It didn't lock on as planned. He eyed it critically. Something wasn't right.

Vincent still looked quite dead, the face colorless. Igor stood unsteadily, grabbing one of two cables hanging overhead. As soon as his damp hand made contact, current zapped through his body, knocking him flat on his back. The jolt caused the head to flop down to lie between the spokes.

Igor turned his stunned skull to come face to face with Vincent's evil stare. Getting onto his shaking knees, he wiped his clammy hands down his pant leg, then pushed himself onto his feet.

Igor reached for the hanging cord, carefully holding it between his thumb and forefinger. He grabbed the second one. He stood, grasping the suspended wires, Vincent's head lying between his feet. Igor looked at the head, biting his lower lip in frustration; the wires were too short to connect. He had forgotten something. *What?*

He sat down, considering Vincent's head. Tapping his finger against the tight skull in front of him, he looked up to see the stand.

Yes! The head had to be on the stand. He lifted the heavy head, propping it on the spike that was there to secure it in place.

The flesh of the neck resisted being pushed in. Igor raised himself, using his fist to hammer in Vincent's head to the spike.

Finally, it locked into place, a rip on the top of its scalp the only damage. Igor squeezed the torn flesh together, nervously looking around, hoping no one else would notice the slight damage.

Next, he yanked the cables, attaching them to either side of Vincent's neck.

He stood holding his own hands out triumphantly shouting, "Behold ... I give you life!"

Vincent remained lifeless.

It should have worked. It did with the hamster.

Igor chewed his lower lip. What was wrong now? *Did I miss a button or sequence?* Igor wondered. He slapped his forehead. *Remember!*

We should have gone over this a few more times, he said to himself. Closing his eyes, he replayed the rehearsal over and over again, his hands fluttering over the cranium, when it suddenly occurred to him. *There was more!*

The electrodes! He forgot to place them below the ears.

Igor clambered over the glass partition, the wheel spokes sliding underneath him. He stumbled back to the control area, opened a drawer to the console and rummaged through until he retrieved the equipment.

He took the black thimble-shaped electrodes, climbed over the partition once again, crawled back to the head, and fastened them onto Vincent's neck.

Igor plunged two hanging receptacles into the electrodes. "See, Vincent; it *is* like jumping a car."

There was a sizzle and the smell of burned flesh. It reminded Igor of *Blud & Guts,* the cafeteria in the hermetically sealed commissary.

Sparks flew from the cathodes, making Igor back away. It fizzed once more, then quieted down. Vincent continued to stare at him vacantly.

Igor cocked his head, considering the gray flesh of Vincent's pale cheeks. The mouth hung slack; the eyes drooped down.

"Your fancy doctor should be here any minute," Igor said, looking at Vincent's ravaged face.

This will never do. He considered his employer—well, he thought with pride, *partner* really. He readjusted Vincent's head, tweaking his nose playfully. He should be more presentable.

Spitting on his grubby hands, he stroked the top of the crown, flattening the hair that stuck up around the wan face, feeling slightly guilty about the torn skin. He hid it underneath some stringy hair. He grunted with satisfaction. Reaching into his pocket, he extracted a plastic comb and groomed the head carefully, making a perfect part over the left side.

Unsatisfied with the result, he combed it over the sunken

eyes, making a new part on the right side. "That's better." Vincent was looking more like himself.

Impulsively, he reached over to pinch the lean cheeks when Vincent's eyes opened wide. The mouth parted in a sneer, then snapped viciously at Igor's fingers, catching the thumb and tearing into it with fury.

Igor yowled, desperately trying to pull his finger from the iron grip of Vincent's teeth. "Vincent, stop!"

The head swiveled mechanically, the jaw working, but no sound came from its purple-tinged lips. It was mouthing words to the hunchback, who stared back in fascinated horror.

"It's alive!" Igor's maniacal laugh went on for a minute too long, ending in a choke. He cleared his throat noisily, then added, "It worked. You are a genius!"

The face stilled, the eyes hot with venomous anger. Igor leaned closer, waiting for Vincent to speak. "What?" Igor moved further in, watching Vincent's mouth form words. "What? Doc ... tor? Oh, doctor? Do you want to know where the doctor is? He's not here."

Vincent gnashed his teeth, his eyes so black they looked like chunks of coals. His mouth rapped out soundless orders. Igor scrambled up, looking around, not understanding what he was mouthing. "What do you want me to do?"

Vincent darted his eyes to the control panel.

"What? Over there? You want me to go over there? Wink your right eye for yes, and left for no."

Vincent rolled his eyes in exasperation and then slowly winked one eye.

"Wait, was that your left, or my left?"

Vincent's eyes narrowed dangerously.

"I know! Wink your right eye for my left, and your left eye for your left. Wait."

Vincent's stare steamed, his eyes turning red, like the fires of hell.

Igor backed away from the center of the circle toward the end of the platform. Clumsily, he fell over the railing onto the floor. He peered up through the glass to see Vincent staring at the ceiling, looking like his patience was wearing thin.

"This is where you want me, Vincent? I'm here."

Vincent's eyes lowered to the control panel.

"Press the button? The doctor was supposed to do that." He shook his head petulantly. "You know I'm not good with my hands." Igor stopped talking when he saw the growing fury on Vincent's face. "Stop that, Vincent. You're going to pop an electrode or something. All right, already. I'll do it. Which one?"

Igor looked at the control panel. *There were supposed to be others doing this, professionals. Where are all of Vincent's people?* He was only expected to deliver the head, and not only did he do that, but he also reanimated it as well. Igor was mightily satisfied with himself. *Wait until Nate hears everything,* he thought with pride.

He gazed inquiringly at Vincent, a stupid smile on his face. He looked for the biggest button on the console. "Ah, ha!" he shouted, then pressed it.

He glanced up to see Vincent's mouth open in soundless horror as the head revolved in dizzying circles.

"No, no!" Igor panicked, pressing all the knobs. The machine was screeching like a banshee, or maybe it was Igor.

Either way, the noise died down when Igor pulled a lever, and Vincent came to an abrupt halt, his mouth hanging open, his eyes still rolling in their sockets. Vincent roared a litany of silent abuse.

Igor flicked a blue switch. The room's speakers erupted with a mechanical voice.

"You moron, you stupid … Wait until I get my hands back. I am going to give you to the zombies for lunch!"

"Vincent! You're back." Igor was elated.

The sound of metal scraping metal interrupted Igor. He spun, then darted into the shadows. Vincent's robotic voice rang out. "Igor. Who's there?"

The giant wheel moved in a jerky circle. Vincent's eyes opened so wide, the pupils were surrounded by the whites. "Igor … Igor …" Vincent screamed.

A steady slap of leather soles on the concrete filled the vast cavern. Vincent looked up to see a face move into the light.

"Took you long enough," Vincent said coldly, then added, "Dr. Frasier."

"I've been busy, Vincent," replied Dr. Frasier.

"Did you activate Plan B?" asked Vincent.

Outside the room, Igor eavesdropped. He cocked his head, wondering, *Activate Plan B? What are they talking about? I activated Plan B.*

"I managed to release W1457 as planned through the sewage systems of Bakerton, Stocktonville, and Henderson Springs, energizing it enough to bring it to you. As you can see ..." The man gestured with his Malacca cane; the gold alien head ornamentation pointed directly to Vincent. "It's working."

"Put that damn thing down!" Vincent spat. "Silly affectation. It feels like Igor rolled my head in a manure pile."

Dr. Hugh Frasier laughed, his slim form shaking. He placed his cane against a console. He was tall, with a head full of iron-gray hair and a distinguished air about him. He was polished and urbane; the suit under his lab coat custom-made in Savile Row. "You do look a bit worse for wear."

"Did they all make it here?" Vincent asked.

"Indeed, all three hundred soldiers, your new Federation Forces have arrived. Worked like a charm, delays and all."

Vincent grunted, his dark eyes gleaming.

"The civilians have no idea," Frasier chuckled. "We used their own underground water tunnels to get the troops here and the sewage systems to dispatch Plan B."

"Why the delays, Frasier?"

"The truth is, Vincent, negotiations have broken down with many of your allies. There was the unexpected coup ..."

Their conversation was interrupted by the shuffle of Igor's feet in the corridor leading to the lab. Igor stopped at the perimeter of the room, listening at the entrance.

Vincent looked up sharply. "Not now, Frasier. Where are the others?"

"Setting up phase two of Plan B right above us in your theme park. Giant vats are being prepared." He observed Vincent's bruised head. "Your body is gone—I had heard. They took it for DNA testing. Lucky for us, they didn't find your brain."

"Damn werewolf," Vincent cursed. "I don't know how he escaped getting a transmitter collar."

"It's not important now," Frasier dismissed it. "We'll find you a suitable donor, as soon as we get this show on the road." Frasier pressed a few buttons on the console. Nothing happened. "Igor! I said, Igor, show yourself! I know you're there."

Igor hobbled into the room, feeling filthy and insignificant compared to the clean-cut doctor. He had a way of making Igor feel like a toad.

Frasier turned to Igor and said, "Password?"

Igor shrugged and said, "What password?"

Frasier clicked a few knobs and said, "Vincent, the password?"

"To what?"

"The WiFi." Frasier rolled his eyes.

"BorisKarloff$$," Vincent said. "One word, no spaces. Capital b, capital k. Money sign, money …"

Frasier laughed as he typed in the password and said, "I should have known. Once I get settled in, I'll see what I can do to make you more comfortable, Vincent. Right now, I've got some work to do. Igor!"

Igor's feet remained planted where he stood. He looked at Vincent, his head tilted, and he asked, "Vincent, didn't I activate Plan B? What is W1457? And what is this coup he is talking …?"

Vincent's head spiraled as he faced Igor, his eyes black with fury. "You don't need to know anything more than I tell you."

Igor turned to see Frasier eyeing him with disdain.

"Come here, you demented little goblin. I have a job for you to do, I-gor." He dragged out the name as if he found it funny. "Last time I met you, your name was Andy."

Igor straightened his spine, making himself as tall as he could. "It was Andrew. Vincent likes 'Igor' better."

"Does he now?" They sized each other up, but Igor found himself withering from the doctor's contemptuous stare. "Know where the bodies are buried?"

Igor ignored the doctor and asked Vincent, "What tunnels is he talking about?" He didn't know about this new development, and he thought he knew everything.

Frasier glanced at Vincent, a question on his face.

Vincent clicked his tongue, and his mechanized voice said, "Go ahead, you can share that information."

"There is a network of tunnels underneath the desert. It was a big public works job started at the end of the last century by the government. When they ran out of money, Vincent took it over. The government was installing it to catch the rain, so it would stop flooding."

Igor shrugged. "So?"

"The water won't penetrate the desert soil, and it causes … it doesn't matter. The pipes are laid out in a network all over the west, and that's how we got here undetected," Dr. Frasier finished.

"Where'd you come from?" Igor asked.

"Where do you think? Area 51." Frasier's laughter echoed in the vast chamber.

Dozens of uniformed guards flooded the room. Each carried a heavy-duty assault rifle. Helmets hid their faces, yet they were intimidating.

Igor immediately realized they were Vincent's army, each with a patch that read Federation Forces. These were his enforcers. They were not US military. Igor wondered, *What happened to Nate's army?*

They made Igor feel as if the room was becoming too crowded. He couldn't breathe for a minute. Two of the goons drew up to either side of Dr. Frasier. Others took places at various consoles. They were well rehearsed and appeared to know exactly what they were doing.

Igor looked at the looming guards flanking Vincent's doctor. The room had filled entirely in mere seconds. A new group filed in. Hundreds of them in beige uniforms, each one bigger than the next. They wore no helmets; many had on lab coats. The room hummed with the buzz of numerous technicians. The soldiers stood silently, waiting for orders. Frasier held out his hand to the guard behind him. The burly man placed the handle of a shovel in his palm. The scientist tossed the shovel to Igor, who caught it deftly.

"Go dig 'em up," the doctor ordered.

Igor looked at Vincent, a question on his face. Vincent stared back with an intensity that bordered on madness.

"You heard the doctor's orders," Vincent sneered. "You know what has to be done." He swiveled his head in the other direction.

Igor had been dismissed.

Chapter 8

"You or me?" Howard Drucker asked Wyatt in a quiet voice, as they stared at Keisha's doorway.

Wyatt looked up from the dashboard, his face incredulous. He watched Barry running from door to door down the street informing people of the pending meeting at the VFW hall. Every household had lost someone in Monsterland. In many cases, no one answered their door at all.

"Are you kidding me? Go in and get her," Wyatt said.

Howard gulped so loudly, Wyatt was sure they heard it all the way to Rancho Cucamonga. In the end, it didn't matter. Keisha was bounding down the walkway. "Never mind, here she comes," he said.

Keisha was a sight, he had to admit. Seeing Keisha made him miss Jade even more. Watching the tall girl race down the steps, Wyatt's chest filled with anticipation to hold Jade's hand again.

Keisha Hall was both the tallest and smartest student in the school. She had coffee skin and bright eyes. Her hair was braided close to her skull, and Wyatt noticed she was wearing dark clothing. She moved gracefully, almost in slow motion. Both boys sighed, watching her elegant stride.

"Are you going to stay in the front or sit next to me?" Keisha demanded of Howard Drucker as she slid into the backseat.

Howard took off his seat belt, then left the car to move into the rear. Wyatt watched as his friend entered the back of the car, sitting alone, as far from Keisha as he could. Keisha rolled her eyes, then moved nearer to him.

"Is that a pocket protector you have in your pocket or are you just happy to see me?" she whispered, her face close to Howard's.

Wyatt met Howard's eyes in the rearview mirror. He glanced at Keisha, then back to Howard.

Howard's knuckles were so white they looked like plaster. Wyatt caught a glimpse of Keisha's expectant face and mouthed the words to Howard, "Kiss her."

Howard looked like a deer caught in the headlights. Keisha clicked her tongue. "I thought we had this all straightened out." She shook her head. "I don't know why I like you, Howard Drucker. I just do." She leaned over, grabbed him by his shirt, and kissed him full on the lips. She pulled back and said, "I missed you. I really missed you." Howard leaned in and kissed her again.

Well, kissing must be like riding a bicycle, Wyatt thought because it looked like Howard Drucker remembered how to do it not only quickly, but noisily as well. He made a bigger racket than the cat that had been outside his window last night. Wyatt regretted ever saying anything; this one had to be the longest kiss in history, and from the looks of it, they had no intention of coming up for air.

Barry jumped into the car. "This street's done." He did a double take when he noticed his brother and Keisha in a lip-lock in the back seat and laughed. "Howie's got a girlfriend."

Howard turned to his brother with a smug expression on his face. He smiled, putting his arm around Keisha and said, "Seems I do. It seems I do."

Wyatt gunned the car, circling around to the next block, where they split up to knock on doors. He could feel the excitement fill him as he spied Jade's house. A stupid grin he couldn't contain spread across his face.

Jade answered the door. She was as beautiful as always. The only evidence of the horrific past few weeks were the dark bruises from many sleepless nights under her eyes. Her bottom lip trembled when she opened the door, then turned into a shy smile. Jade twirled her hair with one finger, then dropped her hand to place it on the screen door. She searched his face with soulful blue eyes. Wyatt put his hand on the screen so their fingers touched each other. He swore he felt an electric current leap from her flesh into his when their fingers met.

"Are you okay?" It was the only thing his sluggish brain could think of saying. He cursed himself for the lame conversation. What he wanted to do was open the door and take her into his arms. It seemed he was as inept with girls as Howard Drucker; only Jade didn't take control of the situation. Instead, he shuffled awkwardly and asked if she wanted to help them notify people.

"I'll get my bag."

"Where do you think you're going?" Jade's father demanded as she opened the door to leave. Her father was enormous, with a bullet-shaped head that looked too small for his body. He walked over, swinging his arms like a wrestler. Wyatt couldn't help but stare at the skull and crossbones tattoo on his bulging bicep. *Wait, does he have tattoos on his fingers too? What does it say?* Wyatt strained to read the letters. *D-E-A-D M-E-A-T? Dead. Meat. DEAD MEAT!* Wyatt gulped, his face drawn to the military buzz cut, feeling vastly undersized.

Wyatt glanced back to the car longingly from his spot on the top step while holding the screen door open.

Jade pivoted to peek at her father, her eyes downcast, her lashes fluttering. Wyatt watched as she went back, making stupid baby noises. She wrapped her arms around her father and gazed up adoringly. "We have to do our part, Daddy," she said with a pout.

Jade's father gave her a tender chuck under the chin, his sausage fingers dwarfing her petite frame. "I'm just worried about you, Jade-Jade."

Jade-Jade, Wyatt repeated the name alarmingly in his head. Her father turned towards him like a Mack truck. "You are going to take care of my little girl, right, Wayne?"

"Wyatt," Jade said.

"Right. Whatever. She's not to leave your sight."

Jade took cute little steps towards Wyatt, burrowing her soft hand inside his larger one. He wished he'd known she was going to do that. He would have wiped his sweaty palm down the side of his pants. With a sweet wave, they headed toward the car.

Wyatt was surprised at how weak his voice was. "Your father has the words *dead meat* inked on his fingers?"

Jade shrugged and replied, "Well, he *is* a butcher. What else is he going to have on his hands?"

She noticed Keisha was in the backseat and squealed so loudly Wyatt was sure it pierced his eardrum.

Is this the same girl that hacked Nolan Steward in half in Zombieville? Wyatt thought. *Maybe chopping meat runs in the family.* Wyatt watched her. Jade seemed different. While he used to think her beautiful blue eyes showed great warmth, today all they seemed to emit was a mindless vacancy. She chattered on and on as if the town wasn't turned upside down and half its occupants gone. Wyatt felt his chest tighten with tension and had to fight the urge to ask her to stop talking.

As they made their way down the walk, Jade rambled about the past few weeks. It was like she wouldn't shut up. Then, of all things, she started babbling about how a werewolf ended up saving their lives and didn't Wyatt agree that werewolves were *"the best monsters ever!"*

Wyatt stopped in his tracks; he was done talking about the more superior monster. *Isn't that what she wanted in the first place?* The Jade he remembered preferred to discuss important world issues, like hunger and containment camps.

He turned to her and said, "You're fan-girling about werewolves?"

Jade's face lit up with a dazzling smile. She laced her fingers with his hand.

They continued down the walkway. Her thighs were brushing against his. She stuck to him like a limpet mine. He wondered briefly what about her had made his heart beat faster this past year in school. He stared in mute shock at her little hands, and he tried to recall, *Did she always act this way? Was I so crazy about her that I never even noticed it?*

Then she smiled again, and Wyatt remembered why he loved her so much.

Keisha came out of the car, dragging Howard. They met at the end of the sidewalk and simultaneously grabbed each other's hands. "I'm sad," Jade said. "I wish Melvin was here."

Howard looked at her and said, "Really?"

Jade shook her head solemnly, "Yes. It's like a piece of all of us is missing."

"I never thought you noticed any of us," Wyatt said.

"How could we *not* notice the three of you?" Keisha added. "You were like a single-cell organism."

They had a moment of silence, as if they were putting the horror of what happened behind them.

Howard shook his head and said, "Things will never be the same."

The thought of Melvin and what happened made Wyatt sad, something had changed in his life forever. He mourned it with the same intensity as when he had to leave his home and resettle here. He shook off the feeling before it would overwhelm him. "You take the north side; we'll take the south," Wyatt suggested, breaking the mood.

"Great," Keisha agreed. "Howard Drucker, you go to that end of the block, I'll do the other end. We'll meet in the middle."

"Sounds like a good idea." Wyatt nodded in agreement.

Jade interrupted them. "I'm staying close to Wyatt. I'm not taking any chances."

Wyatt searched the long block, then back to where she clutched his hand in a vice-like grip. What did Carter always say to him? *Something about being careful what you wish for?* He shrugged, a wry smile on his face. It didn't really matter. He had a job to do, and he was going to get it done.

They canvassed the entire neighborhood, everyone else splitting up to reach more houses. Many were dark with no answer. Wyatt thought sadly about all the casualties. They had all left for the theme park, full of excitement and hope, most never to return.

Jade stayed so close to him, he was beginning to feel as though they were conjoined twins. She complained that her feet hurt, she whined about the heat. They had to stop and find her a bathroom. By the time they reached the VFW hall, Wyatt was wishing Nolan Steward was here and Jade was still his idealized vision of what a girl should be.

Chapter 9

Wyatt met up with his family outside the VFW hall two hours later. His mother stood in a knot of people; Carter was nearby. Wyatt extricated his hand from Jade's grip and told her to go inside. Keisha had seen her own parents and dragged Howard Drucker to meet them.

"Nice turn out. Good job, Wyatt," Carter told him with a smile.

"You sound like it was a school project." Wyatt dismissed the praise. "Mom, Carter." He gestured for them to separate from the crowd a bit. "I have to talk to you." As soon as they moved to an empty spot on the walk, he blurted, "Mom, I'm going to leave town tomorrow. Someone has to go out there and find out what's going on." He exchanged a long look with Carter and said, "We have to tell them about things that happened in Monsterland."

"Tell who?" Gracie's face paled. "The army was here. They know everything."

Carter shook his head and said, "Not yet, Wyatt."

"You don't understand, I want to go back home," he told them. "To Los Angeles."

"We are home." Gracie had two red spots on her cheeks, a sure sign of agitation. "This is our home."

"Not for everybody. I want to go to L.A.," Wyatt continued.

"We're completely isolated here. I have to find out what's going on."

"How are you going to communicate with us? By smoke signals? You have no idea what the conditions are out there," Carter stated. "Until we have a clear picture of where the country stands, I think …"

"I don't care what you think! Stop treating me like a child," Wyatt whispered fiercely, his teeth gritted.

"Just because you strapped on a gun, Wyatt …"

"What?" Gracie shrieked. "Strapped on a what?"

"Grace," Carter warned. "Lower your voice. Look, Wyatt; this is not the time or place to discuss this. I'm working on something; have a little patience."

"There will never be the right time. You can't stick your head in the sand and pretend everything is fine. Sometimes you have to do something."

"What's that supposed to mean?" Carter asked, his voice calm.

"I think you know exactly what it means," Wyatt said.

As if half the conversation went over her head, Wyatt heard Gracie mutter, "You're a child."

"No, he's not, Grace," Carter's voice was firm. "Look, I understand how you feel."

"You can't," Wyatt said.

"More than you know, but Wyatt, we don't know how far this thing has gone."

"I want to do more."

"You may have to," Carter said.

"What does that mean?" Gracie demanded again, her lips trembling. Her face was mottled; her hands clutched in front of her.

Carter was saved from answering when Jade's father poked his head out the door. "They're ready for you, Carter."

"I'm not done," Wyatt said.

Nobody answered him as they entered the darkened hall.

Carter was pale; his arm was close to his chest. Wyatt could see a spot of blood on the gauze to the right of his shoulder where his shirt gaped open. He was standing on the stage of the VFW hall. It was a small auditorium, where his graduation was supposed to occur. The room was dim. There were no lights but for a few strategically placed high-powered flashlights that lit the area and candles in paper cups. It looked like the whole town had turned out to do a vigil, like when Melvin's mother disappeared.

Graduation, he thought again. Somehow, he believed that was never going to happen now. He saw both his mother and Sean enter the room. She was visibly upset; she wouldn't make eye contact with him.

Gracie walked toward the front, taking a seat on the steps leading to the stage. Renee, the mayor's widow, sat on the other side, as if they were Carter's guardian angels.

Wyatt glanced around the room. It was packed with older men. Most of the younger men had gone to the Monsterland opening and never returned. The hall buzzed with low conversations, reminding Wyatt of the atmosphere in a funeral home.

People appeared shell-shocked, their faces bleached of color, their eyes empty. They looked no different from the zombies in the theme park. He felt himself shudder, making Jade look up at him. She was reattached to his hand again, which had gone quite numb a while ago. He unglued their sticky skin.

"What's the matter?" she asked.

He shook his head. "It's too hot in here."

She inched forward, rubbing her shoulder against his chest, suffocating him.

A pall of sadness hung over the room, along with the smoke from the candles in their Styrofoam cups. The town had outlawed those last year, and Wyatt thought inanely if the person who decided to use them would get a ticket. The murmuring grew louder. Carter raised his hand, drawing their attention.

"What's going on?"

"What happened to the electricity?"

"Where are the authorities?"

People were calling out all at once.

"Settle down, folks," Carter said. "As you all may have realized, the power's out from the main source in Stocktonville. The army's pulled out."

There were cries of dismay. One woman yelled, "Who's going to protect us from the monsters?" Wyatt recognized it was his math teacher. This set off the room again.

"There are no monsters anymore, Lori. I saw it with my own eyes. Every living thing in Monsterland is dead, including Dr. Vincent Konrad."

"What about the monsters?" Jade's father yelled out.

"Everything is dead," Carter confirmed.

There were murmurs of approval. "We reached Stocktonville by citizens band radio today. I spoke to an old buddy of mine from the service. He's holed up in a warehouse near the tracks over there. They think for some reason Copper Valley has been leveled, and there were no survivors."

"We're all dead, I tell you!" A man stood up. "The end is here!"

There were a few screams and Betty, Wyatt's school nurse, fainted. The crowd parted, allowing Doc Morris to see to her. A few people helped lift her to a chair in the corner.

"Shut up, Doyle," said Manny, Wyatt's boss at Instaburger. "Carter, we've got to send someone over there to tell them we're okay."

"We need to know what's going on outside of our town," the man called Doyle retorted.

There was the buzz of complaints that got louder, and the crowd grew restless.

"What happened to the CB radio?" Hank, Wyatt's neighbor, asked, his voice rising above the din.

"It's dead," Carter told them. "I tried for over three hours. Nothing, not a soul."

"We're doomed," another resident moaned, then fell to his knees.

"Let's all calm down." Carter nodded for two of the men to help the woman to a chair next to the semi-conscious nurse.

The anxiety level was increasing. Nobody was listening. The heat was stifling, and people were fanning themselves with loose papers.

Carter motioned for some men in the back to slam the doors.

Manny and Father Tim let the heavy metal doors fall with a bang.

The noise dropped, and the room grew quiet.

"Listen to Carter. Stop panicking," Father Tim told them. "We have to come together."

"Agreed," Carter said. "Fear is going to destroy us. We don't have the luxury to lose control; we have things to do. We have to protect both ourselves and our resources."

Betty, the school nurse, got shakily to her feet. Her face pale. "What happened to our government?"

Carter shook his head. "I don't know, Betty. I'm not sure about anything. But we can't stick our heads in the sand and our butts in the air and not think about things like food and water."

"The army will airdrop that to us," Hank responded.

"Yeah, like they did in the Caribbean during the Cat 5 hurricanes. I saw how they took care of those people." Jade's father raised his tattooed fist.

The room became charged. People were all talking at once, trying to be heard. Wyatt saw Carter try to restore order by raising a hand in the air. "Everyone settle down. We have a plan."

Though the crowd calmed, there was still an undercurrent of tension. They looked up to Carter.

"Most importantly, we have to secure the water supply. Doc Morris has someone guarding the drugstore. I need some people to head over to the hospital. They don't have enough help." He looked out into the crowd earnestly. "We need a weapons count."

"Why?" a woman yelled.

"Because we are mobilizing," Manny said. "We have to protect ourselves. There is no one else to do that."

Carter gazed into the rumbling audience as if he were assessing them.

"Someone has to go to Stocktonville," Jade's father bellowed.

"Can't do that now," Carter said. "We'll be spread too thin. We have to secure our town first."

"We'll never know what we are securing from if we don't have an understanding of what the dangers are. We don't have a choice." This was from Father Tim. "Besides, you know we're going to need supplies."

"I don't have any people I can spare to go to Stocktonville," Carter said. Wyatt saw his stepfather looking directly at him, his face thoughtful.

The crowd protested unhappily. A baby cried, and they could hear the mother soothing the child as she rocked her.

Howard Drucker stood up slowly, his voice quivering. "I'll go, Officer White."

There were a few cries of "No." A person in the back laughed out loud and said something about Howard Drucker being a loser.

Carter's gray eyes locked with Wyatt's.

Keisha stood next to Howard. "I'll go too."

All the noise died down, and the air hummed with suppressed tension.

"In what car?" Colonel Drucker demanded. "I'm not letting you take the only vehicle I own."

Wyatt rose to his feet, forcing Carter to make a decision. Wyatt knew the conversation from earlier today was going through his stepfather's mind as it flitted through his own.

Sometimes we have to sacrifice for the greater good of others. Wyatt knew right now Carter was left with little choice. Circumstances were forcing his stepfather's hand and Wyatt's fate.

Jade tugged his hand as if she wanted him to sit back down. "Don't do this," she whispered.

Wyatt looked at her and said simply, "Jade, let me go." He turned to the stage, "I'll drive," he called out and shook off Jade's hold. "I'll take my mom's car." He smiled, thinking about driving his mother's car. His own car was still up at the Monsterland parking garage.

Wyatt watched his stepfather's eyes measuring him. His own face reddened, and for a moment he thought Carter was going to say no. Carter shook his head, slowly then said. "No, you'll take my car. It'll be safer."

"No!" Gracie stood. "It's too dangerous."

"They're just kids," another woman hollered.

"They don't have the luxury of being 'just kids' anymore," Carter told them all.

Wyatt smiled, his chest slowly filling with pride.

"I think we should split up into groups. Gracie and Renee will be assigning jobs. I need a list of residents who are dependent on medicines and what kind they require. The Doc is setting up a dispensary. Benson, Manny, Father Tim, I'll be needing your help." Carter surveyed the group, his eyes settling on some of the thirty-year-olds in the room. "Sandy and Ed Neal, meet me off to the left. You'll be our new police force." Carter's eyes were scanning the room. "Is Terrance Parks here? Where's Amir Mansour?"

"They're gone, Carter. They went to the theme park," someone answered.

"The whole Smithson clan was wiped out. Damn shame." The Korean grocery owner stood.

"Wyatt, I need a moment with you before you leave." Carter motioned to a guy dressed all in black off to the side, propped against the wall, looking mildly bored.

Wyatt followed Carter as they exited the building. Gracie tagged along behind them.

"At least let me change the bandage on your hand," Gracie said in exasperation.

Taking Carter's lead, Wyatt said, "Mom, it's all healed. Don't make a big deal."

"It's not healed," she responded. "I know it's sore."

They both ignored her.

"Damon, you'll go with them," Carter ordered the hulking man.

Damon? Really? Wyatt thought with a bit of resentment. He shook his head. "We don't need Damon, Carter. We'll be fine." Damon Thayer was three or four years older than Wyatt. He worked at the gas station at the edge of town. He was local, a known hunter, and Wyatt knew that's why his stepfather wanted him to go. "I think I can handle this."

Damon smirked.

Carter shook his head. "Damon's going," he replied with finality.

Sean ran over as Wyatt, Howard Drucker, Keisha, and Jade met Carter while he descended the steps of the building.

"I'm going with you," Sean said.

"No!" Both Carter and Wyatt shouted at once.

Carter gave his youngest stepson a warning glance when he opened his mouth in protest.

"I don't have time for that right now. Wyatt, take this group and head over to Stocktonville. You may have to split up. Try to locate Espinoza. Set up a supply exchange with him."

"What about Washington?" Wyatt asked in a low voice.

He heard Carter sigh heavily. "If you can get a transmission out in Stocktonville, try to get a message to the FBI. Let them know we are okay … and let them know about Nate Owens. Remember, Wyatt, your prime directive is to set up a line of communication and get supplies."

"Supplies?" Wyatt asked, sliding into the front seat. "You don't expect this crisis to last long. It never has. Even when the plague broke out, everything was back to normal in a few weeks." He reached under the seat to pull out the handgun. Wyatt placed the weapon on the middle console. He exited the car to be with the group.

The jagged line of the mountains in the distance surrounded the town like a protective wall. It gave Copper Valley a sense of security, as if time could stop here and keep its inhabitants safe. The clouds painted them lilac and deep shades of purple, like an oil painting. For Wyatt, the mountains made him feel boxed in, smothered, rather than safe. He couldn't wait to get beyond them.

"You know this thing really flies when you need it to." Carter was watching him intently.

"In other words, I shouldn't be worried about speeding tickets."

"Don't stop for anything or anybody. You understand?"

"I got it, Carter. We've been through worse," Wyatt said.

"I don't like what Espinoza said. Why would they make a statement that we were all dead? What's the benefit of that? I don't know how long this thing is going to last, but I have a strong suspicion we're going to have to take care of ourselves. So, it's you, Howard, Keisha, and Jade?"

"And Damon," Wyatt said.

"No." Jade shook her head. "I … I can't leave without asking. I mean. I can't go."

Keisha turned to give Jade a look of withering scorn. "Really, Jade?"

Jade's face flushed. She didn't respond. She looked at Wyatt and cried, "Please don't go."

Wyatt sensed the heat of Keisha's exchange and was troubled by Jade's lack of spirit. He felt like he didn't know her anymore. On the other hand, he couldn't help the bubbles of relief shooting through his veins. He didn't have time to examine this phenomenon. He observed Jade take her baby steps to her father who was signing up for a job assignment. Another girl approached them. She held a .22-caliber rifle in her hand. Wyatt tried to place her, his mind coming up blank.

"Lily Tallifer." She nodded to the group, then turned to Wyatt. "We had bio together last year." She was tall with sun-darkened skin, complemented by the broad cheekbones of her ancestors. Her smoky almond-shaped eyes watched him examining her; her mouth twitched contemptuously. She wore ripped jeans and a large flannel shirt two sizes too big, the ends tied around her waist. Midnight hair fell like a waterfall over her shoulders. She threw her head back with defiance, whipping her hair, so it brushed his cheek. It smelled of summer. Wyatt inhaled deeply, catching the fragrance of sunshine, grass, and happiness. Jade scooted back, latching onto Wyatt's hand like a suction cup. She and Lily appeared to square off like two prizefighters. Wyatt felt the tension sizzle between them.

"You're Isaac Tallifer's daughter?" Carter asked. "What's been happening up on the reservation?" Lily's family lived on native land about thirty miles outside of Copper Valley. While they had their own schools, many of the kids went to Copper Valley High.

"Most everybody was invited to the Monsterland opening." Lily swallowed convulsively, holding back a sob. "It looks like only children and some old women are left. I'm here to help, Officer. We are going to have to work together."

"Where's your Uncle John?"

Lily shrugged. "I'm not sure. He may have gone to the opening with my father. I haven't seen either of them."

Carter nodded. "I think you'll have to get out of here now. Fill up at the station before you leave." This was directed to Damon. "Remember, don't stop for anything. Do you know how to use that?" he asked Lily, pointing to her rifle.

Lily smiled. "Been target shooting since I was six."

"Target shooting and where you're going is not the same."

"It's the same to me," Lily told him with a smile. "I'm not afraid."

Jade bristled and said, "Maybe I will go."

Jade's father stomped over, grabbing her hand and pulling her back into the auditorium. She looked longingly at Wyatt and broke her dad's grip.

"I want to be with Wyatt," she pleaded.

He took her by the forearm this time and said, "Over my dead body, baby girl! I let you go to Monsterland with that Nolan Steward kid. I'm not letting you leave this town. Home is where you'll stay with your mother and brother, safe and sound!"

Wyatt watched as her father dragged Jade away. She halted, turned, and said, "Be careful. I'll be here when you get back."

Part of Wyatt felt a sigh of relief that he could concentrate on getting back to Copper Valley with his hide intact if he didn't have to worry about Jade. The other part of him regretted saying goodbye.

Lily moved next to him.

Without responding or looking back at Jade's tear-filled eyes, they watched Damon approach them, a semi-automatic propped against his shoulder as if he were a marching soldier.

They all took their places in the cruiser.

Carter leaned down to speak with Wyatt by the car window one more time before they left.

"I got this, Carter," Wyatt said.

Gracie was slightly breathless and held a few plastic shopping bags in her hands. "Ray Yeong's wife opened the grocery store. I put in a few rolls; they're stale." She shrugged, her face sad. "Everything was spoiled, no electricity. So, I loaded it with those small containers of peanut butter."

"Ugh, I'm allergic to tree nuts." Lily looked at the bag with disgust.

"No worries, Lily," Howard informed her. "Peanuts are a legume, that doesn't fall into the same category as almonds, walnuts …"

"Not now, Howard Drucker," Keisha said.

"Oh," Gracie said with dismay. "I'm sorry, Lily. I could try and get …"

"Mom." Wyatt rolled his eyes. "We aren't hungry."

"Speak for yourself. Thanks, Mrs. White," Howard said. "Did you put in jelly?"

"Good idea! You can have jelly, right, Lily? I'll go and grab some." She turned to run back to the store at the end of the block.

Carter stayed her by grasping her wrist. "Gracie, I need you to assign posts to the residents."

Gracie bent down, her face close to Wyatt. "I threw a couple of cans of Whisp in there," she said with a self-deprecating smile. "Oh, they had that new Whisp-flavored juice pack too. You can stick those in your pockets …"

"That's enough, Grace," Carter said.

Wyatt patted her hand.

"You know how I feel about that poison …" she continued.

"Gracie," Carter interrupted her, his voice exasperated. "They'll be back before nightfall."

Gracie opened her mouth to say something, and Wyatt said, "I'll be home for dinner, Mom. Make something good. Besides," he added with a grimace. "He's making us take Damon Thayer."

Wyatt watched her glance from Damon to him and then his ragtag group of friends.

She mouthed the words, *Love you*, her bottom lip trembling, then ran into the darkened doorway of the VFW hall.

Keisha broke apart the packaging holding the flat packets of flavored drinks and made everyone slide one in their shirt pocket or hoodie.

"You know we still have to have that talk," Wyatt said as he watched his mother return to the hall.

"You've got the extra shotgun?" Carter said as though he hadn't spoken.

"Yup. Can I use the siren?" Wyatt asked with a grin.

"Not unless you want to arrest somebody," Carter replied.

Howard Drucker stuck his head out the window. "We can arrest people?"

Carter's hand covered the entire top of Howard's head as he pushed it back into the interior of the car.

"No, don't draw unnecessary attention to yourself. Don't let anyone take the car. Stay in pairs."

Wyatt glanced at Damon. "We can't, got one too many."

"Damon will be fine. You." He pointed to the teens in the car. "Remember to stay together. Find Sebastian Espinoza. *Him,* you can trust. Ask him to notify the authorities that we are okay here."

Wyatt nodded.

"You know, I'm not happy about sending you," Carter said after a long pause. "But, you're the only person, well people," he said, acknowledging the others, "I trust to get the job done?"

Wyatt patted the gun resting on the console.

Carter tapped the roof with his good hand and said, "Get going."

Wyatt looked at the freeway, his face resolute. "I know what we have to do and when I get back ..."

"Just get back, Wyatt, and I promise we will discuss L.A."

"L.A.? You mean Los Angeles?" Howard shouted. "What are you talking about, Wy? What's going on in L.A.?"

Wyatt pulled out of the parking space and headed down Western Boulevard toward the interstate. He reached up, readjusting his rearview mirror, catching sight of Jade's eyes watching him. She stood on the steps of the VFW hall, looking tiny and lost. She raised a hand to wave to him, but Wyatt turned his eyes to the road ahead.

Chapter 10

"Line 'em up … line 'em up …" Igor repeated the words in his head, sweat pouring down his crooked body. He was exhausted, but couldn't stop. Vincent depended on him. He stood, his hand on his lower back. Igor would work for Vincent until he collapsed. He asked again if he could speak to Nate, but Vincent said they had to have radio silence for now.

The sun baked them, even though temporary canvas tents had been set up covering large swaths of the park. A new army of soldiers had arrived, filling the streets of Monsterland. They were dressed in protective gear, covered from head to toe, showing only their eyes, each sporting a Federation Forces badge on the right side of their chest proclaiming them to be part of Vincent's new army.

Their mouths and noses were shielded because of the horrible smell that hung in the air like a living thing. Igor smirked, even though they were in the desert. The areas under the tents had a weird humidity, like a layer of mold in the air. It might be from all the decaying flesh, he reasoned. Either way, he wasn't as hot as the others in their anti-contamination suits.

No, sirree. He didn't need a suit. He wasn't afraid of a few zombie germs. *What's it going to do,* he chuckled to himself, *turn me into a zombie?* Looking overhead, he waved a hand at the circling vultures. "Away, you scavengers." He shook his fist at them. "No food for you! Or you." He brushed a black cluster of flies from the face of a zombie.

The army bulldozed the dead into mass graves. Even though many of the victims had lost their heads in the battle, they were still squirming. The graves seemed to writhe like maggots on a dead animal. Every so often, a hand would jerk up, fist clenched, the legs twitching. It unnerved Vincent's little soldier boys. A few had fainted. One dropped dead from a heart attack. They didn't bury him, just left his corpse in one of the piles that were filling the tents for the next phase of what only Frasier seemed to know.

Frasier strutted around their new compound, a smug look on his face, almost gloating at Igor who was knee-deep in guts and gore. He kept waving and pointing his cane as he directed people to all the stations set up around the park.

Igor stood, straightening a kink in his back. He could use that cane right now. He looked at it, his eyes narrowing. The grounds were looking like a giant checkerboard of cadavers. Igor considered the rows of decomposing zombies. The doctor was planning something. *What the hell could he do with these useless sacks of humanity?* He pulled another body from the pit. *Germ warfare,* he shrugged. It had to be something like that. He couldn't wait to show his and Vincent's accomplishments to his Nate. Rule the world, they were going to do it together, and now Igor wouldn't have to hide in the shadows anymore.

Igor felt the heat of a gaze boring into his shoulders. He swiveled to catch Frasier staring at him with contempt. He propped the shovel on the top layer of bodies, then casually leaned his arm on the handle.

"You have a problem with me, Doctor?" he asked.

Frasier cleared his throat. "Me? You think I even noticed you?"

"It doesn't matter if you notice me, as long as Vincent knows I'm here for him. Yes, me and my boy, Nate."

Frasier snickered with contempt, "That's rich. You and your boy, Nate. Go back to work, you old goblin."

Around him, he saw soldiers exchanging looks, their shoulders shaking as if they knew a private joke.

Igor's face stung with embarrassment. He turned to scrape

away the mounds of dirt. He hit the shovel hard into the soft bodies under the layers of soil. Losing himself once again to the labor, he had to admit the smell was epic. The coyotes howled from the hills, causing many of the soldiers to look around nervously.

"Just a bunch of coyotes," he assured them, feeling superior once again. "Harmless, nothing like the wolves—I mean the werewolves." A ripple of nervousness went through the crowd. "You want a good fright, head in there." He pointed his shovel at the darkened hotel that was cordoned off by a metal fence from the rest of the park.

"Don't listen to him," Frasier yelled. "He's nothing. A nobody."

Igor grinned evilly at the doctor, and then shook his head, "Pretentious elitist moron." *His day will come.* He decided to go back to excavating. The only person he wanted to make happy was Vincent, and if digging up rotting corpses pleased Vincent, that was what he was going to do.

"Dig 'em out and line 'em up!" yelled Frasier.

Igor dug into the next layer with relish.

"Line 'em up … line 'em up …" he sang to himself, pulling out corpses of dead zombies, their skin flaking off in his hands until all he was holding were bones attached to sinew. He held up a shin bone hanging by the meniscus to a kneecap that rattled when he shook it.

"Hey," Igor called out. He was ignored. All around him, the steady hum of four-by-fours filled his ears. Vincent's industrious army of well-paid mercenaries kept busy cleaning the mess that was Monsterland. People scurried with determination across the small area where he worked, pulling bodies from the mass grave. *Vincent is a genius,* Igor thought. He would be the yard-stick for all future measuring of megalomaniac world conquerors.

Igor looked around for the doctor in whom Vincent put all his trust. He sniffed loudly. Frasier may have designed the machine to reanimate Vincent's head, but whatever his talents, he couldn't fix Igor's body. He couldn't make a hump disappear. He could only imagine what horror they were dreaming up with all these contaminated bodies.

"Hey, Frasier." He waggled the shin bone. "You want 'em like this or do they have to have more skin on 'em?"

Frasier looked at him clinically, as if he were an insect under a microscope. Igor squirmed, the slimy bone heavy in his hand. The doctor had a way of making him feel like a science experiment.

"Take them all, Igor. Take them all."

Igor frowned as he stood in the open grave, surrounded by hundreds of decomposing bodies. The theme park was filled with healthy and straight-backed workers who were walking purposefully to and from the different stations that had been set up.

"A little help here!" Igor called.

Frasier nodded, motioning for a group to slide into the grave to pull the bodies from the next layer.

Igor went back to his song, happier to have extra sets of hands dragging the plague victims into long rows, where another soldier appeared, holding a tablet, taking a picture and cataloging the corpses.

Beyond the walls of the theme park, a beast howled again. The soldiers looked up, shifting uncomfortably.

"I told you, it's just a coyote. All the werewolves are dead."

"Not the wild wolves," a soldier responded.

Igor sidled up to him, looking at his face from his shorter position. "I explained to you *all the werewolves are dead*. Wolves are just stupid little dogs with a warmer coat. Frightened, are you? Of a little wolf, you big, bad thing?" He wagged the shin bone at him. "The wolves are afraid of us now. They're all hiding. Vincent killed their brethren, and they ran off." He started to laugh at the look of horror on the young soldier's face.

Frasier added, "You heard what the little goblin said. All the werewolves are dead." Frasier conferred with another man, then jumped into a golf cart.

Igor watched him disappear as they drove to the entrance of Vincent's tunnel. With Frasier gone, he felt better already. He looked around at the workers slowly pulling the corpses from the grave. They had to get moving, he thought, or Vincent would get angry. The sooner he finished, the sooner he'd be able to share everything with Natie-boy. He couldn't wait to tell him about his day.

Igor repeated what Frasier had said. It made a nice new song for him, and he tried it with a melody, *"You heard what he said. All the werewolves are dead. You heard what he said. All the werewolves are dead."*

There, he said to himself, *that ought to get them moving.*

Chapter 11

The road was deserted. Wyatt drove, keeping his speed over sixty, little chance he was going to get a ticket. *Besides,* he thought smugly, *who was pulling over a police car?* The inside of the car was quiet. Nobody spoke much. In the back, Keisha and Howard stared at each other as if they were starving. They sat closely together, every part of their bodies touching. Damon moved as far from them as he could, silently watching out of the open window. He seemed to have no use for any of them, only answered in primal grunts.

Wyatt heard Keisha clear her throat. She turned to the desolate landscape and said dramatically, "I feel like Persephone being dragged down deep into hell."

Howard Drucker gazed at Keisha the way a parched man stared at a bottle of water and responded, "I think you're more like Athena, Goddess of Wisdom."

"What the hell are you talking about?" Damon muttered.

"Oh, Keisha and her Greek gods," said Howard. "She loves all those Greek gods."

"What's wrong with Greek gods?" Keisha replied. "They're a lot more colorful and smarter than your stupid vampires." She added a teasing smile to soften her opinion.

Howard searched for something, anything to defend his

vampires, but after the Monsterland debacle, he couldn't think of a single thing.

Keisha smirked and said, "It's okay, Howard Drucker. I'll find you an interesting Greek deity to admire."

Wyatt glanced over at Lily, her dark eyes watching the horizon, the wind from the slightly opened window blowing her hair across her mouth. Wyatt's eyes kept going back to her lips. She turned to face him, her long fingers capturing the wild strands of hair and rolling them into a loose bun, putting it behind her head with a rubber band she dug from her pocket.

"I never saw you much at school," Wyatt said to her.

"I'm on a work program," Lily told him. "I am … I mean, I was only there for the first three periods. I work at my uncle's market on the reservation."

"Your uncle is John Raven?" Keisha asked from her spot in the back seat. Wyatt observed she had managed to tear herself from contemplating Howard's pale face. Wyatt watched the two girls size each other up.

"Yeah, so?"

"I read he's an important man in the tribe," Keisha said.

Lily shrugged. "Everybody's important."

Keisha snorted. "Some are more important than others. There's a legend about him."

"A legend?" Howard perked up.

"Nothing. It's all nonsense." Lily looked out the window again. "You're confusing the facts with your mythical Greek gods."

"No, it's not," Keisha insisted. "I heard a story. He's called the *teller of secrets*, you know, like the medicine man or shaman."

"Shaman?" Wyatt asked.

Lily shook her head. "My uncle owns the grocery store; he's not a medicine man. You don't understand our beliefs. The Mohave religion is based on animism. They believe … we believe that Matevilya transformed himself into a fish eagle. You're getting the story mixed up."

"Who's Matevilya?" Wyatt asked.

"Their supreme creator," Howard supplied. "You know, God."

"Right," Wyatt said, rolling his eyes. "After what we saw at Monsterland, I don't know what to believe in anymore."

"Yeah, well, you're confusing reality with fantasy. It's all a big myth," Lily retorted.

Keisha bristled, then said, "I researched dreaming is the source of their power. They go on spiritual journeys."

"Yes," Howard added. "They put themselves into a trance in order to be guided by the spirits."

"Yeah, yeah, the Navajo have their skinwalkers, the Mohave tribe have shapeshifters. They eat peyote and other hallucinogenic things. My uncle dances around covered in raven feathers, so what?" Lily responded.

Damon seemed totally uninterested in their discussion but grumbled, "I can use some peyote myself right now." He tapped his fingers on the backseat.

"Your uncle is a medicine man," Wyatt said. "Like a doctor?"

"No, a shaman," Keisha corrected. "It's like a priest."

"Wait a minute," Howard interrupted. He pushed his glasses up his thin nose. "Your uncle is *that* John Raven?"

"That's what I've been trying to tell you! They say some Natives can take on the persona of a specific animal and shapeshift," Keisha added.

"Shapeshifting." Wyatt exchanged a look with Howard in the rearview mirror. He knew they were both thinking of Melvin. "Do you believe in shapeshifting, Lily?"

"You mean like a person becoming a werewolf?" Lily asked, her eyebrows raised.

"I don't consider that to be exactly shapeshifting in the truest sense. It's involuntary." Howard shook his head. "I'm talking about changing your body at will or by using magic."

"You don't think when a person transforms from human to werewolf is not shapeshifting, Howard Drucker? That is just about the dumbest thing you've ever said." Keisha laughed. "They're both shapeshifting."

"Keisha," Howard said patiently. "Shapeshifters are creatures that are either born or taught how to change their appearance. Some can only morph into one kind of animal, and others are so developed they can do multiple creatures. It's a common mistake to confuse them with werewolves."

"Don't go there, Howard Drucker. You're bordering dangerously close to condescension." Keisha folded her arms across her chest.

"Keisha, is this our first fight?" Howard asked.

Keisha clicked her tongue and shook her head no. "I agree to disagree until further evidence."

"I remember reading they have the ability to transform parts of their body," Wyatt added.

"Okay," Damon interrupted. "Call me the next time you see a bird walking around with a human head. You're a bunch of knuckleheads."

"I can think of some people who resemble the hind parts of the animal, and they don't have to shapeshift into anything at all," Keisha said, her eyes resting on Damon.

"Just because you haven't seen it, doesn't mean it can't exist," Lily said, her voice soft. "The legends say that shapeshifters can change at will." She shrugged, and Wyatt thought she was pretty, the way the wind was blowing her hair. Her dark eyes were serious.

"They can't control that," Wyatt said.

"It's just some old stories the elders repeat to make people feel more special about themselves." Lily dismissed the subject. "It's not any more magic than parting the water of the Red Sea."

"Hey," Damon interrupted. "Moses really did that. I saw it in the movies."

"Hardly," Howard said, ignoring Damon. "Meditation. Magic. Wishful thinking. It's found in dozens of cultures worldwide. I don't care what you call it. It's real."

Damon slumped back into his corner, visibly stewing.

Wyatt knew in the silence that followed, his friends were thinking of Melvin.

"It's not like that," Lily said.

"Then what's it like?" Keisha challenged.

Howard went on, oblivious to the tension between the two girls. "They say, that ... her people, you know, the shamans ... are connected to the cosmos and bring back messages ..."

"Messages from whom?" Wyatt asked.

Lily looked away. "From the gods," she murmured. "It's the old legends. We are just an unfortunate group of people with an intolerance to sugar and a high death rate from diabetes. How could anyone like that have a connection to greater beings?" Her voice had an edge of sarcasm.

"How, indeed?" Keisha asked under her breath.

Wyatt looked out the rearview mirror at the long ribbon of road behind them. He squinted.

"What is it?" Damon demanded, becoming alert.

"I see something behind us. But it's far away."

Damon twisted in his seat. Wyatt heard him curse softly. "Step on it," Damon ordered, his hands moving to pick up the gun resting between his legs. "Put more distance between us."

Chapter 12

The bodies were laid out in rows next to each other. Overhead, buzzards circled. Every so often, a guard took a shot at one, killing the large birds before they could pick at the bones of the plague victims. The sun beat down on the putrid flesh, creating a toxic mix of odors that might have felled a normal person. Igor had stopped being normal years ago, so it didn't affect him. Frasier had returned to watch from a platform far enough away to escape the miasma hanging over the broken streets of Monsterland.

Igor wiped the sweat from his forehead with a filthy rag. "How is Vincent?"

Frasier ignored him. Igor repeated his question.

The doctor looked down at him contemptuously.

"It's a simple question," Igor said with a smile, revealing a mouthful of gray teeth.

"He's resting, building strength," Frasier said at last. "Go back to bringing out the bodies. It's late." The doctor's eyes followed the narrow highway in the distance; then he looked at his watch impatiently.

"What are you looking for? You keep staring at the freeway like you're expecting someone." Igor walked halfway up the steps of the platform to peer at the highway. "Is something coming from Vincent's headquarters?"

"You ask too many questions."

"I have a right to know," Igor said. "You'd still be looking for his head if not for me. You'd be weeks behind."

"There've been reports of gangs taking over the highways, demanding ransom, hanging bodies from the road signs as a warning to anyone entering their territory."

"Gangs?" Igor laughed. "There are no gangs anymore. Nate took care of them and sent them all to prison."

Frasier stopped watching the roadway, smiling down at Igor with an evil grin.

"How do you know what's happening? You've been locked up in Monsterland for weeks."

"I know my son has everything under control. Gangs were suppressed. Most ended up as zombies anyway."

"Well." Frasier poked Igor in the chest with the blunt end of his cane, forcing him to move backward off the steps. Igor felt himself stumble, his foot catching on a skull, his boot crushing it, brains and fluid pooling around his feet. "Maybe regular people are fed up with your son and his government. Maybe people are taking it into in their own hands."

Igor looked up shocked. "How can that be happening? It's been almost a month. My son …"

Frasier looked at him with distaste. "You don't even know what's going on out there. It's chaos … Until we get Vincent sorted out and in charge, we are going to have to let bedlam reign."

"You're crazy," Igor shot back, spit flying everywhere. "Nate has the army, the navy, the air force at his disposal."

"What am I doing talking to a goblin?" Frasier said. "I have a job to do, and I am waiting … ah … and here they are."

A convoy of trucks with no identifiable markings snaked its way down the main artery leading into Monsterland.

Frasier looked down at Igor. "I don't have time to talk to you now. The troops are here. I have work to do."

Igor stared at the trucks quizzically. They were unfamiliar to him. "That's not the army." He pointed to the unmarked vehicles. "My son will provide you with all the manpower you need."

Frasier looked at him, his mouth twisting in a parody of a smile, then said softly, "Your son is dead."

"What?"

"Your son. The president. He's dead. The army took control of the government last night."

"You're lying!"

"Ha!" Frasier laughed. "Washington's been destroyed. There's nothing left. A new provisional government has been created in Omaha."

"Nebraska?" Igor whispered.

"No, Omaha, Ohio, you idiot! Of course, Nebraska. Where else would you have them go?" he demanded. "We march there tomorrow night. That's if you finish doing your end of the deal. Line 'em up!" He placed both hands on his hips, his face gleeful as he gazed at the piles of decaying humanity lying like a carpet across the grounds. "I say, line 'em up!"

Igor threw down his shovel, his face twisting with anger. He ran to the opening of the tunnels, feeling a stitch in his side. He didn't care. His son, Nate, the president. *He couldn't be dead!* Vincent promised them both great things; they were going to rule the world, right at his side. Vincent would have told him if Nate was dead.

His breath sobbed as he ran in the dank tunnel. His arms flailed wildly, his feet slamming against the concrete.

The room where he had brought Vincent was teeming with people, most of them in protective suits. Igor burst breathlessly into the cavernous lab, sprinting as fast as his leg allowed.

"Vincent, why didn't you tell me?" he cried out, his filthy hands flat on the railing surrounding the giant wheel upon which Vincent's head was attached.

Vincent's eyes were closed, as though he was resting, the colored glass panels glowing mauve below him. Their polished glass reflected onto Vincent's cheeks, so they had the flush of life on them.

All activity in the room stopped; a hush swept over the space. There was a mechanized whir as the base spun in a lazy circle.

Igor's eyes followed the movement, feeling lightheaded and dizzy.

"Stop!" Igor urged, his hands gripping the partition. "Vincent, tell me it's not true."

The base upon which the head rested ground to a halt. Igor

looked up, noticing a wall of glass tubes. He watched as a purple foamy substance rose from the bottom of the tubes. Vincent's face looked euphoric. The dark bullet holes for eyes opened lazily. The head rotated on its stand, looking directly at Igor.

"What do you want?" the mechanized voice demanded.

"My son! Nate, President Nate," Igor said.

"Leave us," Vincent's metallic voice spoke with deadly calm. Soldiers paused but didn't leave their posts.

"I said leave us!" he screamed, the voice echoing off the rock walls.

The workers all looked at each other.

"Now!"

Quickly, paperwork was placed on work surfaces, and the team of scientists left the room.

Vincent's calm face moved in a half circle, making sure they were alone. The face turned to examine Igor as if he were a specimen. There was no sympathy or warmth in its features. "It was over in an instant."

"What, no!" Igor screamed, falling to his knees. "You promised he'd be safe. We had a deal; we had a deal!"

"I didn't anticipate the coup. It doesn't matter. I will retake control from here. This is Plan B."

Igor watched Vincent's mouth move, heard the monotone response, his face filled with disbelief. He searched the cold eyes, looking for warmth, friendship … or even pity. His heart lay heavy in his chest, his hands shook. "Nate was to be president in Plan B," Igor said, his voice sounding like a child's.

"Plans change," Vincent said in his robotic voice.

Igor cradled his face as he sobbed, his heart broken. He dragged himself from the room, not caring about Vincent or his new plan. He wanted to crawl into a cave and die.

Chapter 13

Wyatt shifted in his seat, the gun bulky under his thigh. He had placed it there as a precaution when he saw the car miles behind them.

It was an Acura SUV, silver, a regular family car. He didn't feel threatened by it. It was like any other car in Southern California, but he still wanted to feel the security of the weapon.

He squinted into the rearview mirror. It wasn't driving fast, but it appeared to be following him at a steady clip.

Wyatt changed lanes, then watched the car do the same lane change. He looked at the deserted road ahead of him. The area was devoid of life, no movement. Not even animals. It was eerily silent.

They drove with the windows open. Wyatt wanted to conserve gas just in case they had a problem. The hot air gusted through the car, buffeting them.

He heard Lily's cry of dismay as they passed a road sign riddled with bullets. He looked up, gulping when he realized there were three bodies swinging upside down under the sign. Each was tethered to the sign by their booted feet. Blackbirds flapped around them. One was perched on the dead man's chin, feasting on his skin.

"Are those real? I feel like I'm stuck in a bad dystopian movie on cable." Howard's voice sounded strangely high.

"Holy crap," Keisha whispered, then covered her eyes.

The rest stared at the trio of hanging men, all in jeans, their shirttails flapping, the bellies hanging flabbily. Their arms dangled; one of them was so tall, his long fingers grazed the dry grasses.

"Execution style," Lily said.

"What?" Keisha asked.

"They've been murdered. Shot in the head as if it were an execution. I've seen drug stuff like this up on the reservation."

Wyatt slowed the car to a crawl, all of them peering at the neat bullet hole in the corpses' heads as if they had a third eye. "This is crazy ... Why would they hang them like this, like laundry?"

Keisha cleared her throat with a loud gulp that bordered on a sob. "I've read about this in some of the ancient civilizations. It's a warning."

Wyatt's stomach contracted into a hard knot. They craned their necks to see the corpses, except for Keisha, who had now hidden her head in Howard's shoulder.

"What kind of ..." Wyatt paused as the roar of a powerful engine behind him froze the words in his mouth. The vehicle peeled onto the highway from a hill. It was a vintage sports car.

It was old. Wyatt observed the turquoise color of the Thunderbird following them. It was a coupe made in ... he guessed 1957. Wyatt watched it in the rearview mirror. The passengers were clean-cut, like the guys he'd seen earlier in the day cruising through the town, non-threatening looking. Like a couple of dudes out for an afternoon drive, which meant they shouldn't be a problem. He didn't realize he'd spoken it out loud until Lily answered.

"Didn't your mother tell you not to judge a book by its cover?"

"Yeah," he responded. "But that was for, you know, people who deserved it."

"You're an idiot," she told him. Lily twisted around. Her breath caught when she looked out the window to catch the car speed up in what was developing into a chase. They kept a steady distance, but Wyatt felt as if they were crowding Carter's cruiser.

Wyatt narrowed his eyes. "Nothing to worry about, I think." He pressed the gas pedal anyway, making the car speed up.

"Are you kidding me?" Damon growled.

"What, he's wearing a golf shirt and a watch. I think it's even a Rolex," he said, spotting the driver's arm resting on the door of the car by the window. "He looks like a lawyer or something." His words trailed off as the car sped up, tapping the cruiser lightly in the rear. "Hey!" Wyatt depressed the gas, increasing their speed, his eyes opening wider when the car behind them did the same.

"I don't like this," Howard whispered in the tense silence of the car. "That's just plain weird."

The vehicle was almost on top of them, their bumpers nearly touching.

"Can't you make this thing go any faster, Baldwin?" Damon sneered.

"It might not mean anything," Wyatt said. "Who says these are the bad guys? Maybe they feel threatened by us, and they don't like strangers near their town."

"Yeah, they could be an escort to make sure we don't stop here," Howard offered.

"We don't know if they are the ones that killed those people." Even though Wyatt said it, he was having a hard time believing it. He didn't know if he was saying it to make the others feel better or to reassure himself.

"No wonder Carter asked me to babysit!" Damon yelled. "They got onto the highway in the middle of an exit, and they've been eating asphalt as soon as they noticed us. What do you think that means, they want to exchange recipes?"

The car behind them, the Acura, picked up speed as though it was turbocharged, coming abreast of the Thunderbird. Both cars hugged the cruiser's tail.

Four more cars closed on them, seemingly from nowhere. A brand-new BMW, a Subaru wagon, a very expensive Jeep, and a silver Volvo, all in pristine shape. Wyatt turned to see each car was filled with well-groomed people, their hair neat, but oddly their eyes held them with a menacing stare. Wyatt glanced nervously at the growing number of cars surrounding them. Feeling hemmed in, he resisted the urge to close the windows. He had seen every desert dystopian movie under the sun, and he sure as hell didn't remember any Beamers.

"They look like … wait a second, I know that guy," Howard gasped.

Just then, the first shot rang out. Keisha shouted in a horrified voice, "Are they shooting at us?"

"Move over!" Damon started to climb over the front seat. "I'll take over."

Wyatt gripped the wheel with two hands, his foot punching the gas pedal to the floor. "Sit back; I can't see. You're blocking my view!"

"You don't need to see outta the rear," Damon yelled reaching for the front of the car as if he were going to climb over.

Lily elbowed Damon's chest, pushing him backward.

"Step on it, Wyatt." Lily aimed the shotgun out the window, taking a bead on the intruders.

The bores of six shotguns from the car beside them were aimed at the windows of Wyatt's cruiser.

"Duck!" Keisha screamed, grabbing Howard by his shirt, pushing him down on the seat. The entire back windshield exploded in a shower of glass.

The Thunderbird was hugging their tail bumper. Wyatt looked in the rearview mirror, his stomach moving to his gullet. A big dude, wearing dark glasses and a fat cigar dangling from his mouth, was standing in the back seat of the convertible with a semi-automatic rifle. *Apparently, he ascribes to the casual Friday style of clothes when terrorizing the freeways,* Wyatt thought, on the edge of hysteria, noting he looked slightly different from the others. He seemed decidedly seedier. The wind plastered his mouth into an evil smile.

Wyatt made eye contact with the driver of the car for an instant. He had a wicked grin on his face as well. The man gave a friendly wink, then appeared to shout something to the guy standing in the back seat.

With a flick, the big one threw the lit cigar into the brush. Wyatt watched as the sparks landed, igniting a cluster of tumbleweed.

Wyatt looked back at the man standing in the car following

them, realizing the gun was pointed directly at his head. He knew he had to get out of his line of sight.

Wyatt swerved the car, the tires screeching loudly. His spine pressed back into the seat as shots exploded around them, shattering the front window, more glass raining down on them. The car jerked spasmodically.

Wyatt's gun slid onto the floor of the car. There was a stinging pain, and Wyatt felt the skin of his cheek split. He turned the wheel. The car's tires screeched, throwing them all against each other in the back seat. Wyatt fought with the wheel, regaining control of the steering once again. He managed to put some space between them and the Thunderbird.

"Why are they attacking us?" Keisha yelled.

"There's more of them," Lily said.

They all twisted to look back to see at least fourteen more cars speeding down the interstate.

"They must have modified the engines," Howard stated. "They appear to be picking up speed. I estimate they are traveling at about one hundred and twenty miles per hour. At that rate of acceleration, they should intercept us in …" He stopped to calculate, and another shot rang out. "Five seconds."

Damon cursed. Howard counted the pursuers, his mouth moving silently.

"Never mind that, it's fourteen to one," Keisha told him. "We're outnumbered fourteen to one."

"I think you're wrong. I estimate thirteen point six …"

A bunch of bullets whizzed past them.

Damon yelled, "Shut up, you two! Either way, we're dead!"

Wyatt turned around for a second, his face wild. "What are you waiting for? Start shooting!"

Damon pumped his shotgun, blasting away, while Lily leaned halfway out the window, trying to pick off the guy with the semi-automatic.

"Aim for the tires," Wyatt urged, sweat pouring down his face, stinging the wound on his cheek.

The Jeep approached the Thunderbird. The two cars moved to be side by side.

Wyatt gripped the wheel, afraid to lose control. This car

could fly. He felt as though he glided above the asphalt. He had never driven so fast.

The desert sped past him. He bit his lower lip, drawing blood, never even realizing he was holding his breath.

The car filled with the roar of multiple engines. Motorcycles leaped over the small hills running parallel to the freeway, driven by a bunch of bald-headed men.

Where are they all coming from? Wyatt thought. They weren't the scary kind of bald guys, just guys that were losing their hair. They could have been his neighbors. *What's going on?* Ordinary people didn't act this way.

"I know I know that guy," Howard kept repeating, as if it would jog his memory. "I just can't ... oh, my God. That's the guy; that lawyer on TV in those commercials, Brightman, Billingsly, and Buford. You know, 'Had a crash? We'll get you cash!'"

"Shut up," Damon screamed.

Wyatt saw that the sky was black with smoke behind them, the careless cigar having ignited the dry bushes of the desert. The winds were whipping and fanning the flames. He considered turning around. With a glance at the unlikely gang following him, he figured maybe it wouldn't be a good choice. He couldn't jump the concrete median to get to the eastbound lane. He moved his foot on the floor of the car, trying to find the Glock that had fallen there. He was afraid to lose control if he reached for it.

Wyatt squinted, trying to see their faces. The bikers all wore bowling shirts like they were in a league. *This is nuts!* he thought.

The bowling team on the bikes were armed to the teeth, he saw with dismay.

"I think that guy is my dentist," Keisha said to no one in particular.

"They're the welcoming wagon," Damon spat. "Who do you think they are?"

They were older, their faces impassive. They communicated with hand signals, Howard noted with interest. "They seem well-rehearsed, like they've done this before."

"Enough with the commentary! Shoot, damn it, Howard, shoot!" A burst of bullets ricocheted around them.

A rider came close to the driver's side, his face inches from Keisha. She noticed he was raising a .357 Magnum point blank.

Keisha screamed. Howard leaned forward, his arm protectively blocking Keisha. He pointed his gun, blasting the rider into oblivion.

Wyatt saw Howard wince, then grab his shoulder. "Howard!" he yelled.

"Ow, ow, ow," Howard wailed.

"Howard, where are you hit?" Keisha cried out.

"My shoulder. The gun's recoil punched me in the shoulder."

Wyatt let out the breath he had been holding. Lily leaned out her window, her face set. She took careful aim and picked off the tire of the Thunderbird. It burst with a loud bang, and everyone in Wyatt's car cheered. The man standing with the semi-automatic tipped backward, his arms windmilling, the gun flying out of his grip. He lost his balance, bouncing from the back seat onto the highway with a thud.

His weapon, meanwhile, continued to skitter across the blacktop, connecting with a speeding bike, unseating the rider when it hit the front wheel. Wyatt heard tires scream. The Thunderbird was moving diagonally across the road, the driver struggling with the steering.

It smashed into the Jeep, rebounding hard against it, then flipped to land on the other side. Wyatt watched the tires continuing to spin, and he depressed the gas pedal to put more distance between them.

Damon, meanwhile, was shooting out of the back window. Wyatt saw the Jeep zigzagging across the road, evading the blast of the gun.

Wyatt was so busy watching the action behind him, he didn't notice the road signs. He looked out at the vast landscape without any idea of where he was. It all looked the same. He searched for a landmark, but the drab scenery was a monotonous palette of dun and gray. All he could hear was the thundering of the motorcycle engines as they ate up the distance.

He kept moving the car from one side of the road to the other. Lily was hanging out of the window like she was drunk and it was spring break. He heard her gun going off. A Toyota minivan pulled up, hitting the side of his car.

"I feel like I'm drag racing against my grandfather," Lily said.

"Where'd they come from?" Keisha cried. "They're all over the place. What do they want from us?"

Wyatt groped for the gun, which was now lodged under the brake. His hand throbbed with pain, his nearly healed cut had split open. The car swerved dangerously.

Damon ordered, "Pay attention to the road!"

"They got on at Pecos." Lily aimed again, one eye closed, her hair flying around her face. "They don't need an excuse. There's no law right now. It's like the Wild West."

Keisha looked at Lily, then copied her position, leaning out of the window. Narrowing her eyes, she took aim, hitting the minivan, screaming with satisfaction when its windshield evaporated in a hail of glass.

"Good one," Lily told her.

Howard had his weapon sticking out of the glassless rear window, the bumpy ride making his shot go wild.

"Watch out," Lily warned.

The Jeep slammed into them. Wyatt felt the car fishtail. They spun in a complete circle, Lily's gun flying out of her hands to crash through the Toyota's windshield like a javelin. It hit a female driver in the head, ruining her perfect hair, then exploded with a shot that blew a hole into the passenger.

Wyatt recovered so fast his hands were numb. He turned the wheel and pressed the pedal all the way down. The car seemed to burn the asphalt, then rocketed like a bat out of hell. The caravan behind him took off after them.

"I hate minivans," Lily said breathlessly.

"You're bleeding." Keisha gestured to Lily's shoulder. Lily pulled the flannel from her arm, sliding onto her seat.

"Are you okay?" Wyatt shouted at her, taking his eyes off the road for a minute. She was pale as a ghost.

"It grazed me, but man, it hurts."

Keisha groped for her hoodie and threw it to Lily. "Use the sleeve to stop the blood."

Then she pointed her gun at a motorcycle with two riders coming abreast of their car. The passenger was holding a sawed-off shotgun aimed at the back of Wyatt's head. Keisha gave a feral scream as she fired, the man's hand dissolving in a shower of blood and bone. The driver's eyes opened wide, and now he was the one screaming as he lost control of the bike. They watched it do a double flip into a ditch on the side of the road, both riders flying through the air as if they were shot from a cannon.

Damon, Keisha and Howard leaned out the back window, peppering the Jeep with a barrage of bullets. The Jeep went out of control, hitting a sign that broke in half, slamming into the roof of the vehicle and collapsing the bikini top. All they saw as they followed the next turn was the smoking heap of metal.

Wyatt glanced at the dash; he was flying at over one hundred twenty-five miles per hour. Any faster and they'd be traveling back to 1985. His hands held the wheel in a death grip.

"I'm out of ammo," Damon yelled.

"I have two rounds left," Howard said. "That guy is finished. I think we are done."

"Take this," Keisha said, handing out what was left of her bullets.

Lily groped on the floor, her hands blindly trying to locate the Glock, but it evaded her grasp. "Can you kick it?" she urged, wincing as she stretched her arm.

Wyatt used his other foot to push it closer to her. Her fingers scrabbled on the floor, but the gun now slid toward the left-hand side of the car. Lily cursed.

"We're not out of the woods yet," Damon said. Behind them were a row of bikes and a truck barreling down at least one hundred miles per hour. The truck had a steel barrier reinforcement on its front bumper. They all knew bullets would bounce harmlessly off its solid surface.

"What do they want from us?" Wyatt pressed the pedal so that it hit the floor.

"Directions?" Lily said smugly.

Keisha smiled at her from her spot in the corner of the car.

"Eleven o'clock," Howard yelled. Two guns moved to the right, blasting the rider and his bike from existence.

"Faster, Wyatt," Damon said. "I can see the truck driver's unibrow."

"We're not going to outrun it. We're not going to make it!"

Wyatt screamed over the sound of a triumphant blast of the horn on the truck.

Bullets flew off the hood of the semi, the reinforced steel plate acting as a deflector. The car jolted sickeningly when the truck tapped the rear. It was going to crush them. The truck hit them again, with more force. Wyatt felt the cruiser's transmission groan.

"Shoot!" Wyatt yelled.

"With what? We are done!" Damon screamed back, the veins standing out on his neck.

"Wait." Keisha reached down, fumbling with the shopping bags. She tore through the packaging, coming up with handfuls of tiny cups of peanut butter.

"What? You're hungry?" Damon's eyes bulged from his head.

"Take them." She handed Lily and Damon several of the containers. She hauled up the stale rolls. "Throw them out the windows."

"You're kidding, right?" Damon asked.

"Watch!" Lily shouted, taking aim. She pitched her cup like a hockey puck. It hit a thickset biker in the eye. He screamed, grabbing his face. The bike twisted on the highway, three other motorcycles colliding with it.

Damon wound up his arm, throwing the peanut butter cup at the window of the semi. It splattered against the windshield like vomit. Cans of soda followed, exploding like grenades when they hit the truck, the paint fizzling and evaporating off the surface of the vehicle.

"Wow, and you drink that stuff, Wyatt," said Howard Drucker. "Think what it's doing to your …"

"Shut up," Damon yelled as he threw peanut butter cups out the window.

The driver of the semi turned on his wipers, smearing the sandwich spread across his windshield. It covered the entire window with an oily film. The truck started to weave across the two lanes.

They jumped to their knees on the backseat, lobbing the small snack containers at their pursuers.

"Aim for the wheels!" Lily shouted. Both Lily and Keisha

started tossing stale rolls at the moving motorcycles, who swerved to avoid the missiles.

Keisha chucked hers in a high arc. It was sucked into the momentum of a motorcycle wheel, causing it to flip forward.

"See what else is back there!" Wyatt shouted over the noise.

Lily popped open the glove compartment and tossed the car manual to Howard.

Howard began ripping out the pages, letting them fly into the faces of their pursuers.

He cheered when a sheet fastened itself onto a driver's face, causing him to slide into a ditch. "Got another one?"

Damon, meanwhile, took careful aim, flicking the peanut butter cups at the wheels of the bikes, watching in astonishment as a speeding rider was tossed like a rag doll when his motorcycle skidded on the sticky substance.

Wyatt's favorite jacket joined the projectiles and wound itself around the face of a driver of the Mini Cooper that joined the fray.

No matter what they threw, more pursuers joined in.

"Watch out!" Howard shouted, pulling Keisha down onto the seat.

A Mercedes pulled up next to them, a passenger leaning out the window. She was neck and neck with Wyatt, a sawed-off shotgun pointed directly at his head. Wyatt saw the details as if through a long lens; time seemed to stop. His hand groped the floor, his fingers locking onto the Glock. He could swear he heard the woman next to him laugh. Wyatt raised his hand, pumping out three shots in rapid succession. The Mercedes veered into him, apparently driverless now, the passenger half hanging out the window.

Wyatt's bloody hand made the gun feel slippery in his palm. The body hit Wyatt's knuckles, his other hand trying to keep control of the car. He felt the gun fly from his slick grip, smashing onto the freeway. He pulled away from the now out-of-control vehicle, looking up with dismay at the massive truck bearing down on them.

"There's nothing left," Keisha shouted. The truck was behind them again, the windshield smeared, the wipers furiously coating the peanut substance.

Wyatt looked to the right of the road, noticing one of the ramps used for runaway trucks. Pulling a hard right, he jumped the highway, and the cruiser accelerated up the ramp. Keisha turned around to watch them fly upwards, her eyes wide with fright. The motorcycles stayed on the highway, bypassing them, but the truck followed him up the steep incline.

Wyatt felt his car leap over the edge of the hill. There was the sensation of flying, followed by a teeth-jarring crash. Ducking instinctively, they watched the semi coming up fast behind them and then going airborne, the impetus of the heavy weight propelling it over the car to land with a loud crash. He heard the driver shouting something and watched, amazed, as the entire truck burst into flames.

"Move, Baldwin!" Damon bellowed. Blood dripped from a cut on his forehead.

Wyatt stepped on the gas, and the car's wheels spun in the dirt.

"Move!" he ordered.

"Don't you think I want to?" Wyatt snarled.

They saw the motorbikes swing around and circle back. There were three of them left.

Wyatt stamped his foot on the gas; nothing. Lily opened the door.

"Get out of the car," she urged. "Take cover on my side."

They scrambled out of the vehicle, crouching on the passenger side. Wyatt's nose twitched. He looked around, smelling gasoline.

"The fuel is leaking. We're going to be burned alive," Howard told them.

Wyatt looked around the sparse landscape but saw nothing. No rocks, no trees; they were out in the open. The sun burned them from above. Behind them in the distance, the desert was an inferno from the lit cigar.

Sweat dripped down his face. They all stared at each other grimly.

"Any ideas? I'm open to anything." Wyatt looked at Damon who shrugged.

"Once those gorillas come back here and start shooting, either we go out in a bonfire or like Leonidas," Howard said.

Lily looked around, her breath coming in little pants. "This sucks."

"Shhh," Keisha said, her finger to her mouth. All they heard was the crackle of the truck burning.

"The bikes, they're gone."

"Where'd they go?" Howard whispered. He leaned down to look under the car. Shaking his head, he spied three sets of dusty boots.

"Where'd they go?" They heard one of the bikers call out, echoing what Howard had said.

"Don't matter none. I smell gas," the biker laughed, taking out a semi-automatic. Wyatt watched in slow motion as he aimed at the oily puddle. Wyatt's breath caught in his throat; he closed his eyes.

"Look!" he heard one of the bikers yell.

A pack of coyotes, each the size of a baby elephant, jumped from the brush, attacking the three bikers. There had to be at least ten, Wyatt counted. He wondered for a minute if they were wolves, they were so big. It was like Monsterland all over again.

The coyotes tore off the arms of the marauders, blood spraying like a fountain to be soaked up by the dry earth. Their dying screams were cut off one by one as their throats were ripped out.

"What are we going to do when they finish with those three?" Howard moaned.

"They'll be satiated," Lily whispered. "We'll be all right."

"They are the appetizer," Howard informed her. "Look at the size of them; we'll be the main course."

Wyatt's eyes darted around. He wondered if they could outrun the coyotes.

"Don't even think about it." Howard shook his head. "Maybe we can set fire to the car to distract them. Anybody got any gunpowder left?"

"I never saw a coyote do anything like ..." Keisha said, then quieted, knowing they were all thinking about Monsterland and the werewolves. "Do you believe they're a hybrid?"

"Werewolves, or in this case, *coyotes*, always win," said a familiar voice.

Wyatt stood up. "Melvin?"

Chapter 14

Easy to claim a victory when all the vamps and zombies are dead," Howard said with a smile. He ran over to his friend, and they hugged awkwardly.

"I always said the werewolves would take it. King of the monsters, they have a special intuition. The vamps are too self-centered to think about anything besides themselves," Melvin responded, his hand on Howard's shoulder. His auburn hair was wild. He looked more relaxed than Wyatt had ever seen him. Though his stance was slightly aggressive, his face had a boyish charm Wyatt had never noticed. Melvin smiled.

Howard nodded. "I was totally surprised by the vamps' response to danger. All those years I went on and on about their superior intelligence. They were just plain stupid. However, I did learn they could …"

"Spare me, Howard Drucker, you should have been ashamed of your precious vamps. They … never mind." Melvin waved his hand as if he didn't want to talk about it anymore. "You have to admit, it was awesome," he said with amazement, his eyes shining. "I was never prouder of … well," he stuttered a bit. "They ripped the place to shreds. The vamps only cared about themselves, and the zombies were …"

"The zombies acted like zombies." Wyatt reached his two friends. "I'm so happy to see you. We were worried." He raised his fist in the air, ready for a triumphant fist bump, halted by the sound of an ominous growl.

"Stop, Carrie," Melvin ordered, his voice gruff. He pointed to a huge coyote standing by his leg. "She's a bit protective." He shrugged, his face reddening. "Puppy love." The giant beast did a tight circle and lay down close to Melvin's feet.

Wyatt looked at the creature, its snout covered in the blood from her kill. This was like no coyote he had ever seen. He opened his mouth to say something when he heard Lily gasp. "Are you okay?" he asked.

Keisha was binding Lily's wound with a ripped strip of fabric from her hoodie.

"I'm fine. It looks worse than it is," Lily said with a wan smile.

"It's topical," Keisha muttered. "Like your cheek." Her mouth was half full of fabric she was ripping.

Wyatt realized his cheek was stinging. He reached up to touch his face and felt a small cut. "Ow."

"A flesh wound. Lemme see your hand." She proceeded to peel the old bandage off, tightening a new piece of cleaner cloth around his hands. She finished by tying a knot so tight that it made his eyes water when she gave a final tug. "You'll do," she said with a smile.

Wyatt nodded his thanks, then turned to observe his red-haired friend. He looked like he was dressed in an assortment of articles stolen from multiple clotheslines.

Melvin's clothes were, well, not his. He wore overalls without a shirt, his skinny chest slightly burned from the sun. The were-wolf pendant hung around his thin neck, the emerald eyes winking in the light.

"What happened to you? Where have you been?" Wyatt and Howard peppered him with questions.

"Oh, here and there," Melvin said.

"Seriously?"

"Who is this?" Damon demanded, coming around them, then recognizing the third boy. "Oh. Melvin, what are you doing here?"

Melvin held out his hands wide. The pack of animals around him moved restlessly. He ruffled the fur behind the ears of the female who stood next to him. She looked up at him slavishly.

Everybody but Lily backed away from the wild animals.

"Do you talk to them?" Lily asked.

Melvin's eyes lowered to the ground shyly.

"I asked you what are you doing here?" Damon demanded.

"I live here now," Melvin answered. He looked at the canines, who all turned menacingly at Damon, their long fangs exposed. "With them."

"What are you, some kind of jungle boy?" Damon laughed at his joke. No one else responded.

"What happened after, you know, Monsterland?" Howard asked, ignoring Damon's taunting.

"I escaped."

"Did you hear about anything happening in Bakerton?" Wyatt sat down on a boulder. Melvin sat next to him on the ground. The beasts encircled him. Melvin looked down at them fondly, patting one, tickling another.

"Mel … what happened to you?"

Melvin shrugged.

Wyatt heard a series of sounds coming from the animals. *They couldn't be communicating,* he thought.

Melvin gave a guttural growl to his pack. One of the larger beasts huffed, then whined a response.

Melvin continued with his solitary chat; Wyatt turned and said, "Dude, you're weirding me out."

Melvin looked up at him, his face tilted, like … *a dog,* Wyatt thought with a start.

Melvin glanced at Damon as if he were reluctant to talk. "Go on," Wyatt urged. "Never mind him. Tell us what … they're saying."

"Something happened in Bakerton. The people died wherever they stood." He snapped his fingers, then said something in coyote or whatever language he was using. "They said a thing came and sucked the life from every person there."

"A thing?" Howard interrupted. "Like vampires?"

Melvin shook his head. "Not human, or …"

"What do they know? The army probably dropped gas on the town," Damon said, brushing off Melvin's comments.

One of the beasts growled low in its throat. "He says it wasn't gas. And it wasn't the army."

"How does the coyote know? It's just a dumb …"

"Don't say it," Melvin warned, his face in a sneer. His teeth seemed larger, his canines elongated. Keisha's inhalation of breath made Melvin tighten his lips, so his teeth disappeared.

"Did the werewolf bite you?" Keisha asked. "You're different."

"What do you mean?" Melvin balled his fists.

"You look …" Keisha thought for a minute. "Feral." Melvin smiled serenely as if he had a secret. "Tell us about it," Keisha said.

"The werewolf's name was Billy. He was part of the pack that was imprisoned in the Werewolf River Run. Vincent killed them all."

"He put a chip in their necks and exploded their heads, obliterating all werewolves everywhere," Howard informed them.

"Billy understood me." Melvin's eyes were shiny with unshed tears.

"He was a werewolf, Melvin. What did you let him do?" Wyatt demanded.

"It wasn't bad." He looked at Damon, who stared at him with revulsion. "I don't want to talk about it anymore."

"But what are you going to do? You can't run around with a pack of …"

Melvin turned on Wyatt with hostility, and a frisson of fear raced down Wyatt's back. Melvin no longer looked like himself, awkward and goofy. Keisha was right; he looked wild.

"Pack of animals?" He came close to Wyatt's face. "Those animals saved your sorry asses." He snapped his fingers again. "Come."

"No." Wyatt reached out to take Melvin's arm. Carrie lunged, but Melvin stayed her.

"You don't understand. I belong to them now. There is no going back. I've made them like me."

"These are not typical coyotes," Lily stated.

"Not anymore."

"You bit them!" Howard accused. "How could you?"

"Howard Drucker," Melvin said. "Don't judge me. This is my

life now, and I'm never going home." He paused, looking just a bit lost. "I guess this is goodbye."

"Wait, Mel. What do you mean?" Wyatt asked.

"I'm happier here." Two of the larger beasts moved in front of Melvin, as if to protect him. "It's okay, Chucky. Sit, Jason!" he crooned, rubbing their heads.

"Carrie? Jason? Chucky?" Howard questioned. "Movie monster names from a great era, Mel. Intriguing choices."

Melvin shrugged and said, "You can take the boy out of Monsterland …"

"But you can't take Monsterland out of the boy," Wyatt finished his sentence.

Melvin turned to the growling animals and said, "I'm not going with them." He made a gesture toward the group of teens. "The freeway's been taken over by crazy people."

"They were monsters. I'd rather fight the vampires," Howard said. "At least they were honest about what they wanted from you."

"All those thugs wanted was your vehicle," Melvin told them.

"Monsterland changed everything," said Wyatt.

"Yeah," Howard added. "Now we can argue who is the superior creature—lawyers, accountants, or dentists."

"What were you idiots doing out there anyway?" Melvin asked.

"We're headed to Stocktonville." Wyatt pointed to the west. "I guess this is it, then. Do you want me to say anything to your grandfather?"

"Nah, I think it's better this way."

"You've only gone rogue about three weeks," Howard informed him. "Let's head out for Stocktonville."

One of the giant beasts nudged him in the leg. They did their growly communication.

"He says … he told me you can't go to Stocktonville."

"We *have* to go there."

"Well, I wouldn't advise it." Melvin shook his head, then pointed to the biggest animal. "He told me everyone is dead."

"You're taking advice from Wile E. Coyote?" Damon laughed.

The hybrid coyote's fur stood on end as the animals growled.

Its big head studied Damon, its eyes narrowed. Lily turned to Damon angrily. "Do you think you're so superior because you walk on two legs? They have a language, and I believe that they're more articulate than you."

Damon turned to her. "What, did they teach you how to speak to dogs down on the reservation?"

"That's enough!" Wyatt moved to stand between them. He turned to Melvin, adding, "That can't be true. We spoke to some guy there this morning."

"Did you see this massacre, Melvin, or are we going to abandon Carter's orders based on what your pet tells us?" Damon taunted.

Melvin shook his head, a wry smile on his face, as if he knew something Damon didn't. He said, "Look, I'm giving you fair warning. This is bigger than you think." He started to walk away.

Howard stepped forward, his face solemn. "Wait. I sat in your room with you after your mother disappeared. I was your best friend since kindergarten, playing video games with you when everybody else …"

"I know what you did, Howard Drucker. Nobody was busting down doors to be your buddy either," Melvin said.

"That may be so, Mel. I never let you down. We need your help."

Melvin looked at his canine friends, then back at the mountains surrounding them. "Tell me why you're going there."

"Carter asked. He wants us to open a line of communication with some old army buddy of his. He also wants to get word out that we're okay."

The coyote barked, and Melvin responded. "I know."

"You know what?" Wyatt asked.

"He said you're a bunch of morons."

"Oh, did he?" Damon said with menace.

Melvin ignored him and asked, "How far is it?"

"I think … about … maybe three miles," Howard answered.

"Three miles, about an hour's walk," Melvin said. "That should be enough time to finally finish our argument."

Wyatt and Howard grinned back at Melvin, who smiled widely.

"What argument?" Lily asked as they started walking together, their voices raised in friendly banter.

"Which monster is most superior: werewolves, vampires, or zombies?"

Damon shook his head, muttering, "Friggin' nerds."

Chapter 15

Igor sat on the floor inside an abandoned storefront, biting his fingers. He made noises as he chewed, little cries of hurt and anger. His eyes filled. He dashed the brimming tears, thinking of Nate and the lost opportunity.

Vincent promised so many things, he thought bitterly. Hadn't he donned the ridiculous outfit, lured the vamps into Monsterland, performed in the garish show, only to help Vincent gather monsters from all over the world to trap in the theme park?

He'd certainly lived up to his half of the bargain. They had a deal, signed in blood. Nate was to supply the army; Nate would rule the world through Vincent's genius.

Both the werewolves and vampires were doomed from the start. This had been decided. Vamps and werewolves think outside the box, and Vincent wanted to make sure that any rogue personalities would be contained. The humans would have no chance.

Vincent was adamant the werewolves had to be destroyed. They were after all, a hybrid of man's best friend.

If humans figured out the potential of friendship rather than enmity and teamed up with any creature that had superior capabilities, then there was a chance of a paradigm shift affecting who controlled the world. Vincent had to destroy any possibility of that happening.

Vampires operated on the periphery of society, not realizing the power of their charisma. Had they gone into politics rather than the music industry, they would have ruled the world.

Zombies, of course, were the most useful, a built-in police force. Lock up malcontents with the infected and a leader would have zero opposition to their plans. Vincent thought of everything. Vincent was brilliant.

A mass extinction, so there would be only one surviving species of monster. Vincent called it, *survival of the damned.* The zombies were their future. Vincent had planned to use the disease to keep the rest of the world in check. He had doctors to study and isolate the germ. Then the plan was to ransom the world into following his rules. Soon the entire planet would have no choice but to adhere to Vincent's grand plans. He was rich. He had built an empire by using his brilliant brain. Vincent understood what had to be done.

Nate said to do whatever Vincent wanted. It was the only way to bring order to the world. It was chaos, everybody and their stupid ideas. *Isolate the monsters, no, don't isolate them. Live together, but don't let them work. Give them rights, take them away ... the stupid politicians couldn't make up their minds.*

They spouted their promises, then took four years, two of which they dismantled the work of the last guy, then spent the next two years arguing how to deal with the changes, then it was onto the empty promises once more. Every four years, nothing was accomplished. He and Nate had had enough. With Vincent's support, they were going to make the world a better place. They had ideas, good plans to make it right for the planet, to end suffering.

Nate studied Vincent's strategy. He knew exactly what had to be done; he didn't even have to go through an election to accomplish it. He wouldn't continue with the silly bargaining to bring forth a bill, or tailor his plans to meet his party's requirement. In this takeover, they would be really free. They would show the world the futility of democratic rule. There would be no more pretense about who was in charge. Democracy was dead; Igor knew this to be true.

Only now, Vincent had found himself someone new. Hugh Frasier. Igor made a face, thinking of the scientist strutting around in his fancy clothes and poking his silly cane at everyone. Igor sniffed, wiping his running nose on the sleeve of his coat. He hunched his shoulders, feeling alone, stifling a sob. He had nobody now, not Nate, not Plan B and not Vincent.

Igor moaned loudly, falling on the dusty floor, his tears making tracks down his grimy face. *What will happen to all those wonderful programs now? What will happen to me?* He sat up abruptly. He had to leave. He didn't belong here anymore.

He struggled to his knees; nobody noticed him anymore.

Frasier was in the center of the park, his lower face covered by a mask. Huge operation stations with tables were set up around steaming vats. He knew the liquid was the same as the stuff he saw in Vincent's glass tubes. The viscous purple ooze roiled in metal cylinders ten feet tall. Giant spools of linen were being rolled in by Frasier's soldiers. Each of the spools was then attached to wires hanging across Monsterland. Workers in white contamination suits stood on top of tall ladders unwinding the strips into the vats that spat sulfurous smells into the dry desert air.

Igor watched as the soaked linen was fished from the tanks by a long pole with a hook. It was transferred to a team of four surrounding the most intact zombie bodies.

"Begin Operation Winding Shroud," Frasier barked.

Frasier nodded to the soldier, who began rolling the linen strips up the body, feet first.

Igor watched in fascinated silence as the purple-tinted material was patiently wrapped around the body until it was completely covered. The corpse was put to the side, and soon six more were stacked on top of it, each neatly swaddled by the linen. Igor's jaw dropped in shock at the mounting piles of bodies that looked like a collection of kindling.

"Mummies?" Igor whispered. "They're making mummies?"

In the vast crowd of dead zombies, Igor watched Frasier start to laugh. His deep voice bounced off the empty streets of Monsterland, filling Igor's head. Igor slid down, covering his ears. The old man had to get out of here. *They're all crazy,* Igor thought. *What kind of monsters are they?*

Chapter 16

The teens walked on the side of the road, dragging their feet over the hard-packed sand. The dirt gave way to a sidewalk that simmered in the afternoon sun. Abandoned cars littered the highway as they grew nearer.

Most of the autos were half on and half off the asphalt, the sun baking them so they shimmered from the heat. The coyotes stayed clear. When they first noticed the vehicles, Keisha moved close to look inside. Carrie, Melvin's coyote, dashed in front of Keisha, pushing her away from the car.

"I wouldn't if I were you," Melvin warned.

"It appears to be empty." Keisha peered into the dark interior of the abandoned car.

"Maybe so, but she's telling you not to touch it."

"That's ridiculous," Damon spat.

"So, go ahead," Lily dared him, squaring off. "Go ahead and open the door, big shot who knows everything."

Damon and Lily stared at each other, breathing hard, the hot sun bearing down on them relentlessly. It was late afternoon, but the sun baked the desert, bringing everything into sharp relief. Hot, white light glowed from the chrome, blinding them. There was no sign of life, anywhere.

Wyatt looked at the car longingly. It was an old Ford Galaxy, big enough for all of them. They were going to need a way to get home. Between the roving bands of psychos and the darkness, a car would make their return safer.

Melvin must have read his mind because he said something to Carrie, who growled back.

"She'll let you know which vehicle is safe. You're going to need a car to get back to Copper Valley," Melvin told them.

Damon cursed. They all ignored him.

Vultures flew overhead. Lily pointed upwards. "Not a good sign."

"Thanks for the update, Sacagawea," Damon muttered.

"Shut up, Damon," Wyatt said through his teeth.

The streets leading into the town were quiet. The hot wind whipped and eddied loose papers that skidded down the blacktop. The only other sound was their shoes slapping the pavement.

"Hello?" Wyatt called out, startled when his own voice ricocheted back as it bounced off the abandoned buildings. They walked for blocks, but the only signs of life were the circling buzzards.

"Let's head to the tracks. That's where our guy is," Wyatt said, his eyes examining the empty storefronts.

"Was, probably," Howard added. "Where is everybody? Hey Mel, can you ask your friends what they smell?"

Melvin growled a response to the beast, who responded with a soft whimper.

"Death. They smell death," he replied.

"Creepy," Keisha whispered.

"This sucks," Howard said. "Anybody here?" he bellowed in his high voice. "Where could they all have gone? I smell something ..." He sniffed the air tentatively. "What is that odor?"

"I don't recognize it either," Keisha said. "It's not human decay."

"Agreed. It has a sweetness to it,"

"You're crazy, dude—it stinks like sewage," Damon said with disgust.

"Not sewage. Perhaps like burnt hair?" Lily offered.

"Smells like crap, and I'm not kidding." Damon made a face, then held his finger under his nose.

"Look!" Lily pointed to the sewer grate that was flooded with a viscous purple liquid. It bubbled as if it were boiling.

The coyotes started howling, circling the teens nervously. Wyatt began to walk over, but Carrie bared her teeth, grabbing his jeans, holding him back.

The oily fluid expanded, gushing from the sewer grate, the puddle widening at an absurd speed.

"What the …" Damon said.

The beasts started jumping, their saucer-shaped paws pushing the teens across the street. As if the substance had a mind of its own, it rushed to one spot, forming a river that began to move toward them. The larger it became, the faster it moved.

"It's coming after us!" Howard said breathlessly. He grabbed Keisha's hand and shoved Wyatt down the street in the opposite direction.

"Run!" Damon screamed. The teens took off, corralled by the barking canines, attempting to evade the fluid.

They spread out, but the substance pulsed and gurgled, nipping at their heels.

"Get on the sidewalk!" Wyatt shouted.

The group raced toward the curb. Carrie moved closer to Damon, causing him to trip.

Wyatt heard a curse and saw him go down. The liquid made a beeline to Damon's left foot. Wyatt yelled to the others to hurry, made an abrupt about-face and grabbed Damon's forearm, hauling him off the street. The teens turned to see the liquid hit the curb with a splat. The height halted its approach.

"What is that crap?" Damon asked.

Keisha and Howard crouched to observe the river of purple muck as it raced past their spot. The current slowed, turning sluggish. Eddying in tiny whirlpools, it appeared to gather in volume. The circle widened, and soon the purple ooze was building as if there was a dam holding it back. Wyatt looked down the street. There was no obstruction to stop the fluid, yet it stopped to build ominously right before the storefront where they all stood on the curb. Small whitecaps lapped at the pavement. The coyotes were whimpering in fear.

"That stuff is going to jump the curb!" Wyatt yelled. "Into the stores, now!"

Desperately they pushed and pulled the shop doors to assorted storefronts. Nothing budged. The ooze washed over the curb like a small tidal wave, soon covering half the pavement.

The sound of all seven of Melvin's pack howling sent chills of urgency down Wyatt's spine.

Keisha yanked a door to a shop, but it was locked tight. The kids clustered around the entrance, pulling the handle.

Wyatt looked wildly around. He spied a broken parking meter laying on its side. He picked up the metal pole and screamed: "Watch out!" He heaved it through the glass pane display window. Lily and Keisha urgently picked off the remaining shards of glass, and the kids climbed through the opening as the fluid hit the wall beneath them.

They entered the darkened building, finding themselves in a hardware store.

"Anybody here?" Wyatt called out.

"Hello!" Keisha yelled.

Howard sprinted down the aisles. He paused to touch a shelf, wiping a finger along the gray dust coating the metal.

"Don't touch that," Keisha said, coming up to observe over his shoulder.

Howard ignored her, lost in thought. He pressed his thumb and finger together, watching the dry substance flake away. He brought his fingers to his nose, sniffing lightly, then withdrew his hand as if he had inhaled something foul.

"Metallic," he observed.

The group gathered around Howard.

"Let me," Keisha said pulling his hand to her nose. "Reminds me of jet fuel."

"Oh, really," Damon said. "Like when was the last time you hung out at an airport?"

"Keisha interned at NASA last summer," Wyatt said.

The coyotes circled them, whining.

Melvin made a bunch of guttural noises to the animals. He listened to their response, then darted to the window to stare at the bubbling liquid pooling at the base of the storefront.

"They're telling me it's going to follow us," Melvin said.

"That's impossible." Damon looked skeptical. "It would have to rise over four feet."

Melvin responded heatedly, "I'm not arguing with them."

The beasts took off for the back of the store, barking madly.

"What is it?" Wyatt asked.

Everyone followed, stopping short when they found the coyotes clustered around a body.

Howard pushed himself between the restless animals and got on his knees.

"Don't touch it!" Melvin shouted.

The man was laying on his side; his waxy skin was as white as if all the blood had been drained. A line like a seam separated his chest. Wyatt peered over his arm and gasped. The entire cavity of his body was empty, except for his skeleton. He looked like a side of beef he'd seen hanging in the butcher section of the supermarket. All of his organs were gone. The corpse's face was frozen with a look of horror.

One of the beasts—Carrie, Wyatt thought—raised her paw to touch the man's arm gently. It crumbled as if there were nothing inside.

Wyatt cursed; all the teens backed away. "It looks like his guts were, I don't know …"

"Scooped out," Keisha supplied. She had grabbed a broom-stick and was holding the chest open so she could study the cavity.

"I've seen this before," Lily whispered.

"Where?" Howard asked.

Lily nodded toward the west. "On the reservation. The cattle. Usually the remotest parts. They come in clusters. All the blood drained, body parts missing."

"Maybe you can ask your uncle, the bird or whatever he is, what's going on," Damon sneered.

Wyatt moved closer to him. "You got a problem?"

"Maybe," Damon said, puffing out his chest.

Lily forced her way between them. "Stop acting like little boys."

She lowered herself to her knees. The floor was covered by the same residue. Lily picked up a rag, wiping the surface. It came away coated with the fine powder.

Howard poked the body with his pencil. It sounded hollow.

He shook his head. "I'm not sure. It's like he's been dehydrated or something."

"Don't you guys think we should be more worried about that crap trying to get in here?" Melvin said.

"We should get to higher ground." Wyatt moved away to look at the shelves.

Howard stood up. "He's been drained of everything, his organs taken, leaving only a husk."

Wyatt shined a flashlight on the corpse.

"Where'd you get that?" Howard asked.

"Duh. We're in a hardware store."

"Looks like an empty cocoon," Lily said, peering at the body.

"All right," Damon said. "Science class is over. The guy is dead, and it just doesn't matter. There's a gooey thing, and according to Dog Man, it's trying to get in here. Let's head over to the railroad tracks and see if we can find that dude your father wanted us to talk to."

"My stepfather," Wyatt corrected.

"Whatever," Damon said.

The coyotes began climbing, their long legs knocking over merchandise on the shelves. Carrie started to whimper. She nudged Melvin's knee.

"We have to get out of here now!" he said.

"Calm down, Wolf Boy," Damon said.

The room filled with the sour-sweet smell they had noticed out on the street. Lily looked up, a scream escaping her mouth.

The purplish liquid gushed over the opening, coming in through the window.

"How can it do that?" Keisha said with astonishment.

It was heading toward them. As it came closer, it picked up speed, as if it sensed their presence. The entire front of the store was covered in the bubbling mass.

"Move!" Wyatt shouted, pointing to a corridor in the back of the store.

They raced back, the lava-like thing still progressing, faster, in a straight line directly for them.

"Do you think it's intelligent?" Howard called out as they ran.

"Not now, Howard Drucker. Run!" Keisha cried.

They were in a storeroom filled with high metal shelves that towered over them. It was dark inside. All Wyatt could hear was their panting and the occasional thump as they tripped over merchandise. He aimed his flashlight at the ceiling so the light would bounce back, illuminating the room for the others.

The animals were barking, running alongside them, knocking over the shelves so that small paint cans rained down on them.

"Cover your heads," Wyatt cried out as a small can hit him squarely on the ear. He saw stars for a second but pushed through to the rear of the store.

Damon reached the exit first, yanking it open. Carrie bounded around him, knocking him against the wall, leaping into the open doorway. Outside, a sea of purple ooze snatched her back legs like a tidal undertow, dragging her into the alleyway. She yelped, and Melvin raced to the door. Damon slammed the door closed.

They gathered around a small mesh covered window to see Carrie collapse, as the purple fluid overwhelmed her. Her howl of pain cut through the noise of their heavy breathing. Carrie's exposed paws were encased in a puddle of the purple slush. Her limbs were stuck fast; her cries rent the air, growing feebler and fainter as they watched in shock.

She writhed, her fur turning white, the essence of her being sucked out wherever her body was in contact with the liquid.

"Carrie," Melvin cried. "Carrie!"

Melvin wrestled with Damon. He wrenched the door, but both Wyatt and Howard held his arms back. Tears streamed down his face as he struggled against their hold.

"Stop, Melvin," Wyatt said, holding him. "There is nothing we can do." He could feel sobs wrack Melvin's body.

Melvin whimpered, "She sacrificed herself for you." He turned to Damon. "You shouldn't have opened the door."

Damon ignored him.

Wyatt watched a red line appear at Carrie's gullet. As if guided by a laser, it traveled down her abdomen. Horrified, they saw the purple foam sweep through her cavity, disintegrating her internal organs. She crumpled, an empty carcass, like the shell of a wax figure.

Wyatt slammed his fist against the door. "We have to find

another way out of here." His eyes scrutinized the dark room as he shined the flashlight on each of the walls.

Lily turned around. "We better do something. That stuff is moving this way."

"Up," Howard said. "Climb up the shelves."

Lily hauled herself up the metal shelves, while Wyatt pushed from behind. Keisha went up next. Wyatt could hear the insidious sweep of the slow-moving flood as it covered everything in its path.

"You're next," Wyatt told Melvin after all of them had climbed the shelves.

"I'm not going," Melvin said to Wyatt. He shook his head. "I'm not leaving my band."

"I'll help you; we'll push them up."

"Come on!" Lily screamed. The purple ooze was sliding into the storeroom, overpowering the area with its harsh odor.

"Just go. I'm not gonna abandon them!" Melvin dashed a tear from his eye.

"I can't leave you."

"It doesn't matter. Don't you understand? I can never go back!" Melvin pushed Wyatt. "Go!" He pointed to the slanted ceiling, where a dirty window brought in muted sunlight. "There's a skylight. Get out that way."

Before Wyatt could respond, Melvin took off, the pack of animals surrounding him. Wyatt reached for him, but Melvin evaded his grasp. Wild howls of alarm filled the room; the slow-moving slush invaded the store.

Keisha, Lily, and Howard screamed at Wyatt, Howard holding out his thin hand for Wyatt to grab. He closed his palm around Howard's wrist, scaling the metal shelves. His injured hand was on fire with the contact. Still, he fought through the pain. He held on, his feet scrambling up the metal shelves.

Damon pulled a wooden broom handle from a long box. "Get another," he ordered. He aimed it at the skylight, but couldn't reach it. Lily leaped over the shelving.

"Bend down," she ordered.

"What?" Damon asked.

"You're the tallest. Come on! Find stuff to stack," she told the others urgently.

Howard and Wyatt gathered boxes, piling them on top of each other. Howard stepped onto the cardboard. He wobbled on his small stack, falling to his knees. The metal shelf echoed like a bass drum when he fell. The tall shelving swayed as if they were in an earthquake. Wyatt yelled, "Hold on!" He dropped onto his stomach, clutching either side of the metal, his eyes tightly shut until the shelf steadied.

"The cardboard is too weak. It'll never support us." Keisha was up and on her knees already. Her hand pressed the top of the box.

Wyatt glanced over the sea of shelves, his eyes going wide. The purple goo was traveling up the sides of the shelves, enveloping and expanding as if it were alive. "What else can we use?" he shouted.

Damon lowered himself, then pointed to Lily. "Hop up." He patted his shoulders. Lily stared back as if she didn't understand. "*Today*, Lily, hurry!"

Wyatt stood behind her, helping her climb onto Damon's back. Damon braced himself with a wide stance; Lily secured her long legs under his arms. "Hand me the broomstick!"

Keisha handed her the pole. Lily closed one eye, drawing her arm back as if she were throwing a javelin. The wood connected with the glass, shattering it into a crystal rainfall.

Lily steadied herself, then stretched upwards, picking out the splintered glass. She hooked her hands on the skylight frame and hoisted herself up; her fingers gripped the molding of the casement. Grunting from the effort, she attempted to stand on Damon's shoulders. Damon swayed, making Lily lose her grip. Her hands regained their purchase, and she heaved upward, her thin arms trembling with the effort. She dangled for a minute, then pulled herself up and through the shattered glass. They heard the thump of her landing on the roof.

Lily's head popped through the opening. She lay on her stomach, her hand outstretched. "Keisha, you're next." Blood dripped down her fingers from a cut on her palm, pooling on the top shelf. "Hurry!"

Keisha looked at Howard, a question in her eyes.

"Women and children first," he told her. "I'll be right up."

Damon bent over so she could get onto his back. Keisha's

height made grabbing Lily's hand easy. She stood on Damon's shoulders and was through the skylight in an instant, falling with a grunt onto the roof.

Wyatt searched the boxes, finding a spool of rope. He ripped open the carton, calling out, "Look what I found." He held up the coil of hemp triumphantly. A sucking noise drew his attention, and he saw the purple substance moving up the tall shelves. Making a lasso, he called, "Lily, catch." The rope flew through the air, falling short of the opening.

"Let me do it," Damon said, grabbing the rope.

"I can do it," Wyatt said.

"Well, one of you throw the damn rope, that globby thing is almost here!" Howard yelled, looking over the side at the expanding foam bubbling up at them.

Wyatt threw the rope again. Lily caught it, then called out, "I'm tying it to this pipe sticking out of the roof. Come on, you guys!"

Wyatt pulled the rope, watching it grow taut.

He pushed Howard, who looked up at the long climb. "I'll never make it."

"Oh, yes you will," Keisha yelled back.

"I failed gym." Howard looked stricken. Damon pushed him out of the way.

"I'm outta here," Damon said, his strong hands grabbing the rope.

Like his gorilla ancestors, Wyatt thought, watching him shimmy up. Damon moved agilely out of the store.

"Howard Drucker, you look at me. I am not moving from this spot until you get your sorry butt up here!" Keisha shouted, her head sticking through the window.

Howard gulped.

"I'm not going until you go first. I'm not losing another friend tonight," Wyatt told him. The shelf started to teeter with the growing weight of the globs of liquid that crept nearer. "But you may be losing another friend if you don't get moving. I'll be right behind you."

Howard pushed his glasses up his thin nose. Grabbing the rope with two hands, he struggled up toward the opening, his arms shaking.

Wyatt knew Howard's hands were burning. Still, his friend held on tightly, his legs wrapped around the hemp, his ankles crossed and pushing him upward. Lily and Keisha called out encouragingly.

Howard slipped downward, grunted, his thighs stopping his descent. His teeth were bared as he made his way up to safety.

Wyatt peeked over, a gasp escaping his mouth. The purple gunk encompassed the entire room as if he sat on an angry rain-cloud. He saw it slide over the top shelf.

Wyatt looked up to see the rope hit him in the face. His three friends were leaning over the edge, screaming at him. He squeezed his hands, his cut palm sore and swollen. Gritting his teeth, he forced his arm to reach up but was unable to grab the suspended lifeline. Something sucked at his feet.

Wyatt snatched the rope, a cold seeping into his bones. He sighed dreamily, his eyes becoming heavy. One of his arms dropped. He looked down absently to see a slimy puddle around his feet. It sizzled, oozing around the rubber soles of his sneakers. Shivering with cold, he looked at the rope, not quite knowing what to do with it. Howard Drucker was screaming at him, but it sounded far away. Time became syrupy, as if he was suspended in amber. His bones were icy; they felt brittle, his teeth chattered. Wyatt's ears filled with the sound of buzzing, as though he were in the center of a hive. Strange thoughts flitted through his brain.

Once when he was young, he remembered a family vacation somewhere on the east coast. His father had taken him to see an antique nickelodeon on a boardwalk by the shore. He recalled looking through the eyeholes to see the small pages race, creating a sepia-colored moving picture. It was a Roman legion marching. He saw a similar image in his mind now.

He smiled lazily, all the sounds in the room fading. Only the images changed. *There was an army*—he frowned, his eyes closed, his hands weightless—*but they were wrapped in linen. Why would an army be covered in strips of cloth?* A great mass of linen-wrapped bodies was stomping in one direction.

He felt his feet move in unison to their shuffling tread. The drums of thousands of beings pounding the earth together filled his ears, drowning out the buzzing and the cries of his friends. One voice filled the cavity of his brain; however, rather than hear it, he felt it. *Vincent Konrad?* Vincent Konrad was ordering him, telling him to march with the others. His arm swung in an identical movement to the bandaged person next to him. Wyatt turned to look, his half-closed eyelids seeing rows of people, their bodies swathed in purple-soaked strips of cloth that covered them like ... covered them like ... like ...

He shook his head in disbelief, the last vestige of individual thought fighting to remain free. A loud wolfish cry of triumph pierced his brain, breaking into his lethargy.

There was an answering howl from a coyote, filling the room. Wyatt came back to himself with a smile on his lips. Lily was leaning over. He saw her mouth moving, but no words reached his ears. He could barely feel his feet. He glanced down, seeing the strange goop puddled around him. He was standing in it. It was only an inch thick but high enough that it penetrated his sneakers.

He focused on her lips, nodding vaguely. A heat pierced his chest where his ribs met. He cried hoarsely from the pain. He placed his palm on the spot as if to soothe it. Lily's insistent voice reached into his skull until her words began to make sense.

"Wrap the rope around your wrist," Lily repeated.

Numbly, he groped for the hanging cable, twining it around his forearm. With a dawning sense of urgency, he allowed the rope to loop around his arm like a snake, securing it with his other hand. He felt himself being lifted, but his feet stubbornly remained glued to the surface. He heard shouts and grunts, but they were so far away. He watched in a detached manner as Howard leaned over the skylight, his face red with the effort of screaming. Howard was almost hanging upside down through the opening. Something flew from his pocket. Wyatt watched in a disconnected way as Howard's keys, pocket protector and a bunch of number two pencils landed all around him, sinking into the ... what did Howard say its name was? he wondered. He heard a *splat*, watching with dismay as the packet of Whisp splattered on the top shelf where it landed, opening like a blooming flower.

Smoke started to rise from the spot where it broke open, the two liquids combusting when they came into contact with one another. Flames rippled as it dispersed across the surface, seemingly to eat the foam. The purple bubbles shrank where it was exposed, dissolving where Whisp soda mixed with the viscous fluid.

He heard Howard Drucker gasp.

There was a great sucking noise as Wyatt's sneakers tore from the top shelf, held by a sticky web trapping his feet. The Whisp spread and with it, a blue flame melting the purple globules clinging to his soles. Wyatt felt himself being pulled upwards, his body swaying. Once he was separated from the slime, his brain started to function again. He kicked violently, freeing his legs from the weakened substance. The clean desert air hit his face, clearing his mind as he was pulled through the skylight. He tumbled out of the window, his friends collapsing around him breathlessly.

Keisha was at his feet. Howard shouted, "Don't touch it!"

Wyatt breathed heavily, feeling slightly stunned, as if he'd been kicked in the head. Both Howard and Keisha leaned over the open skylight. He heard their observations, smiling sleepily at their discussion.

"Did you see what happened?"

"Whatever's left is retreating." Keisha pointed to the deflating cloud of purple goo. The top burned weakly in isolated patches.

"Reminds me of napalm," Howard said.

"Exactly what I'm thinking," Keisha replied with a nod. "Look, it's shrinking, leaving that dusty residue we saw earlier."

Howard crawled over, his face close. He reached for a pencil, cursing when he remembered he'd lost them all. He patted his pants pocket and found his money clip. He proceeded to scrape the purple dust from Wyatt's sneakers.

"Are you okay?" Lily asked, brushing the brown hair from his forehead. She pressed both her palms on either side of his face, repeating, "Are you okay?"

Wyatt stared dumbly at her smooth skin, the concern in her dark eyes making him feel peaceful in a way he had never felt. He became aware of a burning pain down the center of his chest.

"Ow," he muttered.

"What?" Lily bent close to him.

"My chest hurts."

Lily peeled his tee away from his chest, gasping when she saw a neat, shallow line grazing his ribcage.

"What is it?" Wyatt asked.

Wyatt closed his eyes at the feeling of Lily running her hand down his body. The heat was replaced by goosebumps.

"Is the skin broken?" Keisha asked.

"Barely," Lily replied.

"There's no blood." Wyatt heard Howard's voice. The three of them were bent over his midsection. "Looks like a laser cut." Keisha ran her hand down his torso. "Took a couple of layers of skin off, but no real damage."

"Blood?" Howard bent closer to examine him.

"It's dry," Keisha responded. "A minute or two longer and he would have been gutted."

"Absolutely amazing." Howard's voice was filled with awe.

"Will you all stop talking about me as if I wasn't here?" Wyatt was cranky.

Howard turned to Wyatt as if he just noticed him. "What happened to you down there?"

Wyatt shrugged. "It was weird. I don't know."

"What do you mean, you don't know? We were calling you. You checked out," Keisha told him.

Wyatt tried to collect his thoughts. "I ... it was strange. I didn't care, and it was ... I was cold and ..." Wyatt scrambled to a sitting position, his head swimming. He glanced through the skylight at the interior of the store. "Where are the ..." He glanced around frantically. "There were mummies."

Lily put a hand on his shoulder preventing him from his rising.

"Mummies?" Keisha shouted.

"Yeah. I was marching with them, and it was like ... like we were of one mind. I heard Vincent."

"Vincent Konrad?" Damon asked.

"No, Vincent Price, dummy," Howard said, finally in his element. "Sounds like that goop caused a hallucination, because we all know Vincent Konrad is deader than a doornail."

"I know. But it wasn't a dream, Howard Drucker. I was marching with them. It was real."

Damon scowled and wandered away to check the rest of the roof.

Howard considered the purple dust on the end of his money clip. "Fascinating." He sniffed the substance, and the strong smell made him jerk his head away.

Keisha moved close, sniffing it as well. "It has a distinct odor. I remember it. I've smelled it before, but I'm not sure where."

"I've never seen a substance multiply and expand the way this did," Howard said, almost to himself.

"That's all very nice, Mr. Spock, but we have to get out of here," Damon said as he moved back to them.

Keisha ignored him, caught up in the examination of the foreign substance. "It doesn't act like anything I've ever seen."

Wyatt watched Keisha touch it with her forefinger. The flesh on the tip froze as if frostbitten. She rubbed her skin to make it warmer. "Howard Drucker, what do you think it is?"

"Maybe it's an alien," Damon said. "Like in the movie *The Bl*—"

"Don't even say that." Keisha rounded on him. "That was a stupid film. This is real life."

"So, what do you want to call it?" Howard asked.

"I vote we call it like that creature in the movie, ya know, *The Blo*—" Damon said from his spot on the roof.

"Stop it. This is really happening. You can't call it something so flippant," Keisha retorted.

"It has no personality, no soul. While it appears to be intelligent, it was seeking us out like infrared," Howard said.

"English, Howard Drucker," Wyatt said as if in a daze. He moved his knees. His legs were still numb.

"It was attracted to our heat. Once it can't feel it, it retreats."

"Aren't *we* lucky? I still think that's what we should call it. It looks like a blob, acts like a blob, smells like a blob," Damon said.

"That's it!" Keisha shouted. "That's where I've smelled it before—NASA."

"What?" Howard asked.

"The Blo ... oh, the substance, the globby thing."

"That's what we'll call it then, The Glob," Damon said. "Come on." He gripped Wyatt under the arms, dragging him up.

They walked to the front of the roof. Below them on the

street, they watched The Glob contract, retreating to the sewer where it came from.

"Look." Howard pointed to a group of coyote corpses on the road, their fur almost translucent, their appearance flat. A neat line ran from chest to groin, opening their bodies. All their organs had disappeared.

They heard a single howl. Wyatt shaded his eyes. He saw a coyote, a lone figure walking beside it. Man and beast broke into a loping run, disappearing down the deserted streets.

"Melvin's okay."

"He got out on the backs of the coyotes," Lily said.

"How do you know?"

"Look at their bodies. They made a line. They sacrificed themselves to create a walkway for him."

Wyatt looked at the formation of the corpses. They were indeed in a straight line. Every beast, except for one, who had somehow managed to escape with his friend.

"Good for Melvin," said Howard.

"Screw Melvin," Damon interrupted. "It's getting dark. We have to get out of here before The Glob decides to come back and finish what it started."

Chapter 17

The buildings were connected, and they climbed over the rooftops. The late afternoon sun beat down on them, making them uncomfortable in the heat. Wyatt turned to stare at the horizon, wondering how they were going to get home. Waves of heat shimmered from the sand, turning the landscape muddy and indistinct. He wondered briefly about Melvin, sorry he'd left, hoping he got out of Stocktonville safely.

"Come on, Baldwin," Damon called.

Wyatt caught up with them. Damon was pulling on another skylight. It gave with a loud groan that seemed to reverberate through the empty town. Damon let it drop, where it shattered when it hit the roof.

"It looks like a grocery store," he said, peering into the darkness below.

"I'm thirsty," Wyatt admitted. His throat felt dry as if he'd swallowed sand.

"I'm hungry," Howard added.

"How could you be hungry after what we just saw?" Keisha asked shaking her head.

"It's a market," Wyatt said. "I'll go in first."

He shimmied into the opening, his feet searching for something to stand on. He landed, the metal shelves creaking with his weight.

Wyatt inspected the floor. "That gray dust is here." He peered around the room. "I don't see the purple junk. It's safe."

One by one, his friends dropped into the store. They were like kids in a candy shop. Keisha grabbed a few reusable canvas bags by the checkout so they could load them up with food that could travel.

Wyatt found Keisha by the sandwich spreads.

"Looking for more peanut butter?"

"It makes a good weapon." She grinned.

A display of Kickers Kandy Bars brought a smile to Wyatt's tired lips. They reminded him of Melvin. They were his favorite candy. He shoved a few bars in his pocket.

Wyatt ran to the beverage section, grabbing a couple of cans of Whisp soda.

"Water is a smarter choice. That crap can take paint off a truck," Howard advised.

"Sometimes nothing but a Whisp will do," Wyatt sang the words to the ad. Lily smiled at him, taking more cans for her bag. The two others melted into the shadows. Wyatt found himself alone with Lily. She was leaning against a counter, her face weary.

Fatigue shadowed her dark eyes but didn't dim her loveliness. Wyatt stared at her face, marveling at the way nature sculpted her features. He considered her beauty to Jade's prettiness. It was like comparing classical art to graffiti. There was no doubt that Jade was an attractive girl, he realized now, but, he thought, she had no depth. Lily had a power that made you realize her attractiveness was in every pore of her body. He closed his eyes, blinking hard, trying to hold on to Jade's image instead, but it scattered like dry leaves, and he saw only Lily before him. He reopened his eyes and realized with a start she was quietly watching him.

"You okay?" he whispered.

"Yeah. It was scary. Much worse than I could have imagined," her voice choked.

"You were so brave. You were the first to start shooting on the freeway. I don't think any of us would've done anything until you began." Wyatt opened a can of soda for her; the whisper of the carbonation escaping somehow making the mood more intimate. *In another time or place, this could have been a date*, he thought.

"You know, I always liked you," she admitted.

It was as if she could read his thoughts. She took the soda, their hands touching. She didn't pull away. Wyatt let his fingers linger near hers.

"You were obsessed with Jade," she said with a soft laugh.

Wyatt thought of Jade and how she consumed his every waking minute in twelfth grade. He was a different person before Monsterland. Since that night at the theme park, and all the crazy things that had been going on, he realized he didn't have time to think about her much at all. With a start, it occurred to him that he had been as obsessed with the thought of her as he was with zombies, and now when the world was spinning out of control, Wyatt knew that what he felt for Jade was superficial and childish.

"Are you cold again?" Lily asked, her face concerned.

Wyatt couldn't talk over the lump in his throat. He shook his head, whispering, "No, not cold." The world narrowed to the two of them sitting on the dusty floor in the dimmed store. Wyatt only knew that his life had changed, and from now on, he would be living moment to moment. He swallowed, then added, "I wish I knew … before, in school, that you … you know." He shrugged. "Liked me."

They stared at each other for a second. Lily leaned forward, her eyes sliding shut.

Wyatt felt his body move toward her as if they were magnetized, his heart beating like a drum. He heard her put the soda on the counter, allowing the gap between their faces to narrow to nothing. Wyatt took a deep breath, his eyes closed. His lips grazed hers, with a gentle brush. Now his breath seemed trapped in his lungs, and he felt her own mouth respond with the lightest touch. Wyatt sighed deeply; it was as if he was finally home. He felt nothing but peace. Reaching out, he pulled her close, their kiss deepening.

They leaned against the counter; the can of soda fell and exploded as it hit the floor. They jumped apart, watching Damon glower at them in the gloom. "Is this really the time or place?" he said through his teeth. "Now you know why Carter sent me with you."

Wyatt tensed, but Lily's gentle hand stayed him. "He's kind of right." Her face was crimson. "But I have no regrets," she added quietly for Wyatt's ears.

"If you two are done, I'd like to find Espinoza and get the hell out of here." Damon stormed to the exit, to join Keisha and Howard on the street.

Lily turned to Wyatt and said, "Let's go."

"It came from there." Keisha pointed to the sewer grate.

"It appears dormant. I'd like to take a closer look," Howard said.

"No!" came a chorus of replies. They were all standing at the entrance of the store, watching the innocent-looking sewer grate.

"How far to the tracks?" Damon asked, searching the deserted avenue.

"Not sure," Wyatt responded. He could feel Lily right behind him. He noticed a narrow street and walked toward it. He ducked around a side alley.

"Where you going, Baldwin?" Damon shouted.

Wyatt was at the corner. He spied a vehicle and ran toward it without answering. The car was half on the sidewalk, as if the driver had pulled up and then abandoned it. Wyatt opened the door, the reassuring sound of the pinging bell letting him know the keys were in the ignition, and the battery still worked.

"I got a car!" he yelled back at them, the sound reverberating off the bricks.

He looked around; the street was devoid of life. He heard the scrape of rock, then pivoted, his eyes going wide.

Wyatt surveyed the empty streets; the only sound was his harsh breathing in his ears.

He heard the caw of a bird. He closed the car door quietly, walking in the direction of the sound. A huge raven was perched on a fence, its beady orange eyes observing him curiously. They stood as if in a stalemate. Wyatt shivered involuntarily thinking of that old Hitchcock movie, *The Birds*. He watched it with his father when he was five, and it somehow stayed with him. Since then, birds gave him the creeps.

He waved his hands. "Shoo."

The raven continued watching him calmly, then gave a wild caw that made him jump backward.

He heard running feet, and his four companions rushed at him, stopping short when they saw the bird.

Damon picked up a stone, aiming it directly at the raven.

Lily screamed and hit his arm, so the rock hit the fence below the bird. The raven shrieked, then took off, its big black wings stretching, blotting out the sun.

"What's the matter, you think it might be your uncle?" Damon jeered.

"Stop it." Wyatt turned to him.

"You're an animal," Lily sobbed. "That bird did nothing to you."

"Let's get out of here," Wyatt said, leading them to the car.

Chapter 18

Igor held the can of warm soda in his hand. He loved Whisp. He and Nate used to drink it instead of coffee in the morning. He drained the last of the can, and the flat beverage still had enough fizz to burn the back of his throat, or maybe it was the artificial ingredients that raked his tender gullet. He put the can behind him, careful not to make noise. He was sprawled on an outcropping of rocks on a level above Vincent's lab.

Since Vincent had been hooked up to the machine, his movements became stronger. He whirled in dizzying circles, barking out orders to the soldiers in that maniacal voice. Igor noticed that the fluid in the cylinders started out mauve, but changed to a darker purple as Vincent's strength returned. The more active Vincent's face was, the more the foam churned and boiled behind him in the glass tubes.

Igor stretched his neck to peer at a large television facing his former boss. Frasier's face filled the screen, answering Vincent's demands. Behind them, the soldiers worked steadily in their weird bandaging of the dead zombies.

What was Vincent planning to do with thousands of useless mummies? Igor pulled his lower lip, deep in thought. He knew he had to round up the bodies, that was the plan, but Igor was sure it was so that Vincent could harvest the disease and use it to control the world. A super weapon; germ warfare. What was the purpose of wrapping the bodies up like a gift? *Maybe they were going to drop the bodies like bombs somewhere? The ultimate Trojan Horse.*

"How much longer, Frasier?" Vincent's clipped voice demanded. "You said once the bandages touch the bodies, they will …" He shouted to a large screen where Frasier responded, knee deep in corpses on the surface of Monsterland. "Frasier! I am talking to you!"

Frasier straightened his back, his face tight with fury. Igor watched the scientist successfully control his anger.

"I know what I told you, Vincent. But, I'm not sure how long it will take. The test rats we used were not zombies and had much smaller body mass. That is … what I meant to say … we don't know exactly how the substance will react to the corpses."

"You don't know!" The purple vein on Vincent's temple stood out under his pale skin. "What do you mean you don't know? I paid for you to know. You and your gorilla-sized assistant are supposed to know! I've been paying you two and the rest of your colleagues from Area 51 for years to know exactly how the fuel will interact with the zombies!"

The purple foam roiled in the tubes behind Vincent. Igor watched spellbound as it bubbled over, spilling onto Vincent's wheel. Several of the lab-coated soldiers reacted as if the fluid was nuclear, and they used some special vacuum to suck up any leakage. He noticed they were careful not to touch it.

Back on the screen, Frasier bristled, his face mottled with suppressed rage. "We were operating under the eye of President McAdams. With his death and the chaos of the coup, we were able to arrange the transport of the alien fuel." He pointed his finger at Vincent. "We know that it's growing in strength. Reports from neighboring towns indicated the fuel's mutation from the energy of the living would …"

"Blah, blah, blah …" Vincent cut him off. "I know that part worked. I feel the fuel growing stronger."

Igor watched the pulsing purple foam in the glass tanks glow brighter, bathing the whole room in an eerie light. *What were they talking about?*

"You were supposed to be watching Igor. You should have found him. It's dangerous to let him escape," Vincent whined like a petulant child.

"I told you I don't know where the goblin went," Frasier's harsh voice broke into Igor's thoughts.

Igor trembled with indignation. *Nobody should be called a goblin.*

"He was my assistant," Vincent snarled. "He was my assistant," he repeated, and Igor thought Vincent looked a little lost.

"He's a crazy old thing, Vincent. Don't waste your precious thoughts worrying about the likes of him. Why, he's probably buzzard bait by now." Frasier laughed. "If you will turn your attention to the San Simi pipeline of Copper Valley, the energy from the population should be enough to move into phase two of Plan B."

Vincent attempted to turn, but nothing moved. Igor watched his face redden with anger, and counted down on his fingers to the coming explosion. *Three, two, one, and blastoff!*

"I can't move to the left! You and your idiot staff! They've done something to my machines!" Vincent raged, his dark eyes were directed to a cluster of techs in lab coats. "Fix it! Fix it now!" It appeared as if the purple stuff was foaming at his mouth. It dripped down his chin, staining it. Vincent's eyes looked like they would pop from his face. He wheeled his head around, the purple foam flying from the connection near his severed neck. "Do something!" He was livid.

Frasier's voice bellowed over the loudspeaker. "You heard him! Nichols, fix the damn thing before he blows a gasket!"

Apparently, Nichols reacted. He separated from the group, approaching the console cautiously.

He pressed a few buttons on the board, and Vincent's head did a graceful semicircle then circled in the other direction. It looked like a ballet. Igor shook with silent laughter. *They should pipe in some Vivaldi for atmosphere,* he thought.

"How does this feel, Dr. Konrad?" Nichols asked as he fiddled with a knob.

The disembodied head rotated quickly from right to left. "Stop, you fool. Enough!" Vincent moved his head experimentally, then scowled at Frasier on the monitor. His eyes seemed unfocused, rolling in their sockets. "If I had a stomach, I'd throw up, you moron!"

"Fortunately, we don't have to worry about your other

organs, Vincent. I have work to do," Frasier said. He turned to face the ongoing activities behind him, ignoring the steam rising from Vincent's electrodes.

Vincent watched the screen, his eyes narrowing. Igor chuckled thinking of the impending outburst. Vincent wasn't done yet, and Igor knew it.

"Don't underestimate someone because of their size," Vincent told him.

Now Igor wondered who exactly Vincent was talking about. Perhaps being relegated to the size of a football was something of a disadvantage.

Frasier turned to face the camera slowly. "I'm sure I don't know what you're talking about."

"Igor … you think he's harmless." Vincent's eyes were like the bores of a shotgun.

"He was a silly little man," Frasier insisted with a negligent wave of his arm. He gestured impatiently to his own assistant, a giant that towered over Frasier. He handed him a tablet, clearly done with the discussion.

Vincent's eyes silvered with heat. Igor crawled on his stomach closer to the end of the rocks, watching the fury build in Vincent's face. He recognized the undiluted hatred by the flush of hectic red staining Vincent's cheeks. The wall of tubes behind Vincent bubbled violently again, the purple substance boiling as if it were a volcano ready to burst.

Igor heard cries of dismay coming from the large screen. He jockeyed for a better position to watch.

The huge monitor showed crowds of Vincent's Federation Forces backing away from the central plaza. Some fell over discarded limbs in their haste to leave. He could see their panicked faces, their eyes bulging with fear. *What are they seeing?* Igor wondered, his own eyes glued to the monitor. Frasier cursed as a wall of soldiers bumped into him in a frantic attempt to escape.

Terror, it seems, is contagious. Igor watched as a stampede created a cloud of red dust to obscure the screen.

The cavernous room filled with cries of horror.

"Vincent! Stop! We're not ready yet. You'll ruin everything!" Frasier was yelling; his terrified face blanched of all color. "The fuel hasn't had time to soak into the surface of their skin. Don't rush me!"

Igor knew Vincent Konrad waited for no man or beast, and, watching the wild scene taking place above them in the theme park, apparently he waited for no monsters either.

"Stop him!" Frasier blubbered to the technicians, his face filling the screen, his eyes wild.

Techs ran to consoles, frantically pressing buttons that appeared to be powerless. Vincent let out a peal of maniacal laughter.

Igor stood, his jaw dropping. Frasier backed off, revealing that the vista behind him was filled with a mass of wiggling bandaged mummies, formerly the zombie population of Monsterland. Hordes of them were shakily rising to their linen-swathed feet, stumbling blindly around.

Igor could hear Frasier screaming something about not being ready yet. He took a healthy swig from a new can of soda, marveling at the endless mummy army.

Vincent's rapt gaze was pinned on one particular mummy; his jaw clenched with intense concentration. The corpse dripped with purple foam; it moved jerkily but steadily toward the burly assistant standing next to Frasier.

In the control room, every person's face was glued to the screen. The tall assistant dodged to the left but found himself surrounded by a new wall of mummies. They closed ranks, blocking him from his colleagues. The biggest of the wrapped-up monsters approached as if he was a sleepwalker, his hands reaching out.

Vincent commanded, "Now!" The soldiers watched in disbelief as the mummy grabbed Frasier's assistant by the neck, squeezing until the breath was choked out of him. Frasier clutched the bandaged arm of the killer, his face the same color as the goo covering the bandages. He gasped, releasing his hold, only to stare at his frostbitten hands.

"Stop. This is madness! He's my assistant," Frasier pleaded. He moved to stand behind his subordinate, trying to separate him from the mummy's merciless grip. "Do you know how long it takes to train one of them?" the scientist sobbed.

Vincent turned his head slightly. "You eliminated my

assistant. I am eliminating yours." He jerked his head, and two new mummies moved in spastic unison, tearing Frasier off his struggling assistant, releasing him to fall to the floor.

The victim's eyes rolled backward, his face graying. Vincent nodded to the screen, and the mummy walked behind the sagging body of the man, grabbing his head, then giving it a twist. It separated neatly from the body. The head fell with a thud to roll in the dust, stopping next to Frasier.

Vincent laughed loudly in the shocked silence and said, "Bring me the body!" Then he added as an afterthought: "You don't have to wrap my present, either, Doctor." Vincent's raucous laughter filled the room.

Igor chuckled silently. He had to admit; Vincent Konrad had quite a sense of humor.

Chapter 19

Wyatt gunned the car down the street toward the tracks. All around them they observed the carcasses of humanity, their bodies sucked dry, split down the middle, their internal organs gone as though evaporated.

"That foam. It destroyed the people."

"What, the Glob thing?" Damon asked.

"Stop calling it that!" Keisha demanded. "You minimize it by likening it to a fifties movie alien."

"And a bad movie alien, at that. *The Thing* was much more menacing," Howard said, as he removed his glasses and tried to clean the dried gray flecks from the lenses. "This stuff is like concrete."

"Shut up, nerd," Damon cut him off. "This thing is worse than *The Thing.*"

Wyatt rolled his eyes. After spending the last few years arguing the merits of zombies over vampires and werewolves, he wasn't going to start fighting over the superiority of a walking vegetable and a dishwasher soap, or whatever it was.

"Guys," he implored. "Cut it out. I was closest to the … the …"

"Call it the Foam," Keisha suggested.

"The Foam," Damon exploded. "You make it sound benign. It killed the freaky coyotes your freaky friend hangs with. It took out the population of a whole town, leaving corpses like dried corn husks."

Both Keisha and Howard turned at the same time to stare at each other, their eyes open wide. "Cattle mutilations."

"What are you talking about?" Lily asked.

"There is a place; it's called the Alien Highway, it's … let me think." Howard tapped his temple with his forefinger. It knocked his glasses, so they sat crookedly on his nose.

"It's on the 37th parallel. There are always cattle mutilations. They find hollowed-out bodies, all their organs and blood are missing," Keisha said.

"Like what I told you about earlier," Lily replied, nodding. "The tribal elders thought it was the vampires doing it."

"They don't eat organs, just blood," Damon sneered.

"Organs are filled with blood," Lily said through her teeth.

"Enough!" Wyatt stepped on the brakes. "Hold your thoughts."

The car was stopped. All five passengers looked around. They were in an alleyway, the train tracks behind a row of steel buildings with massive cargo doors. A lone man stood on top of a stack of wooden boxes, an AK47 in his hands. He wore a camouflage jacket, boots, and a peaked cap. A scarf was wrapped around the lower half of his face. He looked like a vigilante from a video game. The gun was aimed directly at the car.

Howard leaned forward, pointing to the muzzle of a shotgun propped on top of a bus, parked perpendicular to the garage door. "Over there," he muttered.

"There's another one," Keisha observed on the other side.

Wyatt placed his hands on top of the steering wheel. "Hold your hands above your heads," he warned the others. "Keep them visible." He gestured to his door; his palms opened wide.

"Don't get out," Keisha moaned. "There's at least ten of them."

"They make those guys back on the freeway look like the *Mouseketeers*," Howard commented.

One by one, the men revealed themselves. Mohawked and pierced, they were tatted up like a group of prisoners on a chain gang.

"Looks like San Quentin let the inmates out," Damon added.

Wyatt heard the whine of a big engine. Damon pointed to a metal box the size of a Mack truck. "These dudes have a serious generator going."

Lily leaned forward, her eyes huge in her face. "You're not thinking of getting out?"

Wyatt didn't hear her. He gulped. *This is it,* he thought reluctantly. *This is what Carter entrusted me to do.* His feet felt leaden. He tried to move them, but they didn't budge. They seemed glued to the floor of the car. Wyatt closed his eyes, breathing heavily through his nose, letting oxygen energize him. His heart was pounding in double time. *Well, here goes nothing.* Wyatt opened his door slowly, wincing when the lock clicked like a gunshot in the street. He stepped out of the car, rotating in a circle, as slowly as his feet allowed. Sweat trickled from his forehead, making a trail down his cheek. "Sebastian?" he asked. "Are you Sebastian Espinoza?"

"Who wants to know?" a man called from a rooftop. He had a semi-automatic pointed directly at Wyatt's heart. Wyatt raised his hands higher.

"We talked to him this morning. He gave us his location." He swallowed. "For trade and ..."

"What do you want?" Another man on the top of the loading bay interrupted, his gun following Wyatt's movements as he edged away from the vehicle. A dozen other firearms matched the movement. Wyatt took this as an invitation and moved forward, stopping abruptly at the sound of twenty guns being cocked. The man nodded for him to speak.

"My stepdad, Carter White, spoke to Sebastian Espinoza this morning. He's the provisional sheriff at Copper Valley."

The man pulled down the scarf hiding his face. He was older than Wyatt expected. Wyatt asked, "You're Espinoza?"

The older man smiled, revealing a mouthful of tobacco stained teeth. "Yup. I served with Carter in Afghanistan during my last tour."

"I thought you'd be younger," Wyatt blurted.

Sebastian's expression became less harsh. "I've been around awhile." He made a short movement, and the guns simultaneously relaxed. "I'm Espinoza. Copper Valley?" He started to climb down from his perch. "Maybe he *was* the provisional sheriff." He jumped down, landing in a pile of debris. He glanced at the grayish residue on Wyatt's shoes. "You step in the purple garbage?"

Wyatt glanced at his sneakers and nodded, then looked up, his skin tightening. He asked, "What do you mean, *was* the sheriff? I know what the news has been reporting, but we're okay there."

The man shook his head. "Come on in." He pulled the large door open, gesturing for Lily to drive the truck inside. "You better bring it in. Marauding lawyers, accountants, and dentists have taken the roads. They're stealing everything."

"Care to explain?" Wyatt asked, his voice breaking with panic. He had to trot to catch up to Sebastian's long stride. He felt like a kid tagging along.

"The world as you knew it is gone." Sebastian watched the others leave the car. "The government's closed down. No one knows what's happening. New president's dead."

"President Owens?" Lily asked as she exited the truck and caught up with them.

"Yeah, they said the army took him out, but no one's stepped forward. Then the purple stuff started bubbling up from the sewers. Killed more than half the town. The other half of the folks were eliminated by bands of crazies roving the roads. No law and order." His crew of men filed in, surrounding the newcomers. "The world, you know. It turned upside down." He took off his cap, then sat down tiredly in an old office chair.

"If the government isn't operating, who is in charge?" Wyatt asked, thinking that even if he could get in touch with somebody about Nate Owens' alliances, it really didn't matter. The traitor was dead.

"We heard they set up in Omaha but it's not true. Gus here"—Sebastian pointed to a large man with his shaven head sporting a tattooed image of a spider web—"heard something's been organized in Los Angeles, with the army. They mobilized at the Hollywood Bowl."

Wyatt looked around at the group of misfits. If anyone was terrorizing civilians, he'd have figured it would be this motley bunch of guys. "You said lawyers? I saw that guy who does those legal commercials. He was part of the gang attacking us."

"Yeah." Sebastian lit up a cigarette. "Never expected that." He laughed. "They massacred the motorcycle gang over in Shirley." He gestured to the other men in the room. "This is what's left of them. Those upright citizens stole their bikes, came here, demanding our supplies as if they were negotiating a class action lawsuit."

"What did you do to them?" Damon asked.

Sebastian nodded to a younger thug who opened a fridge, grabbing a bunch of cans of Whisp. He put them on a makeshift table. "Take one," Sebastian offered.

They each took a beverage. Wyatt nodded. It was icy cold and relief on his parched throat.

Gus grabbed a can of the soda. "What do you think we did with them?" he asked, his voice a deep rumble.

"Made a settlement?" Howard squeaked.

"Yeah, we settled it fair and square." He smiled, revealing a diamond grill. He moved closer to Howard, towering over him. "Wanna see where he's settled permanently?"

"Leave the kid alone, Gus," Sebastian said, straddling a chair. "I know Carter White. He was a fair guy."

"What do you mean he was ..." Wyatt asked, but Damon interrupted him.

"Any idea about The Glob, I mean the purple foam?"

Sebastian grunted. "Ha, I like it, The Glob." He looked at Lily. "You from the reservation?"

Lily nodded.

"Where's your CB radio? I need to speak with Carter." Wyatt stood up, looking for the equipment. He saw it on the counter against the wall and started walking over to it. Sebastian's words made him pause.

Sebastian clicked his tongue. "Don't touch it. I don't want to waste the power. I told you, they aren't answering anyway."

"Just because they aren't responding doesn't mean anything happened to them," Wyatt insisted, coming back to the circle.

Howard sank down on the floor, his face chalky.

"They'll be okay, Howard Drucker," Keisha said. "Carter will keep them safe."

Sebastian turned to Lily. "You look a bit like John Raven. Any casualties there?"

"He's my uncle," Lily admitted. "He went missing after the opening of Monsterland."

"He'll turn up," Sebastian said.

"You know him?" Lily asked.

"We worked together."

Lily put down her soda. "You worked in Area 51?"

All conversation stopped as they turned to look at Sebastian. Sebastian didn't answer.

Wyatt spoke again, his face red. "Look, this is all very interesting about Area 51, but I want to know what do you mean when you said Carter *was* a fair guy?"

"You better sit down, kid." Sebastian nodded for one of the men to bring over a plastic lawn chair. Wyatt sank down into the seat, his legs shaking.

"You saw the fuel?"

"Fuel? Are you talking about The Glob, um … I mean, the purple foam?" Wyatt asked.

"It's alien fuel. Back in the last century, in '47, a ship crashed."

"Roswell?" Keisha said, her voice soft. "That's ancient history. It was proven to be a weather balloon."

"That's what they told the mainstream media." Sebastian pulled out a bottle of bourbon to add to his Whisp. He held it out to Wyatt.

"Anyone want Brutal Juice?" he asked, pouring the liquor into his soda.

"Brutal Juice?" said Howard. "If you say it three times fast, doesn't the devil appear?"

Sebastian downed another shot and said, "Oh yeah, you gonna see the devil all right."

"I'm driving," Wyatt said, shaking his head, then added, "back to Copper Valley."

"Suit yourself." Sebastian shrugged and threw back another swallow.

Sebastian offered it to Wyatt's friends, who declined. The bottle made the rounds with the former motorcycle gang.

"Go on about the spacecraft," Howard said, leaning forward.

"Yeah, well, the ship crashed, and they recovered it. Government's been working on it for decades."

"Were there aliens?" Howard was breathless.

"Only dead ones. I worked there with her uncle, John Raven, during my first tour of duty. I saw them dead little suckers with my own eyes." He pointed to his eyes. "They're preserved. Like pickles."

"Like pickles!" Howard exclaimed. "They're green. I knew it!"

"Skin's violet like the damn fuel." The cigarette hung from Sebastian's mouth while he spoke. "The purple stuff, the army's been experimenting with it for years. Some annoying physicist named Hugh Frasier runs the program. They figured out a way to make it, you know, expand."

Howard nodded. "It all makes sense now, the cattle mutilations over the years, the empty carcasses. Crop circles?" He looked up at Sebastian.

Sebastian laughed. "You think the crop circles were road signs? Naw." He shook his head. "It's something else entirely different."

"Gotcha," Howard said, going back to the discussion about alien gasoline. "The Glob sucks the energy from life forms and transforms it into fuel."

"It turns organic matter into fuel to feed an engine. It's really no different from using fossil fuels," Keisha added.

"It's an issue when you're the fossil," Wyatt said. "Let me try your CB to reach Copper Valley."

"I told you, kid. There ain't no one left." Sebastian ignored Wyatt, then pointed to Howard and Keisha. "You're bright kids. Yeah, the substance is inactive, but when it's mixed with the energy from our bodies, it becomes fuel again."

"So, when they came here to explore the Earth," Keisha said, "they killed animals to refuel? Are you saying that on top of Monsterland, we have to worry about an alien invasion?"

"The aliens are dead," Sebastian said. "They're no threat."

"Then, where is The Glob coming from now?" Howard asked. "If the aliens are dead …"

The biker named Gus stepped forward. "It's coming up from the sewers."

Wyatt demanded, "How did you survive?"

"No sewers here," Sebastian shrugged. "We only have

cesspools, so we're not connected to the town's sewer system. You know, the sewer system put in by Vincent Konrad in the San Simi pipeline public works project."

"Vincent Konrad?" Howard repeated.

"Vincent Konrad is out of the picture. He's dead, remember?" Wyatt said. "So where is all this coming from?"

"The sewer systems are connected to Monsterland. The fuel has wiped out every town in a fifty-mile radius." Sebastian looked right at Wyatt. "Including Copper Valley."

"No!" Wyatt stood defiantly.

Keisha gasped and stood. "We have to go home."

Damon nodded his head in agreement. "You got any gas for us? Let's get outta here."

"Sorry." Another man separated himself from the shadows. "I was there a few hours ago. Copper Valley's a ghost town."

"I want to go home," Keisha repeated, taking Howard's hand.

"There have to be survivors," Howard insisted.

"What makes you think you're so special in Copper Valley? It's a town like any other town. Look at this one," Sebastian told him.

"You survived," Wyatt said, then added. "You all survived!"

"The kid's got a point," Gus said.

A loud banging interrupted him. All of them turned to a metal door, where they heard a crash and the sound of paws scrabbling on concrete.

"What's that?" Wyatt asked.

"We caught ourselves a pet," Sebastian smirked.

There was a long, drawn-out howl that froze the air in Wyatt's lungs.

"Melvin?"

Chapter 20

Igor packed his few belongings in an old shirt, tucking it under his arm as he walked through the underground tunnel. The desert sun baked the land above him. Sweat poured from his face, but he pushed on. He wanted to get out of this place. It had gone so horribly wrong. Vincent was out of control, and Frasier's ideas were ruining all of Igor and Vincent's well-thought-out plans.

Gritting his teeth with anger, he felt his skin go hot with shame. Igor had to perform with vampires, pretend to be enthralled with their cheesy rock bands. He took to his role, placating his son to work in close collaboration with Vincent. He was supposed to run the West Coast for them. He would finally be allowed to shine in the light and prove that ugliness can hide a great mind.

Ignored his whole life due to his misshapen spine and club foot, he made sure his son reached for the stars. He didn't expect ever to marry, but found his mail-order bride in the back of a muscle magazine, and brought her over from Slovakia.

She didn't stay with him long, but just long enough to give birth to Nate. Igor never realized he could love somebody as much as he loved his son. Nate was perfect. Igor wiped a tear from his eye.

Igor worked to put him in the best schools, and expose him to the right kinds of people. Nate did as he directed, even while Igor retreated into the background. Nate worked his way patiently up the political ladder, while Igor stayed out of the spotlight.

Councilman to Congressman to Governor. When Nate was chosen as McAdams's running mate, the campaign manager suggested strongly that Igor disappear. Igor made the staffers nervous, scared off potential voters. His demeanor, his afflictions, ruined the perception of the party, consequently affecting the numbers in a campaign based on making America beautiful again. Igor melted away, but Nate never forgot his father's contribution. He landed him a position as Vincent's confidant.

Vincent didn't mind Igor's odd looks. Igor smiled as he reminisced. He had to admit, while Vincent's mercurial temper could be off-putting, his determination and vision seduced him.

Memories fluttered through his mind. Meeting Vincent, feeling needed, important, vital to Vincent's strategy. He started to miss their camaraderie. Igor would have climbed the highest mountain for Vincent Konrad.

Soon, Nate and Vincent had a greater vision, and a new world order was planned. With Vincent and Nate, the fractured parties would unite, cleansing the globe of violence and illness. Standing at Vincent's right arm, Igor would be his counselor, his *consigliere*, like in all those old mob movies.

Except that damn Frasier came on board. Igor found himself minimized by the intimidating man. Oh, it wasn't as though he actually worked with him, but he stole Vincent from Igor, with interminable meetings and business trips to who knew where.

Igor had gotten used to being included, and the old feelings of being isolated surfaced. *Well, old Frasier is going to learn that I serve an important purpose,* he snickered. *An angry Vincent is an out of control Vincent. Nobody knows how to calm the doctor like me.*

Vincent and Igor had gotten close over the years, like an old married couple. *Ha,* he thought, *a regular Heckle and Jeckle.* Igor laughed. He anticipated Vincent's fits and started heading off volcanic explosions by solving issues before they reached cataclysmic proportions. *I'd like to see you how you handle this Mr. Scientist,* Igor thought.

Igor stopped short. What was he doing? He belonged with

Vincent, even if Vincent didn't realize it yet. How was he going to do that? He looked back into the endless tunnel. His stomach rumbled noisily. He was almost at the end.

First, a stop up in civilization for a bite to eat, then restored, he'd return and make it right with Vincent. It was what Nate would want him to do.

"A plan. I need a plan." He snapped his fingers. "Plan C! I will make a Plan C … Plan C," he repeated. Mumbling to himself, he held up his hand as he made a list. He needed to get back into Vincent's good graces. *It's what Nate would expect.*

He had to get rid of Frasier and his stupid mummy army. He needed to get Vincent alone. *But, first, I need to find something to eat,* he thought, both his steps and his heart light again.

He walked for another mile under the ground, his feet scuffing the grayish residue left by whatever Frasier was cooking up.

Igor stared ahead at the entrance, his eyes squinting from the block of sunlight pouring into the drain tube. He was coming to the end of the pipe.

He slowed his steps, noticing the belongings of the bums and vagrants that lived in the underground sewer system. Clothing was scattered all over the floor.

At the mouth of the opening, three lumps lay in the middle. He approached cautiously, realizing first that they were bodies and second, they were quite dead.

They were lying on their sides, their skin waxy. There was no other decay, as if the bodies had all the moisture sucked from them. Igor noticed their midsections were split open, the black hole revealing empty carcasses. He peered down, wondering what had happened to all their organs.

He rummaged through their belongings, not a candy bar or soda in anything. He threw down a dusty bag with disgust.

Sighing, he rose and continued outside in the bright glare of day. He needed to bring something back for Vincent. *A gift will turn him around.* His stomach gurgled again.

Pursing his lips, he looked at the road signs. "Eenie, meenie, miney … moe," he whispered, pointing to the different directions, finally landing on … "Well, I guess Copper Valley it is," he said, heading west.

Chapter 21

Melvin was in human form, with a black, leather, spiked collar around his neck. It was attached to a heavy chain leash. He strained against it as Gus pulled him out of the room.

"Stop, he's our friend." Wyatt ran over to snatch the leash.

Sebastian nodded for Gus to release Melvin.

Melvin struggled with the collar. Wyatt pushed his hands away. "Let me. What happened?"

"They caught me as I tried to leave town," Melvin spat.

"He's a werewolf," Gus sneered.

"No, he's not," Wyatt protested.

Melvin faced the angry man. "Actually, yes I am."

Gus lunged for him, but a curt order from Sebastian halted him. Wyatt heard a low growl that sent shivers up his spine coming from Melvin, his mouth revealing long yellow teeth. Wyatt gasped at the sight of those canines. Apparently, whatever Melvin did to himself had ruined years of painful and expensive orthodontic work.

"Cut it out, Mel," he ordered. Melvin stopped growling, but his stance remained aggressive. The coyote hit the wall from the other room.

"Let my animal go," Melvin snarled.

"I don't know, man. I never saw a coyote that big," Gus said with a growl that sounded more like Melvin.

"That thing isn't a coyote anymore," Howard informed him.

"What is it then?" Gus towered over Howard.

"It doesn't matter." Howard stood up to him like David against Goliath. "Listen, we're not enemies here. We came on Carter's orders. He wanted to set up a supply exchange."

"Doesn't matter. We're attacking Monsterland at dawn." Sebastian came over to diffuse the situation. He placed a hand on Gus's broad chest.

"Sebastian!" Gus yelled. "Don't tell them anything!"

Sebastian looked at Gus and shook his head. "They're not the enemy. We're gonna need every spare hand we can get if we're gonna shut that place down." He turned to Wyatt. "You should join up with us here. All of you, except the wolf boy."

Wyatt shook his head. "He's with us." As if to confirm this, Melvin yanked the chain from Gus's hands and walked to stand next to Howard. "Besides, we're heading back to Copper Valley first," Wyatt said with a determined voice.

"I told you, it's a fool's errand. No one would have survived."

The six teens remained resolute, their faces grim.

Sebastian inclined his head slightly. "Don't have such high expectations. We all lost somebody."

"But there are survivors here. There has to be some at home too," Wyatt said. "We have to go. We've only been gone since this morning."

Sebastian considered them, and something changed. His stance relaxed, and his face became less hardened. He looked at his band. "They don't have enough weapons."

"They'll never make it past the gang on the 15," Gus muttered.

Sebastian gave them all a long stare, his eyes softening when they fell on Lily. "I liked your uncle."

"Stop referring to him in the past tense. He'll turn up. He always does. You said it yourself," she retorted, her stance defiant.

Some of the men chuckled. Gus walked over to Sebastian, his bare arms like tattooed hams.

"What, Gus?" the leader asked.

"My kid. She reminds me of Zoe," he said. "I'm going with

them." There was a little rumble around the room. "I'll meet you in Monsterland."

Wyatt grabbed the opportunity. "Copper Valley's five miles from there. Once we make sure our families are okay, we'll help in the fight at Monsterland."

"You never know how many we could pick up in the town. It could triple our numbers."

"We will be heading to Monsterland," Wyatt said, his heart heavy. He couldn't believe something had happened to his family or even Jade. He'd feel something if it did, he knew it. "If The Glob did attack Copper Valley, it has to be stopped before it does more damage."

"I was thinking the same thing." Sebastian picked up a shotgun and threw it to Wyatt, who caught it deftly in one hand. "Who's in?" There was a chorus of cheers. "Give these kids some weapons," Sebastian ordered.

Wyatt moved to get into the truck he'd taken.

"Leave it, kid. We don't have enough gas. You'll ride in the back of my pickup. Let's go visit Copper Valley," he told the rest of the men.

"And then we're going to Monsterland," Wyatt confirmed.

Chapter 22

Copper Valley was a ghost town. Igor walked down the streets, peering into vacant windows. Nothing worked, of course, since there was no electricity. His lame foot dragged a trail through the gray residue. The late afternoon sun baked the empty pavement, gilding the houses with its waning light.

Cars lay at odd angles, abandoned haphazardly in the streets. Igor had never learned to drive; he couldn't sit comfortably behind the wheel.

He paused, the wind ruffling his stringy hair, the silence so profound it actually hurt. Igor shifted the lumpy bundle he carried, his back and right arm aching.

Wearily, he sat down on the curb, taking the shoe off his left foot, shaking the small pebble and sand into a pile on the asphalt. *Damn,* he shouldn't have left. He should have stood up to that scientific bully, he thought angrily.

He rested his hands on his knees, feeling smaller than he had in years. He felt himself shrinking, becoming part of the sidewalk. The world seemed different, colder, foreign. He felt like an interloper. He missed the security of being with Vincent.

A cat skittered past him, and he found himself holding out a shaking hand. He wanted to touch it, feel it purr, hold it against his bony chest. He realized with a start he was lonely.

He looked around at the vacant homes feeling lost. He

missed his world. He meowed like a cat, his face breaking into a smile. He felt the drool pool in his mouth. The cat, a feisty calico, hissed viciously, then darted up a driveway.

Sighing, he remembered his youth. He was old invisible Andrew, relegated to the corner, an embarrassment to his parents. People only saw his crooked body, dismissing his intelligence. He left home and traveled a bit, getting gigs, cleaning basements, and washing dishes in small restaurants.

Nate was never going to disappear into the woodwork. Igor worked three jobs, sending his son to the best schools, where he rubbed shoulders with movers and shakers. Igor stayed out of his son's life, afraid his appearance would frighten prospects.

Lucija, Igor's former wife, had run off with some guy she met. He never cared much for her anyway, but she served an important purpose—she gave him Nate. Everything was for Nate, and his son proved the effort had not been wasted. *How could Vincent let something happen to him? How could he be so careless?* he thought bitterly. *Vincent didn't have a child; he didn't understand the bond between father and son.*

Somehow everything went all wrong. Now that Nate was gone, he felt himself disappearing again. His whole identity was bound to Nate's success, or Vincent's. Without his child, he was nothing; a speck of dirt on the earth. His heart ached. He needed to belong again.

Igor shook himself, his hips protesting the long walk. He was getting maudlin. He needed to lie down for a bit, take a nap. A door squeaked on rusty hinges. Igor looked up at the shabby bungalow. The screen door moved slightly, the wind tugging at its ancient springs.

Igor pushed himself to his feet, swaying for a minute. He shuffled toward the old house. Igor wanted a shave, a drink, and some sleep. He wouldn't mind taking a … He didn't finish the thought. His eyes adjusted to the dingy interior. It was run down. He had lived in a million places like this. He looked at the cracked linoleum, imagining Nate's little feet running around. His eyes stung with the memory.

He moved toward the kitchen, his skeletal fingers leaving a trail in the light dust covering the countertops.

The old enamel stove had a pot on every burner, the food

long since congealed into grayish lumps. The cookie jar was missing a lid; it lay shattered on the counter. Igor peered inside the crockery container; even though the cookies looked fine, the thick gray residue surrounding it made the idea of eating its contents unappetizing.

There was a supply of Whisp next to the fridge, he noticed happily. He popped a can and took a satisfying gulp. His throat was dry.

Leaning against the counter, he let his eyes take in this model of suburbia. The house was well used, covered with that strange film he knew was not a natural occurrence. He opened the fridge, cringing when the ghastly odor of rotting food hit him.

Slamming it shut, he reached for a cabinet, taking out a box of cereal. *Fruited Fiber,* he liked that. He munched contently on the pellets that smelled faintly like cat piss.

He sniffed again, detecting the odor of something stronger. Taking a leisurely stroll toward the back of the house, he stumbled over the body. Leaning down, he touched the slick surface. He recoiled from the taut feel of her desiccated skin.

"What?" He peered closer, narrowing his eyes, all hunger gone. A line bisected her middle from neck to groin. Every organ and drop of blood was missing.

Not just the bums, but a town. "Oh, Vincent," he said in a panicked whisper. "What mischief are you up to?" Igor dropped the cereal. It landed with a dull thud, carpeting the floor. He ran wildly from the room, his feet smashing the little circles of multigrain into smithereens.

Chapter 23

"Stop fidgeting," Damon warned, stabbing his elbow in Melvin's ribs. "Move that stupid coyote thing to the other side." He was yelling, his voice lost in the wind as they barreled along on the highway in a pickup truck. The sun had gone down, and, in spite of it being early summer, it had gotten decidedly cooler. A steady wind blew from the north, chilling them.

"Did I snore?" Wyatt asked. He was uncomfortably crammed in the back of the truck bed with all his friends. He had his knees up, his arms resting on top of them. Lily was squeezed close to him, Howard and Keisha on the opposite side of the truck bed.

"Like a chainsaw," Howard laughed.

They had been traveling for almost three hours, taking detours when they sensed trouble. Sebastian and his group knew their way around the desert. Wyatt guessed he'd slept for most of the time. He felt sluggish, weary to the bone.

Keisha opened a cooler filled with sandwiches made from stale bread, which they washed down with water they'd refilled in soda bottles.

He'd noticed Melvin's worried frown the minute he opened his eyes. His friend squirmed as if sensing some sort of anxiety. The coyote that traveled with him panted noisily, then turned in a tight circle, sitting down practically on Damon's lap.

"What's this one's name?" Wyatt asked, trying to distract his friend. "Melvin! What's your ... I mean, what do you call this one?"

"Freddy," Melvin responded after what seemed to be a long time. He was glancing nervously at the convoy that surrounded them.

Wyatt stretched up a bit to look at the group of cars. They rode as if in a presidential cavalcade. Sebastian drove them in a black pickup. All around them were different cars and a few bikes, each loaded with armed passengers.

They were now entering the area where they had been attacked that morning. In the distance, he could see the charred remains of burnt brush where the fire had raged. Wyatt noted, "Looks like the fire exhausted itself."

Howard smiled and said, "It ran out of fuel. No trees in the desert."

Wyatt felt Lily shiver against him. The sun was slowly dipping into the hills; the horizon lit up behind them. Stars made their appearance, dotting the crystal sky like diamonds.

"Cold?" he asked Lily.

Lily's eyes lowered shyly. Her shoulders shrugged. Wyatt put his arm around her back, pulling her into the warmth of his embrace. Her head grazed his cheek, her dark hair whipping behind her. She fit differently under his arm than Jade. She was more substantial; he could feel the toned muscles in her back. Even though she was resting, Lily was coiled with tension. Jade had more of a nervous energy, and while Jade had impressed Wyatt when she hacked her zombie ex-boyfriend in half and prevented him from killing them in Monsterland, it felt more out of character. With Lily, he sensed survival was in her DNA.

He caught Melvin starring at him, his eyes hostile. Wyatt inclined his head. Melvin looked away angrily; his jaw worked as if he were clenching his teeth. *What's up with that?* Wyatt wondered. "Mel?" he asked. Melvin ignored him.

Melvin looked back again, this time his eyes narrowing on Lily, with a final glance at Wyatt. Wyatt turned to Howard, raising his eyebrows, then motioned to Melvin.

Howard shrugged, and Wyatt watched him awkwardly stretch his elbows with a wide yawn, placing his arm around

Keisha's shoulders. Keisha wiggled closer to Howard; her face remained tense.

The group had barely spoken, all thoughts on getting home. He heard Damon curse as Melvin stood, his eyes turning golden as the day became night. The top of the three-quarter moon showed behind the mountain range.

Melvin was holding onto the side of the truck, his face contorted.

Wyatt stuffed his hands into his pocket and felt the crushed candy bars he'd taken from the grocery hours earlier. "Here." He held out his offerings to Melvin. "Take it; you're probably hungry."

The coyote started howling, its mammoth paws next to Melvin on the side of the truck bed, and to Wyatt's surprise, Melvin opened his mouth with a wild cry. His shoulders undulated under his borrowed shirt, becoming wider. His face narrowed, his cheeks changing into a snout. Hair exploded from his limbs, thick and silvery.

Damon scrambled away, crawling over Wyatt, and screamed, "He's morphing!"

Howard said, "That's impossible, it's not a full moon."

Damon looked at him and said, "You don't understand, you don't know what you're talking about. They change at will!"

"That's bull," Howard replied, his rapt gaze on Melvin as he observed the changes in his friend.

Keisha interrupted them and replied, "No, it's not. It all depends on the mental discipline of the human, or if they're uncontrollably angry."

"This is Melvin we're talking about, Keisha," said Howard, turning to her. He pushed his glasses up the bridge of his nose.

Keisha turned to look at Howard full in the face and said gently, "He's not the Melvin you remember." She laid her hand on Melvin's trembling flank. "There's a rare breed of werewolves called Lycans that can transform at will." She peered at Lily through the darkness. "A shaman can teach someone how to do that."

All eyes were on Melvin, his wolfish face baying at the large yellow moon now glowing in the sky.

His paws leaned on the sides of the truck. Wyatt dropped the candy bar, climbed over, grabbing him around the middle.

"Don't do it, Mel. Hold on; we're almost home!"

Melvin turned his huge head around, baring long feral teeth. Saliva dripped from them, staining Wyatt's arm. Wyatt held him tighter, feeling them both trembling as if they were freezing.

"Get away from it! It's going to bite your head off!" Damon grabbed a fistful of Wyatt's shirt and tugged.

Wyatt felt his eyes smart, but resisted wiping the tears gathering there. He pulled out of Damon's grasp. "Stop! This is my friend. He's not a monster!"

Wyatt buried his face in the coarse fur. "Don't go, Mel," he whispered.

Melvin's massive snout turned, his eyes meeting Wyatt's moist ones. Wyatt looked into the dark depths and saw Melvin. He knew his friend was still there.

"I must go." The words were torn from Melvin's throat like a growl.

Howard crawled over. "No, it's not safe. Stay with us."

Wyatt held onto the thick torso.

He felt the hard muscles bunch under the fur, as if Melvin was ready to leap.

Wyatt whispered, "Head for Copper Valley, you'll be safe there."

"Get away from that thing. Stop! Werewolf!" Damon screamed, banging his fist on the cab of the truck.

The werewolf, for surely Wyatt couldn't think of this thing as Melvin anymore, growled a response. The savage eyes softened. He felt a cold nose touch his cheek.

Wyatt heard shouts; the truck was slowing. He looked up to see Damon pointing the barrel of his gun directly at Melvin's head.

"No!" Wyatt yelled. "Jump!" He hit Melvin on the flank, watching in awe as he leaped off the truck bed, over the car traveling next to him. The coyote followed Melvin, vanishing into the desert landscape.

He shoved Damon backward with both hands; the shot from the gun went wild. "What's wrong with you? He's our friend!"

"Don't you understand, he's not human anymore! He'll kill you." Damon's voice was raw.

"You don't know what you're talking about, Damon!"

Damon grabbed Wyatt by the shirt. "You stupid kid, that's what my father did to my mother! He loved her, and he ripped her to shreds. You can't trust them. You don't understand monsters!"

Wyatt backed away, stunned, and stuttered, "I'm sorry, I didn't know."

"Nobody knew what hell I lived with." Damon wiped a tear from his cheek. "Once someone is bitten, they're not the same person you know. They're a monster."

Other shots rang out, but Melvin zigzagged across the asphalt, leaping over an incline before disappearing into the darkening desert. Wyatt smiled. He was heading toward Copper Valley.

Wyatt and Howard stood, watching the beasts melt into the darkness.

"Everybody knows werewolves are the superior monster," Howard said.

Keisha moved next to him. "I thought you believed vampires were smarter and stronger."

Howard shook his head. "Not anymore."

The rushing wind roared in their ears as the truck moved down the freeway. They could barely hear each other talk.

"Watch out!" Lily screamed. The rogue gang appeared out of nowhere, jumping onto the freeway in the middle of the exit, some on motorcycles leaping over the median like professional riders.

The teens crouched down, bullets whizzing past them, pinging on the metal sides of the truck.

"I knew I should have insisted they let me drive the Chevy," Wyatt yelled out.

Wyatt watched a bullet hit the driver in the next car, sending it into a tailspin.

They propped their guns on the sides of the truck, loaded them with shells, and began firing.

"Aim for the largest part of them," Damon ordered, while he took a spot in the rear of the bed.

The largest part? Wyatt aimed his gun. He'd be happy if he hit the side of a barn. With the truck moving at the speed of light, he would be lucky if he managed to get off a shot. He glanced at Lily, calmly and efficiently squeezing off round after round. Wyatt closed one eye and tried to focus on the marauding thugs behind them. The teens spread out.

Howard stood against the front cab of the truck, Keisha next to him. Lily took one side, Wyatt the other. Damon was firing away from a corner.

Wyatt knew he was not effective. His shots bounced harmlessly off the hoods of the approaching cars. He watched the advancing group with horror, knowing they were toast.

One by one, Sebastian's cars were overtaken by the gang members. They could barely see them; their headlights were off. But they could hear the screech and groan of metal colliding with metal. The freeway was littered with both body and car parts.

Damon yelled, "Douse the flashlights!"

As if on cue, all of Sebastian's team extinguished their headlights, throwing everybody into velvet blackness.

Wyatt blasted away, imagining the horror of bodies erupting into a spray of blood and bone. His gorge rising, he forced himself to not think about what he was doing, as much as why he was doing it.

Another of Sebastian's cars careened off the highway, hit the concrete median, then exploded in a fireball. They heard cheers from the attackers; their own fleet was dwindling.

The truck jerked, sending Wyatt over the edge; he felt someone grab the back of his pants, pulling him into safety. He turned around to see Damon, white-faced and sweating, steadying him.

"Thanks, man," Wyatt said.

Damon responded, "I got this side, you take it there. Incoming, two o'clock."

A bike pulled up; a thin man wearing a yellow satin graduation robe with a sash around his waist grabbed the rear of the pickup, jumping in.

The intruder lunged for Lily, catching a handful of her hair.

He pulled out a knife, placing it against her neck. A thin line of blood trickled down her throat.

Wyatt surged forward, and the biker slashed at him, catching it on Wyatt's shirt. It tore through, grazing the skin of his stomach, leaving a stinging trail.

Howard swung his shotgun and hit the attacker on the chin with a satisfying thud. Graduation guy dropped the knife with a scream, going down on one leg.

Wyatt aimed, but the truck took that time to swerve from a cluster of oncoming motorcycles. The weapon slipped out of Wyatt's hands. He scrambled for it, but the other man grabbed it first. The intruder fired, the explosion whistling past Wyatt's face. The heat of the bullet burned his cheek. Shoving Lily out of the way, his ear was deafened by the blast of another gun. Keisha's shot missed the attacker by a mile. She jumped high, swinging her leg in an arc, slamming the man in the midsection. The attacker flipped over the side of the truck, landing on the blacktop.

Wyatt watched the pursuing cars run over his body. His eyes widened, and he pointed over Keisha's shoulder, his voice not working.

They heard loud squeals as tortured brakes ground the chase to a halt.

The truck skidded, stopping dead in its tracks, sending the teens to the front of the vehicle bed as they swerved wildly.

Wyatt scrambled across the truck bed to the side. He leaned over. His jaw dropped.

A mass of marching mummies was surrounding them like a purple tide.

Chapter 24

Howard gulped. "Mum, mum, mummies," he stuttered. "I hate mummies. They're nothing more than corpses wrapped in toilet paper."

"Where are they coming from?" Lily cried.

The stumbling army of corpses reached the stragglers on the fringe of the gang. The mummies glowed with a fluorescent radiance, the gauzy material lighting up the dark desert.

The teens watched the attackers pick riders off their bikes by the neck, swinging their bodies around as if they weighed nothing. Cars were overrun, screams muffled by the linen wrapped around the hands of the monsters silencing their voices forever.

"Keesh," Howard said. "Do they look purple to you?"

"Look." Keisha pointed. Wherever the mummies touched their victims, the flesh turned the same pale color as the people who came in contact with the alien jet fuel.

"Holy crap, I bet they took a bath in The Glob," Wyatt said. He ran to the front, banging on the cab. "Move!" he yelled. "Sebastian, we have to get out of here!"

"Shoot!" Wyatt heard Damon yell.

They fired into the line of oncoming mummies. The bullets penetrated the cloth with small puffs of dust, but the mummies were unfazed.

"The bullets!" Howard screamed. "They're useless. I knew it!"

He heard a curse and felt the truck lurch forward. They were trying to cut through the mass of mummies that surrounded their vehicle, stalling the chase.

The mummies were almost upon them. One by one, the creatures overwhelmed the other cars, moving in a steady stream toward the stationary autos.

Wyatt could feel the earth tremble from their united steps. They marched as if they had one brain, their movements identical. It stirred a memory. He bit his lip, his eyes going wide. *I've seen this before*, he thought. *It was when The Glob almost killed me.*

What was left of the biker gang faded away as the new threat increased.

One linen-wrapped hand latched onto the tailgate. Lily pounded it with the butt of her gun. The truck started to move slowly; the mummy held on, the body dragging on the asphalt.

Keisha cried for Sebastian to drive faster. Wyatt smashed his gun against the corpse's head. It was like hitting solid stone. Nothing was stopping it.

The mummy continued to climb onto the bed of the vehicle. It was half on and half off. Its long legs dangled over the rear.

The truck was picking up speed, moving through the crowd of creatures. They could feel the vehicle bounce over the bodies, but as soon as they were released from the punishing wheels of the truck, the monsters would stand and resume their pursuit.

Still others hung on.

The mummy grasped outward, grabbing Lily's leg. She shrieked when its wrapped hand held her thigh in a punishing grip.

Lily's pink lips turned a waxy blue. Her face lost all animation; she started folding like wet laundry.

Wyatt heard Damon yell his name. He turned to see Damon clutch the mummy. The creature grabbed him by the shoulders and pushed Damon with a volcanic force across the rear of the truck. His body slammed against the cab window, shattering the glass.

Wyatt rushed the mummy, struggling with the iron grip it had on Lily's prone body, not caring when he felt the familiar lethargy fill him. He fought it, gritting his teeth, pushing his fingers underneath the wrapped ones trying to disengage the creature from Lily. He was light-headed and working on autopilot, unsure of what he was doing. He only knew he had to save her. Wyatt headbutted the broad shoulder, which was the equivalent of smacking heads with a moose, he thought hazily.

Wyatt watched in a dreamlike state as Howard twisted and screamed for Keisha. Using their shotgun butts as leverage, they were slamming the mummy's shoulders. They pounded with enough force that the mummy slid back, its feet hitting the rushing pavement.

"The linen!" Keisha yelled. "Keep pushing, Howard. The pavement is shredding the linen."

Wyatt heard Howard agree, the relentless hold easing.

"It's disintegrating!" Howard shouted. "Look! That's zombie flesh underneath the wrapping."

"Yes," Keisha said. "I can see the green tinge of its skin. I think those are the zombies from Monsterland."

Wyatt was sure the stars he saw weren't in the sky when the steely fingers completely loosened, and the mummy fell away. With a shocked realization, Wyatt muttered, "They're coming from Monsterland."

He grabbed the tailgate, his head clearing. He watched in a mixture of astonishment and joy as the feet of the mummy dissolved from the friction of being dragged by the truck.

As if in slow motion, the purple-tinted linen arms cartwheeled and the mummy fell backward. This action seemed to affect the horde, and they stumbled around the unwrapped body in confusion.

"Step on it!" Wyatt screamed to Sebastian.

The truck picked up speed, but the transmission slipped, and they listened with dismay as Sebastian struggled with the engine.

The mummies were sloughing away like dead skin, the movement of the truck unraveling the material. Wyatt shook his head, clearing it, to stare at the monster lying in the middle of the road, its bottom half frayed and unwound, leaving the decaying carcass of a dead zombie.

"Why would anyone saturate them with The Glob? It should draw the life out of them," Wyatt said, breathing heavily.

"The road shredded the linen. It looks like they lose their power when they aren't in contact with The Glob substance," Keisha said, wiping her face with her shirt. "It must be animating them, so it sucks the life from us and gives it to inanimate objects."

"It can't siphon the life out of something that is already dead," Howard explained, then added helpfully, "All we have to do is unwrap them."

"Right," Wyatt replied. "You hold them still, and I'll do the unwinding." He turned to Lily. "You okay?"

"It was an out-of-body experience," she said, her voice husky.

"What did you see?" Wyatt whispered.

"I saw a world covered with The Glob."

"We'll stop it, Lily."

The truck was moving now at a steadier pace, putting some distance between them and the monsters.

"Guys," Keisha's voice was small. "Look at Damon."

Wyatt scrambled on the bed of the truck, searching for his flashlight. He grasped it and illuminated the area. Wyatt looked over to see Damon in the corner; his head was slumped forward, his eyes open in surprise. Crouching down, Howard held his wrist, shaking his head when he failed to find a pulse. All four of them clustered around Damon's body.

Wyatt's eyes smarted. Gently, he shut Damon's lids, cursing with regret. "I wish I had known about his life earlier."

"It didn't help when he acted like a bully," Keisha added.

"Everybody's got stuff," Lily said simply.

Wyatt grabbed an old tarp, placing it over Damon's form. He heard Lily choke back a sob.

The army of mummies had formed a square. They were following the truck again, their speed picking up. Wyatt studied them and noticed there was no leadership. Wyatt leaned over the tailgate. "Who's commanding them?"

Howard turned and watched the advancing horde. "I don't know."

Wyatt yelled, "Hey!" Not one mummy acknowledged him.

"That's odd." Howard's gaze scanned them. "I don't see anyone directing them."

Wyatt shook his head. "Hey, you!" He clapped loud and waved his hands. "I think they can't see or hear."

"Technically, no." Howard bit his lower lip. "I don't know much about them. Never thought they were an intelligent creature. See," he said, pointing with his muzzle. "Look at them. Not a brain cell to be found among any of them. Waste of a good monster, if you ask me."

Wyatt looked up to see Keisha and Lily watching Howard like he was an insect.

"Shut up, Howard Drucker," Keisha said.

Wyatt observed the mummies marching in unison; their heads didn't turn, they followed in a straight line. "They can't see or hear!" Howard exclaimed.

"Seb, get off the road!" Wyatt shouted through the rear window. "I bet they won't follow."

They felt the truck jolt as Sebastian made a hard right off the highway into the desert. The tires kicked up a wall of dust. They watched the mummies continue their march, oblivious to the truck's detour.

Howard commented, "Good thinking, Wyatt."

Wyatt saw Keisha slip her hand in Howard's. "I didn't think things could get worse …" Keisha whispered, too afraid to even voice what she was thinking. "Do you think Melvin is okay?"

Balancing, Wyatt stood, exchanging a long look with Howard. He nodded. He added with conviction that sounded hollow to his own ears, "I told him to go to Copper Valley. I know he'll be waiting for us there."

Wyatt shivered, for the first time worried about what they were going to find when they reached home. He hoped Melvin made it there safely. His eyes rested with regret on the covered lump of Damon's body and wished things could have been different.

The teens watched the creatures disappear as they marched in a file down the freeway.

"Where are they headed?" asked Keisha.

"The reservation is that way," said Lily, her voice small.

Wyatt touched her hand and repeated, "We'll stop them, Lily. I don't know how we're going to do it, but the answer has to be in Monsterland."

Chapter 25

Gus had jumped out of the cab before the truck stopped. He peered over the back and looked from Damon's body to Wyatt.

"You guys okay?"

Nobody answered.

"I nearly crapped my pants when I saw them mummies," he told them. No one responded. Wyatt knew they were all worried about what they'd find, now that they were back in Copper Valley.

It was dark, no lights anywhere. Gus handed out a bunch of glow sticks, the kind that snap and glow bright colors. After they all cracked their sticks, their faces blazed in a variety of shades Wyatt remembered from when he was a little kid at a circus show. Pastel pinks, blues, and greens swung as they slid off the back of the truck.

Wyatt leaped from the rear, with his glow stick. It lit up the area around his worried face. They were a few blocks from his home. The town was silent. Not a dog barked.

"I'm this way." Keisha pointed in the other direction with her green stick.

"I'll go with you," Howard offered.

"Don't you want to go to your home first?" Keisha asked.

"Your house is closer." Howard took her hand. Keisha seemed to hold back.

"What about Jade?" Keisha asked.

"She's around the corner from me. We'll hit up her house after we've been to mine," Howard said to Keisha, but his eyes were locked with Wyatt. Wyatt nodded.

Lily looked at Keisha. "I'll stay with Wyatt."

Keisha agreed, then took off with Howard trailing, holding a blue light to illuminate their path.

Wyatt searched the windows of the houses in the town, looking for a sign of life, his breath still in his chest.

He heard both Gus and Sebastian walking behind them, holding the flashlights. Turning the corner to his house, he noticed the screen door open. He took off in a trot, a sob welling in his chest.

Sebastian urged him to slow down, but he didn't care. He felt tears running down his cheeks. Wyatt slammed into the porch, stopping dead in his tracks. Holding up his stick, he peered into the room with growing panic, seeing the thin coating of dust on the surface of the furniture.

He ran a finger along it, dread filling every cell of his body. He heard the others enter behind him, followed by Lily's gasp at the mess.

The sound of something dropping in the kitchen made him yell with relief, "Mom?"

He heard feet moving with an uneven gait. He ran to the kitchen, his light casting a faint reddish glow on the flapping material of a black jacket. It disappeared around the doorway. Reaching out, he grabbed a fistful of material, his sore hand protesting the punishing hold.

He pulled hard, his face registering surprise when the light revealed the face of the hunchback from the show in Monsterland.

"What are you ..." The words died on Wyatt's tongue when he spied a shoe peeking out from the next room. It was attached to the remains of a leg, purple coated, but with a pale, waxy shade he recognized too well. He dropped his hold on the intruder. Wyatt fell to his knees, his mouth open in soundless horror. The light revealed the carcass, huddled in a fetal position.

Lily tumbled down next to him. "Wyatt?"

Wyatt shook his head. He heard the rapid footsteps of Gus and Sebastian taking off after the old man.

"She didn't suffer. Just remember that. You know it feels peaceful, not painful," Lily whispered. She took Wyatt's hand in her own, sitting silently in the darkness.

Wyatt couldn't say if he sat four minutes or four hours on the filthy floor. His numb legs couldn't lift him. Vaguely, he heard Lily walk through the rest of the house, then she leaned over, her soft hands brushing the hair from his flushed face.

"There's no one else here," she said quietly.

Wyatt wiped an errant tear, ashamed he hadn't thought to look for his brother. He gave a shivery sigh of relief, biting his lip with the realization he had to be cautiously optimistic. If his brother was alive, he would be with Carter, and he would find them. He looked at his mother's carcass. He wanted to lie down and never get up.

The door slammed; Howard's white face floated into the darkness. He was holding Keisha's hand. She walked like a zombie.

Wyatt stood on rubbery legs, holding out his arms. The three of them entered into a hug. He pulled Lily into their group embrace.

"You?" Howard asked.

"My mom," Wyatt said tonelessly.

"Both of Keisha's parents. They were in bed. It looks like they never knew what hit them."

He looked into Howard's brown eyes with the silent question.

"I don't know," Howard said, reading his thoughts. "They left a note." He held up a crushed Post-It note in his hand. "They headed for my dad's old base."

Wyatt took a shuddering breath and said softly, "Jade?"

Howard shook his head slowly. "The house was covered in purple residue."

The four of them stood silently for a moment, taking in the enormity of the situation.

"Are you going after your parents?" Wyatt asked.

"Not until we finish what we have to do." Howard's answer was so low, Wyatt had to strain to hear him.

"I don't even know what we have to do," Wyatt said, his voice cracking. "We should look for Melvin."

"There's nothing left, Wyatt," Howard said. The only sound in the room was their collective breathing.

"Monsterland," Wyatt said, his voice devoid of emotion. "We must destroy it."

Wyatt could feel Keisha's shoulders shaking with suppressed sobs. She stopped crying, her face full of pain. Keisha said, "I wish ..."

"What do you wish?" Lily asked.

"I wish I could find the person responsible and make them pay."

"Keisha, don't let the hate take over who you are," Lily begged.

"Why shouldn't I?" Keisha asked, full of rage. She didn't look like herself anymore. Her analytical mind was gone, replaced by white hot fury.

"Because then they win," Lily continued.

"What a crock, Lily. They took everything from me."

"Not everything," Howard said. "You still have me."

"And me," Wyatt added.

"Me too. You're not alone."

Wyatt watched Keisha struggle through her pain. She sighed gustily, the heat of her grief dissipating. "Okay then, I wish ... I wish ... I wish I was Medusa, and when they look at me, they would turn into stone where they can suffer frozen for eternity."

"Does that make you feel better?" Lily asked with a slight smile.

"Like it's going to happen," she said with a grimace. "I get it. One can fantasize."

"That's better than the hatred."

The cawing of a bird broke the tense silence. Lily pulled away, running to the window. Wyatt followed her. Parting the curtains, they observed the outline of a huge raven perched on a fence post in the darkness.

She walked outside onto the back porch, Wyatt behind her. The raven eyed her speculatively from its spot on the railing. It cawed again, then flapped its giant wings. The raven's black feathers melted into the background of the inky sky.

"Where?" Lily said in a soft voice.

"What?" Wyatt asked, incredulous at the notion she was talking to the bird.

"Stop!" Lily commanded, holding out her hand to silence him.

The bird squawked a few times, then took off toward the west.

"You weren't talking to that bird," Wyatt said with a shake of his head.

"And what if I was?" Lily asked.

"Let me see," Howard said, "on a scale of one to ten, one being a normal boring day in Copper Valley, ten being the strangest day ever, where does this fall in the weird zone? We fought vampires, werewolves, and zombies at Monsterland, and today we made contact with an alien jet fuel that siphons the living energy of its victims turning them into empty husks, along with battling with an army of angry mummies. Really, Wyatt, you think conversing with a bird is weird?"

Wyatt considered this for a minute, then said, "Well, all right then. What did it tell you?"

"Head to Instaburger," Lily said.

The four kids turned at the sound of crunching gravel. Gus was dragging Igor by one arm, and Sebastian had the other.

"Sorry about your family, kid," Sebastian said, shoving Igor in front of him. "We questioned him but got nothing. Are you kids ready to head out to Monsterland?"

Lily shook her head. "We have to make a stop first."

"That wasn't in the plan," Gus said. "Who told you?"

All four of them exchanged looks; Lily responded, "A little bird."

Chapter 26

Wyatt covered his mother's body with a thick quilt, silently promising he would return to take care of her remains. Keisha had done the same thing, she told him. Wyatt leaned through the window of the cab from the flatbed of the pickup, giving directions to Instaburger.

They rode in silence, all eyes watching their surroundings, the dark road stretching out behind them like a silver ribbon. The desert was silent, and the Copper Valley mountains bore down on them, making Wyatt feel like he was underwater. It was desolate, the muteness profound.

He rested his head on his knee, a well of despair closing over his head, making him feel suffocated. The world was unrecognizable.

A little less than a month ago he had traveled this same road, ready for an adventure of a lifetime with his brother, Howard and … Melvin. He had been on his way to fulfill the dream of seeing real zombies, Howard was going to experience a live vampire concert, and Melvin … well, Melvin wanted to prove his beloved werewolves were superior in every way. Wyatt's only wish was to win the heart of Jade; and now everything was changed. "It was all wrong."

Howard perked up. "Vincent made the park attractions into monsters. They were victims of their conditions. His ambition and greed made him no better than Dr. Frankenstein in the Mary Shelley novel."

"Frankenstein was the monster," Lily said.

"No," Keisha shook her head. "Frankenstein made the monster. The monster never had a name. Dr. Frankenstein reanimated it."

"Dr. Frankenstein referred to his creation as the creature, or the wretch. I like to think of the monster as a behemoth. You know, something extremely large and powerful …"

"No, Howard. A behemoth would be more like a giant lizard destroying a city," Keisha replied.

"I can see your point. However, a behemoth is a generic term …"

"Please, stop," Wyatt whispered. "I can't listen to this stuff anymore." His breath came quick and fast for a minute, his chest muscles constricting as if a stake was going through his midsection.

Lily looked at him, her voice gentle. "I agree with Wyatt."

Wyatt started to respond, his throat clogged, and firmed his lips into a straight line. He nodded slightly, afraid that if he opened his mouth to say something he would start to blubber. Lily touched his hand. "I'm sorry about your mother and Jade."

Wyatt let her fingers lace with his. *This is the essence that makes us human,* he thought. He looked down at their clasped hands and felt her palm pressed against his own, anchoring him.

The touch of another human made him feel that he wasn't alone. He took a shuddering breath.

Lily's bird had apparently flown the coop, leaving Wyatt to wonder if they were on a wild raven chase. His gut told him to head straight for Monsterland and stop whatever monster was originating or generating from there. Were they doing the right thing by detouring to Instaburger?

"Lily," he whispered. "Was that really your uncle?"

Lily brushed her hair from her face. Shrugging, she said, "Would you believe me if I said it was?"

Wyatt sat back, not sure how to answer, but he somehow understood that the way he responded was important to Lily. "If you say so, I believe you."

She nodded, a faint smile on her lips, saying nothing. He cleared his throat loudly.

"Someday I'll tell you about it," she said.

"Not today?" he asked.

Lily shook her head. "No, Wyatt. Not today."

Instaburger was located on the 5, not far from the heart of the town. Nestled in a small dip in the road next to a gas station, it had a large parking lot in front with the typical white and red signage, livened up with yellow accents. It was dark; no lights illuminated the building. He knew from his time working there that Manny had a powerful generator he used during blackouts.

Its huge glass windows were usually lit up by hanging pendant lamps of an industrial style that practically baked the people sitting underneath them.

He leaned forward, looking for a telltale stream of smoke coming from the pipe from the frying station. Nothing. He shook his head. Instaburger was as quiet as a tomb. Truthfully, he didn't expect to find anything there, but didn't think it was wise to question Lily's ability to understand bird.

They pulled into a spot on the other side of the parking lot, behind the building. Wyatt jumped out, running for the door. As he expected, it was locked, but a movement caught his eye. Cupping his hands around his eyes, he peered into the unlit interior. He banged on the window with his fist. He saw an arm. He'd recognize that arm anywhere.

"Manny! Manny, open up!" Wyatt screamed. He pounded harder. "Open up; it's me, Wyatt, Wyatt Baldwin."

He saw the white shirt of someone rushing to the door, heard the lock click, and was grabbed in a bear hug of an embrace. Wyatt couldn't believe the rush of emotion, his eyes stinging. He was dragged into the store, breathless, words stuck in his throat, too afraid to emerge. As if sensing Wyatt's greatest fears, he heard the sentence he was so desperate to hear.

"Sean is okay. He's here and safe." The voice sounded broken.

"Carter," Wyatt said, his voice just as choked.

"I didn't know if she was in danger … I would have never left her alone."

Wyatt squeezed Carter's shoulder. His stepfather looked ten years older, his face lined, his color pasty.

Wyatt shook his head as if that was enough. Carter had both hands on Wyatt's shoulders. Despite trying, Wyatt couldn't stop the fat tears that leaked from his eyes.

"You're okay?" Carter asked in a rusty voice.

Wyatt nodded, still too overcome to speak. He was buffeted by another body that broke from the shadows. He heard his brother's muffled voice telling him he was so glad to see him. He embraced Sean with his other arm, regretting that his mother wouldn't see the three of them together. He smiled at the thought; she would have liked that, she would have liked that a lot.

Wyatt saw Carter turn and notice Sebastian for the first time. The two men embraced. Carter asked, "How bad?"

Sebastian shook his head. "It's bad, Carter, really bad."

"Why are you still here?" Howard asked. "I mean, like, alive?"

Wyatt looked at the group surrounding them. Manny, Liz, Jade's father, a few others, all looking shell shocked. His neighbor Hank watched the front door, a shotgun in his hands.

Manny shook his head. "Don't know. That crap crept into every building except Instaburger."

"We were here, having a meeting," Carter said. "I would have never left her." His voice cracked.

"The whole town is gone," Manny interrupted. "We never even knew it had happened until the meeting broke and they returned home."

"Jade?" Wyatt asked her father. Jade's dad looked deflated. Not nearly as threatening as when Wyatt met him earlier in the morning.

Sucking in a breath, the older man lowered his gaze and replied, "I locked her, my wife, and son in the attic. I thought they'd be safe. They must have tried to outrun it. I found my son and part of my …" He turned to the wall, and Wyatt watched the huge shoulders shake. Wyatt walked over and placed his hand on the older man's back. "It's not a painful experience. I know, I … that stuff almost got me."

Wyatt felt a great lump in his chest. He couldn't believe that

Jade was dead. He knew that he'd always love her in a special way. She'd forever own real estate in his heart, and he bit his lip thinking he should have known somehow that she was gone.

"There are no other survivors?" Keisha whispered.

No one responded.

Sebastian and Gus shoved Igor into a seat, blocking his exit.

"What are you planning to do?" Keisha asked.

Carter glanced at Igor, then turned to the group. "There's only one thing left to do; we will be heading to Monsterland. We have to stop whoever released this thing on us." He looked at his watch. "At daybreak. That gives us about six hours. Everybody should try to sleep."

"Who do you think it is?" Wyatt asked.

They both looked at Igor, who had refused to talk, no matter how persuasive Gus tried to be. Igor sported two black eyes.

Carter slid into a booth, motioning Wyatt to join him.

"I know you're tired, but I need to know what happened."

Wyatt quietly recounted the past twenty-four hours, the flight from the unlikely gang from the neighboring town. Carter's eyes lit up when he mentioned finding Melvin, frowning when Wyatt told him how Melvin jumped out of the truck in his new form as a werewolf.

"He transformed? It's not even a full moon."

Wyatt shrugged. "Apparently, there is more to being a … monster than we ever knew."

Wyatt told him about his experience with The Glob.

Carter questioned him about the alien jet fuel, calling it everything from substance to fluid to bubbly stuff, steadfastly refusing to give it an identity.

Wyatt related the story of Damon's death sadly and added that it had been a smart idea to send him, because he did indeed save Wyatt and Lily's life. Wyatt put his head in his hand, wearily, finishing with their flight from the mummies.

"You're saying they didn't notice when you left the freeway?"

"Yeah," Howard joined them. "It's like they operate with one brain that has little to no reasoning skills. We can take them."

"But remember, you can't touch them. They'll suck the life out of you. That is, if they don't strangle you first." Wyatt shuddered.

"A monster of little intelligence, then? Vampires still reign supreme, Howard?" Carter asked with a smile.

"When I used to compare monsters, Carter," Howard said, "I saw them as benign, harmless, a mere fantasy. I have learned that anything with a deadly intent is a monster and should never be misjudged. Evil is as evil does."

The group settled into sections of the restaurant. Manny motioned for Howard. "We might as well eat what's left. Let's get the burgers on the grill."

Howard went behind the counter. "Are you finished with your reunion? I could use a little help here," he called out to Wyatt.

"Bring me some Whisp," Sean demanded.

"Mom hates ..." Wyatt started, then shrugged. He could use the caffeinated boost as well. "How are you fixed on soda, Manny?" Wyatt asked.

"The tanks to the fountains are full. We didn't have much going on. You might as well use it up." He started for the rear door. "I'm going to turn on the generator."

The level of noise increased in the small restaurant. Carter sat with Sebastian, catching up on old times. The bullet heads of Jade's father and Gus were so close together, Wyatt couldn't tell who was who. Others sat in small groups. Lily and Keisha joined them behind the counter. Sean manned the fries. It felt strangely like any other Friday night. Wyatt considered the resilience of the human spirit. For the first time in weeks, he started to feel hope.

Carter looked up, motioning Lily to join him. He heard Carter ask her about her uncle; her reply was drowned out by Hank's shout.

Hank cursed from his spot by the window. "Are these the mummies you were talking about earlier?"

"Ugh, not the mummies again," Howard mumbled.

Carter rose to look at the mass of bodies stumbling toward the building. "I would welcome any ideas right now."

"Are they for real?" Jade's father asked.

"Yes, they're real," Sebastian answered. "And deadly."

"Stay here with your brother," Carter ordered. "Hank, Sandy, Ed, Manny, Sebastian." He pointed to Gus. "Follow me. Father Tim, you take your group, protect the rear of the building. The rest of you stay inside."

"Carter," Wyatt shouted. "I told you, guns don't work!"

"I have to work with what I've got." Carter shrugged. "The noise may disorient them. We may end up being hand-to-hand." He showed a clenched fist in the air. There were murmurs of approval. "Manny, you have any knives around the place?" Carter called out.

"Carter, you can't touch them," Howard said. "Knives aren't going to be effective."

Carter responded, "You got any other suggestions?"

When Howard didn't reply, Manny ran into the back, returning with an assortment of cutlery, a meat cleaver, and a pair of scissors. He handed them out to the group clustered by the doors.

Carter directed Lily to guard Igor. She had the only gun left in the building.

They followed Carter through the entrance, lining up in front of the restaurant, weapons ready.

There was a blurry line of monsters heading toward Instaburger. While they marched in perfect synchronization, their movements were choppy. They trudged over the sandy desert, a faint purplish glow shading the cloth they wore. Wyatt heard Carter's quiet commands through the glass.

"Aim for their heads. Wait for them to get close. Don't waste bullets, and remember, don't let them touch you."

The sound of shots filled the air. Wyatt and his friends gripped the hard plastic of the seats, watching the mummies move toward them, seemingly unstoppable. The bullets whizzed right through the mummies without effect.

"The bullets aren't working!" Sean yelled, his voice cracking. His face was pressed against the window.

"They're dead zombies wrapped up in linen soaked in alien fuel." Howard shook his head. "I don't see a solution."

"What are you talking about?" Sean jumped to his feet. "We have to do something. They're going to be massacred."

"Vincent's reanimated them with linen soaked from The Glob," Keisha told him. "How do you stop something that has no known antidote or natural enemy?"

"Everything has a weakness," Lily added.

"The fuel powers them. We can't stop it until we get into

Monsterland and find the switch to its power," Howard explained.

There was a flurry of shots. Wyatt ran to the window. "No!" Gus was thrown in the air by two mummies. He landed with a crash. A mummy walked jerkily over to him, placing its hands around his throat. Gus struggled for a moment, then went alarmingly still.

"Bullets won't work on The Glob either. We're doomed." Wyatt sat down; his voice was hopeless.

They heard screams through the windows. The mummies had reached their defenses.

Outside, the defenders were swinging their weapons, after realizing bullets were useless.

Carter wielded a cleaver. Using the tip of the blade, he was chopping his attackers in wide arcs, trying to unravel the cloth by tearing the fragile linen. The mummy fighting with him had streamers of ripped cloth trailing behind him.

Sebastian stepped on a piece of the fabric, then with two sticks twirled the creature around until it unrolled like a runaway paper towel, leaving a decomposed zombie to fall powerless onto the hard earth.

Hank's back was to the building, purple linen hands around his neck. His eyes turned vacant, his skin a waxy hue. Manny picked up a huge stone, slamming it against the mummy's head. The corpse turned, lifting Manny by the shirt and throwing him into a cluster of thorny bushes.

The glass shook as Sandy was grabbed by the neck and flung against the giant window. It cracked into a spider web, the back of her head blooming with blood.

"You're just going to sit there?" Sean screamed. "If we are all going to die, we might as well go out in a blaze of glory!"

"Blaze!" Howard yelled.

"You don't know what you're talking about!" Wyatt shouted back. "When that slime touches you, you can't think, you surrender, your brain is gone, it's …"

"Blaze!" Howard shouted. "Whisp!"

"What? What are you talking about?" Wyatt looked at him.

"Howard!" Keisha stood up, her eyes bright with excitement. "The soda, remember?"

"I have to go out and help!" Wyatt ran for the door.

"Stop, Wy. Let me think of a way. We can do this. I … the soda, don't you remember?"

"No, I was barely conscious."

"The packet of Whisp fell from my pocket and opened. When the two substances made contact, it ignited, and The Glob retreated."

"That's what saved you. Instantaneous combustion," Lily said, standing up. "Get all the cans from the fridge."

"Soda." Wyatt ran to the back room.

"Wyatt, where are you going?" Howard yelled at him.

"No, follow me. I have an idea. I need the hose."

Wyatt raced around the storage room, pulling and pushing supplies out of the way. "Garden hose. Where's the garden hose?" he asked.

Howard stared at him blankly, his glasses sliding down his sweaty face. "Mummy cleans the patio with it … I mean Manny. It's by the back door. Oh, I know what you're thinking. Got it!" he shouted, holding it triumphantly.

"I'll start unscrewing the soda fountain coupling. See if you can find the nozzle. It'll have a longer reach."

"Are you crazy?" Sean screamed.

"Wait, Wyatt, are you thinking …" Keisha said, her voice rising with excitement.

"Hurry! Sean, find the ladder. Manny keeps it in the storage room," Howard ordered.

Wyatt went to the soda fountain, his slippery hands trying to disconnect the handle. He couldn't make his fingers work properly. Outside, he heard the thumps and grunts of the battle raging.

His hands fumbled, then he stopped, took a deep breath, and unscrewed the fountain coupling.

Howard raced back with the hose, then positioned the ladder Sean brought in. "Attach the nozzle to the hose," Wyatt ordered. "I'm going up there." Wyatt grabbed the hose. "You think this is going to work?"

Howard paused, "I can't think of a better idea." They heard shots being fired again. "I'm not a hundred percent sure. At the very least, we'll have surprise on our side."

Wyatt raced up the ladder, dragging the hose with him.

There were hundreds of mummies, moving in unison, in a sloppy, disjointed way. Carter and his crew were still fighting. The battlefield was littered with casualties. The corpses made no sound, but for the shuffling of their linen-shrouded feet. Wyatt pushed himself to the very edge of the roof. He heard Howard climb onto the building behind him.

His heart pounded in his chest. He could hear the wind blowing, whipping up as much dust as the monsters' shuffling feet. He heard Carter's shouts of encouragement, along with grunts as flesh was pounded with ruthless intensity.

"Carter!" Wyatt called.

His stepfather glanced up, his face furious. "Are you crazy? Get down from there, Wyatt."

"Trust me, Carter. If this doesn't work, nothing will. Turn it on!" Wyatt shouted to Howard, who relayed the order to Sean.

The hose jumped with the carbonated soda. Wyatt took aim, starting at one end of the line of monsters and moving to the other.

The soda hit the creatures with what looked like gale force. The linen soaked up the liquid like a sponge. Wyatt stared at the bandage-wrapped army, watching for a reaction, when he heard Howard shout with joy.

Flames erupted anywhere the liquid touched the material. The mummies broke line, aimlessly walking into each other, their careless contact setting off the monsters next to them.

Wyatt sprayed the area, watching as the mummies lit up the dark night. The smell was atrocious. He gagged as the odor wafted upward.

Howard joined him, pointing him to any invaders he might have missed. "Make a puddle, spray the trees."

The sugary drink pattered as it landed on the fine needles of a Joshua tree. Soda dripped like a light rain. As the invaders walked beneath the branches, the steady *pat, pat, pat* of the droplets turned into a crackling roar of fire.

Keisha and Sean grabbed cans of soda from the storeroom, opened the door and shouted to their friends. Keisha threw one to Carter, who caught it. Manny crawled from the bushes, holding out his hands. "Here!" he shouted.

"Shake 'em up," she ordered. "Pop 'em and aim."

Carter shook his can of Whisp vigorously, snapping it open so that it exploded like a rocket. The soda flew in a high curve, landing on the arms of a mummy choking Jade's father. The limbs ignited like a torch. The mummy wobbled into the next monster, setting fire to the whole group of bodies.

Soon, they were all shaking and shooting the soda, watching as the invading army collapsed into a bonfire of roasting linen and inert bodies.

The group cheered as the last one fell. Wyatt sat on the edge of the roof, feet dangling, Howard Drucker next to him. He aimed the nozzle at any movement, watching them burst into flames and oblivion.

Wyatt took a look at the dripping nozzle. "I'm never drinking this stuff again."

"Sugar, man," Howard agreed. "We were only missing one thing."

"What?" Wyatt asked him.

Howard pushed his glasses up, his eyes searching the distant hills. "Melvin," he said quietly.

"Yeah, Melvin," Wyatt agreed.

Chapter 27

Smoking strands of linen were stuck on branches; some scattered on the dun-colored sand.

"It looks like a toilet exploded." Howard observed the swaying strips of material stuck on the twigs.

"Remember what we did to the tree in front of Nolan's house last Halloween?" Wyatt responded. They exchanged looks, then laughed out loud.

Carter banked the bonfire of mummies, watching the embers begin to die. The sun was out now, though the air was heavy with the haze of the smoke.

The defenders sat on the ground outside the restaurant, Lily and Keisha using Manny's first aid kit to treat the injuries. There were casualties: two dead that were buried behind the restaurant. The rest were bruised, a bit stunned, but recovering.

"What now?" Wyatt asked Carter, who sat down beside him.

Carter considered the answer for a while, then shrugged. "Not sure. I have no idea who is in control or why. They could have …"

"Hundreds more." The man appeared out of nowhere. He was tall, with long, black hair as dark and shiny as a raven's wing. He had a group of men with him. Each one was carrying a bow and a quiver of arrows.

"Uncle John!" Lily dropped a gauze pad to run into the

man's arms. He hugged her and said something in a language that Wyatt didn't understand.

Lily buried her face in John's shoulder, with quiet sobs. Wyatt knew it was news about her father.

Carter stood, holding out his hand. "Glad to see you, Raven." They shook hands warmly. Carter nodded an acknowledgment to the rest of the men. "You were saying?"

"He has hundreds more of those creatures."

"We're just about out of soda," Wyatt said, joining them.

"The soda worked, I see," Raven said, a smile in his dark eyes. "Instant combustion? How did you figure it out?"

"An accident, of course." Howard Drucker walked over. "Some Whisp dropped on The Glob …"

"You mean the fuel," Raven interrupted him.

"Yeah, I want to ask about that. Anyway, some dropped, and it burned on contact."

"Yes," Raven told them. "Alien fuel. There is a supply of it in Area 51. It is inactive until it takes the energy from our life forces. In other words, aliens have been filling up on cattle for the last millennia when they pop over for a visit."

"So, all Earth is …" Howard interrupted, "is an alien truck stop?"

"The mutilations are a result of their need for energy to power their return trips."

"The more lives it takes, the more power it builds?" Keisha asked.

Raven shook his head. "Vincent is there."

"Vincent Konrad? Impossible," Carter responded. "We saw him die. A werewolf ripped off his head."

"That may be true, but with the supply of fuel, they were able to reanimate his brain, and he is attached to machinery keeping him alive."

"How do you know that?" Jade's father demanded.

"You wouldn't understand if I told you," Raven responded flatly. He gave a slight shrug. "We overheard two workers talking."

"You were able to get that close?" Carter asked.

"We were well disguised." Raven looked at Lily, his dark eyes piercing.

"Can you get us in there?" Sebastian asked.

"No, too well guarded. He's got an army creating additional troops."

"That's crazy, man! It sounds like science fiction!" Manny shouted.

"Well, it's become science fact now, Manny," Howard said.

"Crazy but true," Igor said from the door, speaking for the first time. "The fish stinks from the head."

"Now you're talking?" Gus was standing, but he was shaky on his feet. His shirt was open, and he now shared the same faint line down his torso that Wyatt had.

"Hey, didn't you speak with a lisp at Monsterland?" Howard directed the question to Igor.

"Oh, thilly boy!" Igor laughed. "That was just an act to make the public think I was harmless." His voice normalized.

"Who cares?" Hank said.

"This makes no sense." Gus rolled his eyes.

"Now that you know Vincent's alive, I don't mind talking. You wouldn't have believed me."

"He has a point," Manny agreed. "Seriously, if he told you Vincent was responsible, you would have beaten the crap out of him."

"I did that anyways," Gus admitted.

Igor pressed his dirty hand against his swollen eye. "It does hurt a bit."

Wyatt tensed. Carter halted him. "Wait. Let's hear what he has to say. Tell us more."

Igor nodded, a grotesque smile on his face. "I can get you in there. I know a secret way."

"So, what good will that do, if we still face an army of mummies and The Glob?" Carter asked.

"As I said, get the head, and the military fails. Once Vincent is disconnected from the fuel source, his army has no power."

"What the hell is he saying?" Jade's father yelled.

"He said that once we get rid of Vincent, it will be over," Raven explained.

"Why would you help us?" Lily asked.

"I've seen the error of my ways," Igor said hanging his head in shame. "After all, Vincent betrayed me."

Wyatt watched him, not sure if he was genuine. He didn't know if he believed this strange man. There was something sinister about him. "How can we know if we can trust you?" he asked.

"Do you think I'm a monster? Just because I'm ugly, doesn't mean I'm bad." Igor smiled, revealing a mouthful of gray teeth.

"Who said monsters were ugly?" Keisha asked.

"The vamps were beautiful … and evil," Howard said.

"You have no choice, dear boy," Igor said in a slimy voice.

"I'm not your dear boy." There was something about Igor that filled Wyatt with dread. He was correct, though. They had no options and, for that matter, a limited arsenal. "What can we use as weapons? The soda supply is just about used up."

Raven held up an arrow. "Simple, but effective. Can we dip the arrowheads in what's left? We have more at our camp." He motioned for two of the men and gave out curt orders in the same language he spoke earlier.

"Dip the knives in the liquid as well," Carter ordered, then asked Igor, "So, what's this secret route of yours?"

Chapter 28

"Any idea what's going on with the government?" Carter asked Raven, as the ragtag group made their way toward the underground route that would get them into Monsterland.

Wyatt stood next to Carter; Lily was beside Raven. Another boy hovered near her side. Wyatt bristled, twice moving in her direction. Each time, he was interrupted by Carter to do something. He tried to hide the grimace that tugged at his lips. Much as he liked the idea of Carter depending on him, he wished he wouldn't ask for stuff when the other dude was hanging around Lily.

Everybody was going. They made a detour to a cave, where bows and quivers of arrows were distributed. Most of the older tribesmen knew how to use them, and after a few practice tries, they showed they were competent. Wyatt's attempts were less successful. The guy who seemed to hang around Lily snickered at his lame display of archery.

Still, Lily patted his shoulder and told him to do his best. She patiently showed Wyatt how to pull the bow, but despite her counseling, it didn't recoil and loose the arrow to fly at the hastily painted target the way hers did.

He had a sharpened steak knife under his belt that had been coated with Whisp soda. Between his soda-dipped arrowheads and the knife, he could smell the overwhelming sugary fragrance.

Keisha and Howard walked behind them. There had been a debate about leaving the teens behind. The kids kicked up a fuss, reminding everybody that without their help, all of them would be sporting a linen wrapping and marching in the mummy army.

Raven said, "Government's been shut down. We heard over a wireless there had been a coup, the new president was assassinated, and some general I never heard of has taken over, but the information couldn't be verified. I figure we're on our own. The cavalry hasn't decided whose side it's on."

"You know, Nate Owens was Vincent's puppet. They planned to take over the entire globe by wiping out all the world leaders," Carter said.

All movement on the path stopped, and everyone turned to listen to Carter.

"What?" Hank said.

Father Tim was shocked. "I campaigned for McAdams and Owens. I believed in them."

Raven's lips firmed into a grim line. He nodded once and said, "I respected Nate Owens too. I'm disappointed in the man."

Wyatt turned and saw Igor watching them intently with narrowed eyes.

The little man yelled, "Nate Owens was a good man!"

"Not if he was colluding with Vincent Konrad," Wyatt shouted back.

"Vincent Konrad is a genius," Igor stated. "While his methods can be painful, the pleasure of his planned outcome will be worth the strategy of this catastrophe."

Keisha looked straight at him. "Vincent was the monster. Make no mistake; he's pure evil."

"It doesn't matter," John Raven interrupted, diffusing the situation. "Vincent succeeded and damn near put us into a war with Russia. Russia's a mess. The zombie population exploded there. The infection is running rampant. Thank heavens the Russians are having a hard enough time trying to contain them, let alone thinking about fighting with us."

"Why would Vincent want to do this to the world? He portrayed himself as a philanthropist," Wyatt said, still feeling foolish for falling for Vincent's propaganda. "I don't understand his motives."

Carter made a rude noise and said, "It's all about power, Wyatt. You know, absolute power corrupts absolutely."

They started their slow trek down the road again.

Wyatt shrugged but went on. "He seemed to really care. I believed Vincent wanted to find a cure, make the world a better place. I still can't wrap my brain around it. How could such good intent turn foul? Monsterland was supposed to make everyone safe. How did he fool the whole world?"

"That was his intent," Igor said. He was walking between Carter and Raven, his hands tied together. "Vincent Konrad wanted to eliminate the red tape, get rid of those politicians who abuse their power with empty promises."

"I understand why he wanted to eliminate the politicians, but why did he kill the entire werewolf and vampire population? They did nothing to society." Howard asked.

"A monster's sole power," Igor said, "is in the hands of people who know how to use them. Vincent had to destroy the werewolves and vampires to stop them from being used against him. Don't you see, if all he had to worry about were zombies, and he controlled them, that made the world his oyster."

Howard Drucker nodded. "Vincent became the apex predator. Top of the food chain. With no natural enemy that could defeat him. Zombies and the alien jet fuel makes him invincible."

John Raven held up his soda dipped arrow and said, "Not anymore."

"Vincent Konrad was a megalomaniac. He wanted to destroy freedom," Carter responded.

"You don't understand him!" Igor spat when he spoke. "He planned to save the world."

"I thought you didn't like him," Gus growled.

"You don't have to like someone to agree with their policies," Igor responded quietly.

"Shut that guy up. He's giving me a headache," Jade's father shouted.

"See." Igor pointed to the hulking figure of Jade's dad as he trudged behind them. "It's people like that Vincent was eliminating. Big bully."

"No one should have the right to get rid of someone because they disagree with their point of view," Carter said.

Igor shrugged. "I don't have to agree with everything Vincent did, but there is a method to his madness. Sacrifice for the greater good."

Wyatt looked at Igor sharply.

"Greater according to whom?" Carter shot back, and the clouds cleared for Wyatt. "You can't have one voice decide for everybody."

"Is that why you didn't like him?" Wyatt asked Carter.

"It was a big part. He was so sure of his intent, so convinced his vision was the only way the world could be. That's why we have a democracy. Everybody has to have a voice."

"Sometimes people need to be led," Igor sniffed.

"I don't trust you. Sounds like you support Vincent," Gus grumbled. "I say we get rid of him. He showed us the way in. We don't need him no more." The crowd murmured. Wyatt heard a few voices agree with Gus.

Carter turned, stopping the group from moving forward. He looked directly at Gus. "That's a job for the court to decide."

The group surrounded them menacingly. Carter placed himself in front of Igor, as if to guard him.

"There are no more courts!" Gus shouted back.

"Then we'll make one. I fought for this country to defend your freedom. I will fight just as hard for justice. Anyone who touches this man will personally answer to me."

Wyatt watched the hard angle of his stepfather's jaw set defiantly. His broad shoulders straightened as if he was ready for a battle right now. Wyatt stopped dead in his tracks, looking at Carter as if he had never seen him before.

All this time he thought of Vincent's noble intent, he had been fooled by beautiful speeches. He never understood the quiet sense of duty that was the backbone of Carter White, his ability to cut through hyperbole to do the right thing. He was distracted by the celebrity and excitement of Vincent, never seeing him for who he really was. Yet Carter lived and was willing to die for his principles. He looked up at Carter to find the older man's gray eyes watching him. Wyatt smiled at him, a genuine smile. Carter returned it warmly.

Nodding, Wyatt said, "I think Carter is right. If you kill Igor, then you're no better than the monsters inside there." He pointed in the direction of the tunnel leading into the park. "I stand with Carter." Wyatt moved to his stepfather's side. Keisha and Howard followed. Lily was next, along with her uncle and his band. Manny, Hank, and even Jade's father reluctantly agreed.

Sebastian shook his head at Gus. "I'm with them, man. You coming?"

Gus grumbled, then shrugged his shoulders. "Democracy?"

"Majority rules," Keisha told him. "It's better when we all have a voice."

The group turned to trudge toward the tunnel entrance. As they neared it, they heard a howl.

Gus raised his gun, and a few of Raven's men stretched their bows. Wyatt leaped before them.

"No!" he shouted holding out his arms. "Melvin?"

Melvin walked out from the inside of the tunnel. He was filthy; his red hair was so coated with dust and debris it looked gray.

Wyatt reached forward to hug him, stopping when he felt the tenseness of Melvin's body. Melvin stood aloof, his face closed.

Howard ran forward, stopping short when he saw Melvin's expression. "Dude, did you go to Copper Valley?"

Melvin hesitated and said, "I was there. Then I came here. I had to regroup. My whole pack sacrificed themselves for me."

"What are you doing here?" Wyatt asked.

"We've been hiding in the tunnels." Melvin looked at the others watching them. "What's going on?"

"We're attacking Monsterland," Wyatt stated. "What do you mean, 'we'?"

"I'm not alone anymore." He looked at Wyatt, his head cocked. "I didn't plan for this to happen."

"Plan for what?" Wyatt questioned. His brows lowered in confusion.

"I know, and you may not be happy." He turned to the tunnel and whistled softly. "Come out," he called gently.

There was a shuffling in the dark recess of the tunnel. Wyatt watched as Melvin's companion walked toward the entrance.

He heard a loud curse behind him, then found himself staring at Jade's dirty face. She was wearing random bits of clothing and had Melvin's werewolf's head pendant around her neck, the green glass eyes glowing brightly.

Chapter 29

"Jade!" Wyatt and her father shouted in unison.

Lily's eyes narrowed. Jade moved closer to Melvin, who seemed a lot taller than Wyatt remembered, as well as more menacing.

Wyatt stared at Jade, touching his breastbone, wondering why his heart wasn't beating faster, like it had in the past when he used to see her. She looked different; she was disheveled, as if she had slept in an open field. Wyatt had never seen her with her hair out of place or without a perfectly matched outfit. Her eyes were softer, though. Her small hand was enveloped by Melvin's larger one, and she inched into him. Wyatt could see that Melvin liked when she attached herself, as if they were a single unit. Wyatt cocked his head and thought that they looked … good together. As if they always belonged to each other.

Melvin growled deep in his chest, baring his teeth.

Jade's father backed away. "Jade-Jade," her father said.

"I'm not a little girl anymore, Daddy," she told him, and her voice seemed different, more adult.

"What are you doing here? I went back to look for you. I thought you were dead."

"You sound disappointed she's alive," Melvin accused.

"You locked us in the attic and left," Jade spoke to her father,

her voice angry. "The purple thing came and we ran out to escape," she choked. "I watched Mom and Jagger drown in it."

"Do you know what he is? What he'll change into?" He pointed to Melvin, his face filled with loathing. "I heard what happened to him. How could you go with him?"

"You're not listening to me!" Jade spat. She moved closer to Melvin, who put his arm around her. "Melvin saved me, not you. He was just in time."

"I would have rescued you," Jade's father said, his voice small.

Jade responded, "But you didn't. You were off protecting the town, instead of me and the rest of our family. They're all dead, and only because Melvin came in and grabbed me just in time, I survived."

"Come to me. Come home, Jade-Jade."

Jade looked at her father sadly. "I can't come home anymore. I'm with him. I like him. I always liked him." She turned to look guiltily at Wyatt. "I'm sorry, Wyatt."

Wyatt opened his mouth to say something, but nothing came out. He felt his stepfather's presence behind him as Carter's hand came to rest comfortingly on his shoulder. Wyatt's thoughts roiled in his head. He had loved Jade with every fiber of his being, and realized he had been just a boy who loved the *idea* of Jade. He stared at his best friend's face and saw something in his eyes that he had never seen before. Melvin was finally happy. He knew he genuinely loved Melvin as a part of him, and if she made Melvin happy, then he was fine with it.

"What?" Howard Drucker yelled. "You never even noticed Melvin in school. You liked Wyatt." He sputtered with outrage over Jade's betrayal.

"You don't understand, Howard Drucker," Jade said. "Melvin saved my life."

"Wyatt saved you in Zombieville!" Howard argued.

"No. *I* saved Wyatt's life. I killed Nolan Steward. Melvin makes me feel like a woman. He takes care of me."

Wyatt heard Carter murmur, "You okay?"

"Yeah, I'm okay. She's right, Carter. I was a boy then. I'm not that boy anymore. I understand what she means."

"There's a bro code," Howard said.

"It doesn't matter," Wyatt told him. "Considering everything that has happened in this world, if they're happy, that's all that matters." He turned and locked on Lily's eyes and said, "I'm okay. I'm really fine."

"But he's a …" Jade's father shouted, the veins standing out on his neck.

"So am I," she responded.

Jade's father's eyes popped from his head. "Why, I'll kill …" Four men grabbed and restrained him. He struggled against their hold.

Melvin sneered, revealing long yellow teeth; his eyes turned golden. Both Wyatt and Howard stood protectively in front of him, and Jade moved closer, taking his hand. "Calm down, Mellie. Daddy just has to get used to the idea. Don't you, Daddy?" She looked up meltingly at her father, who deflated, the fight going out of him. She shuffled over with baby steps, tugging on his arm. "You're going to love him, Daddy. He's so loyal."

Jade's father shook off the hands holding them back. Wyatt wasn't sure who was growling louder, but the biggest threat right now seemed to be gone. They walked past each other, their eyes wary, their stance belligerent. Jade moved to Melvin's side. He put a possessive arm around her shoulders. "See, Daddy. Isn't he cute?"

Carter pushed past the group. "Let's get moving."

Chapter 30

As they approached the tunnel, Melvin halted them by the entrance. He whistled, and a pack of large creatures that looked like coyote-wolf hybrids filled the mouth of the opening.

They were twice the size of an average coyote, with longer teeth. Their light gray hair bristled while they crouched low, growling.

"Are those coyotes?" Carter asked.

"Not anymore," Melvin responded.

"You didn't waste any time!" Howard said.

Melvin shrugged. "I had to do what I had to do. Jade needs the protection of a pack."

Melvin turned to see John Raven watching him speculatively. Their eyes seemed to lock, and the older man nodded. Melvin relaxed. Wyatt could tell he wasn't feeling nervous anymore. They entered the massive pipeline.

Wyatt had brought an old camping lantern from Manny's back room for illumination. He held it out, so the light created elongated shadows along the smooth concrete walls. He noticed Melvin's shadow towering over his. He elbowed Howard, who looked from Melvin back to the oversized shadow.

"Don't look at me; I can't explain it." Howard shrugged.

The coyotes brushed against them, their hulking bodies coming too close for comfort. Their panting echoed off the walls.

Every so often, one whimpered, and Wyatt watched Melvin respond with a comforting scratch behind the complainer's ears. Jade was glued to his side, her hand laced in Melvin's freckled one. Wyatt avoided making eye contact with her.

They walked together through the dusty passage. Empty carcasses littered the way.

Wyatt heard Jade's hushed whispers and Melvin's gentle responses. Jade's father plodded behind him, his face closed. Wyatt swore he could hear the older man's teeth gnashing.

Raven stopped walking. He looked at his niece and said, "Do you feel it?"

She nodded once, her face grim.

Carter asked, "What? What is it?"

Wyatt moved closer to Lily. "What is it you're feeling?"

"There's an energy here. It's a bad energy. It's still quite a distance, but we both feel it."

"Vincent Konrad is the bad energy," said Keisha.

Melvin shook his head. "Nope, it's something bigger than Vincent."

Raven said, "It's in the mountain. It's been here longer than us."

Keisha looked at him, head tilted in question, "Are you talking about ancient spirits? Are they here? Now?"

"Some places never let a spirit go," Lily whispered.

"I always wondered why he chose Copper Valley for Monsterland," said Howard.

Raven shook his head. "He has The Glob for his power. No, this is something even Vincent Konrad can't control."

"Are you saying that Vincent placed his theme park on top of a power that dwarfs his?" asked Howard.

Raven gave a hollow laugh. "You so-called civilized people. You think you're mightier than the spirits." He shook his head. "You have no idea."

The coyotes became restless.

"Move out," Carter ordered. The group shuffled on without saying another word.

Multiple corpses lined the tunnel's path. The air was so dry, it hurt to swallow. All the moisture had been sucked from the atmosphere. The coyotes surrounded them protectively, as if they were herding them like sheep.

Wyatt laughed about that and shared the observation with Carter. Carter looked at their formation and grunted a response. They made a detour around a group of desiccated bodies.

"The mummies did this?" Carter asked, pointing to the dry husks.

Howard shook his head. "Nope, the mummies overpower their victims. They strangle them. This looks like the bodies we saw back at …" Howard saw Keisha's face freeze with horror, then finished quietly. "This was definitely The Glob."

The group kept together, their differences no longer an issue. The beams of light from the different flashlights created a criss-cross of illumination. Their voices hushed in the underground walkway, as if they were in a sacred spot, their feet making scuffing noises on the dusty concrete.

"What is this place?" Gus asked.

"It's an underground drainage system installed by Vincent in his public works projects. They have them networked all over the southwest. It collects the rainwater to prevent flooding on the surface," Sebastian said. "Stops the flash floods."

"Looks like it collects bums, too," Gus replied.

"The Glob took care of that problem." They passed another cluster of hollow shells of humanity.

Wyatt walked faster, catching up to Lily, who was next to her uncle. They had an unhurried stride, and Wyatt noticed Raven leaning down to listen intently to Lily.

"I was cold, very cold, Uncle John. If Wyatt hadn't …"

Her uncle cut her off. "Lily, why didn't you change …" He stopped as he realized they weren't alone. He looked at Wyatt, his face unreadable.

Wyatt stared back, wondering what her uncle could have expected her to do.

"Lily, what …" Wyatt started.

"Shhh, everybody, be quiet." Igor's voice sounded hollow in the tunnel. "We're nearing Vincent's laboratory." Igor pointed to a split in the passageway. "He's right through there." He gestured to the left-hand side.

"Where does this tunnel lead?" Carter pointed to a doorway carved into the wall of rock veering to the right.

"Oh, that's the entrance to get into the Copper Valley Inn. Over there"—he pointed to a path moving upward—"is a balcony of sorts. It's where I hid from them. But you have to be very quiet."

Raven turned to Carter and said, "The old Copper Valley Inn?"

"Yeah," Wyatt responded. "The miners' hotel. Vincent bought it and was planning to turn it into a resort."

Carter bit his lip. "It wasn't finished, right?"

"No, it wasn't ready when Monsterland opened. It looked like they were refurbishing it."

Igor interrupted and said, "Don't go in there."

"Oh, Igor," Howard cracked. "How cliché of you. *Don't go in there.*"

Igor's face emerged from the shadows. His smile spread across his face but stopped short of his eyes. His uneven shoulders shook with mirth, but somehow Wyatt knew whatever he was laughing at wasn't funny. "You stupid little boy. We called it *Vincent's Folly.* He bought the entire valley, including that damn mountain, thinking to harness the power, but *they* rejected his plans. There's a reason he never finished the hotel." Igor laughed again, a small demonic cackle.

Wyatt watched Carter consider the hunchback for a long minute. "I'm thinking, Raven, we should scope it out."

"I'll go with you," Raven said.

Carter turned to Sebastian. "You're in charge; wait for us. Get 'em positioned, the younger ones in the balcony, the muscle on the ground. If we're not back in an hour, you know what to do."

Sebastian nodded his head in agreement. "I know what to do."

Carter looked at Wyatt, his hands on his hips. "Let's go. Wyatt, bring the lantern."

"Me too?" Wyatt asked, his eyes wide with excitement.

Carter didn't respond. Wyatt rushed after the two older men.

Chapter 31

Wyatt followed Carter and Raven up a small incline toward a recessed door that looked as if it were carved into the rock wall. The walls were narrower, and Wyatt felt his insides grow taut with nerves. The air itself hummed with an energy that made his skin crawl.

"Carter, why are we going to check out the hotel?"

Carter pushed the door, which gave with a groan and opened. Wyatt watched his stepfather's face pale from the effort. "I don't trust that guy Igor. He was Vincent's lapdog."

Raven was ahead of them. Wyatt observed that he walked silently, as if not to disturb his surroundings.

"I could have done this alone," Wyatt said, stepping through the door.

"I wanted you to come with me."

A simple sentence. Wyatt realized Carter was usually direct, unlike his father. His father knew how to talk—it was a gift—but his words were always empty, and he never gave a straight answer. It had frustrated the hell out of him when he was younger. Carter's responses filled him with a sense of peace. He had never realized that, while he appreciated his father's ability with language, he felt more comfortable with Carter's quiet presence.

They walked together. Raven added softly, "Keep moving and keep a lookout."

"For what?" asked Wyatt.

"Believe me, you'll know when you see it."

"You expecting something weird?"

Raven didn't answer, but Carter responded, "Weird? The whole situation is weird. I miss plain old crime."

Gravel crunched under their feet, their sibilant voices echoing off the rusty stone walls. Wyatt held up his lantern. He pointed to the end of the corridor; another door blocked their path.

"Get ready." Carter motioned to the gun Wyatt held in his other hand.

Raven approached the door, putting his shoulder to it, and opened it as quietly as possible.

The door moved inward, a vast blackness yawning before them. Raven slipped through first, disappearing into the gloom. Wyatt shined his lantern. It opened into a lobby.

He rotated the band of light. The room was enormous, a monument to the Gilded age. Overstuffed Victorian sofas were arranged in pairs, waiting for guests to use them. Above them, a giant chandelier swayed as if pushed by an invisible breeze.

Carter turned to Raven and asked, "Anything?"

Raven gestured to the balcony, then placed his finger in front of his lips, indicating they should remain silent.

Wyatt searched the landing but saw nothing.

They all moved into the main hall, their footsteps muffled by the Turkish rugs. Wyatt glanced around. "Why didn't Igor want us in here?"

"Because the little man doesn't understand the power of the spirit world," Raven said.

"Are these spirits you speak of good or bad?" Wyatt asked.

"It's all about perspective," Raven answered.

"That makes no sense," said Wyatt. "If it's so powerful, how did these spirits let Vincent build Monsterland in the midst of it?"

Raven looked directly at Wyatt, his eyes piercing. "Who are you to decide what's right and what's wrong? How very pompous of you. They see our world through a different lens. Only they know the real truth."

"Are you saying Vincent is good?" Wyatt demanded.

Carter interrupted. "As much as I'd like to debate the actual meaning of good versus evil, I think we have something a little more pressing going on."

"All I'm saying," Raven continued, "is that good and evil can only be decided by your point of view."

"Right now, I don't really give a crap about things like that." Carter walked around the perimeter of the room. "Stay close to the walls."

Wyatt kept his back against the wainscoting, a chill running up his spine. "Where are you going?"

"I want to see what's happening outside," Carter said. "Raven, take the other window."

Tentatively, Carter approached a bay window. He leaned into the drapes, motioning for Wyatt to stand closer to him. He parted the thick material, then looked outside. "He's got a friggin' army."

"I'm guessing he's got about a hundred. Paramilitary?" Raven said.

Carter agreed and replied, "They're definitely hired."

"How can you tell?" Wyatt asked.

"Look at them. There's no one under six-foot-four."

"They're wearing a patch." Raven squinted and read, "Fed … Federation Forces."

"Never heard of them." Carter's voice was grim.

Wyatt peered outside, his jaw dropping. They looked superhuman. Dozens of soldiers milled around the broken Monsterland streets. Wyatt could make out the hulking shell of the Werewolf River Run, the flumes darkened, the glass cracked and broken. He pointed to the opened gate of Zombieville, the street deserted of monsters. The stores had been ravaged by the US Army the buildings pockmarked with bullet holes.

A group in hazmat suits was working near the entrance of Vampire Village.

"There's not too many of them," Wyatt stated. "We can take 'em."

Raven let the drape drop from his fingers. "With the zombies activated into mummies, there will be hundreds more of them. He will replenish his army. We can't."

"That's where they're making the mummies," Carter whispered, gesturing to the open theater that used to house the vampire show. The vast arena was now a holding pen where the corpses were stored. "Efficient."

"Looks like something is going on over there," Wyatt said, pointing to a guarded entrance that seemed to be carved out of a rock wall.

"It must be leading them into the underground chamber," Carter agreed.

Something tapped Wyatt's shoulder, and he jumped, making the drapes sway.

"What are you doing?" Carter hissed.

"Did you feel that?"

Carter turned, and Wyatt could see his gray eyes shining as they searched the dim interior. "What?"

"I don't know; something touched my shoulder."

Carter looked at him and then at Raven, who was standing on the other side of the room.

Wyatt felt his heart settle into a steadier rhythm.

"I don't see anything. Wait here. I'm going to check out the other window," said Carter. "I want to see if we can get into Vampire Village and destroy their mummy factory."

"Carter, I think we're going to have to destroy the power at its source," added Raven.

Carter darted to the other side of the room. Wyatt saw a flash out of the corner of his eye, as if something was suspended in midair. He blinked hard, his eyes searching the balcony.

"Come on," Carter called to him. Wyatt followed the sound of his voice, and crouching low, heading in his direction.

"Carter," Wyatt whispered. "There's something in here."

"Human, vegetable, or mineral?" Carter said, his voice distant.

"I'm not sure." Wyatt laughed nervously. He waited for Carter's voice. "Carter?" Wyatt shined his light into the void. "Raven?" he said a little louder. A hand reached out, grabbing his wrist. Wyatt dropped his lantern, a scream cut off by a palm over his mouth.

"What the hell is wrong with you?" Carter demanded. "I told you to stay close."

They crept out of the lobby toward the rooms. "I don't understand it. What did he want with this place?"

"He needed a hotel for guests," Wyatt said, his breathing normal once again.

Carter grunted a noncommittal response.

Carter parted lacy drapes that covered a window. It was facing the rear garden of the building. There was a maze of hedges, and in the center, they could make out the rotors of an Apache helicopter.

"How convenient," Carter commented. This time Carter gasped. He spun. Wyatt's skin pebbled, the air around them icy.

"You felt that?"

"Yup."

"Something is here, in the hallway with us," Raven said, closing his eyes. He hummed a few words, his voice low.

Wyatt heard the sound of feet running past them. He turned in time to see Raven's body go rigid. Raven recoiled as if he were punched in the midsection. There was a loud roar as a freezing blast of wind swept through the hallway.

Raven was sucked backward, as if a vacuum was pulling him into the center of the lobby. He crashed onto the floor, flattened, his arms outstretched, his eyes closed. His mouth never stopped the chanting.

Wyatt's vision narrowed and his head felt light. Something tugged on his pants, pulling him down the darkened hallway into the Victorian lobby. He heard a cackle, but when he opened his mouth to call Carter, a great weight descended, smothering sound and cutting off his air. He tried to cough, but wheezed, the lights dimming peripherally.

He clawed at his face, unseen hands holding him captive.

Carter rushed at him, his fist swinging like an avenging angel.

Wyatt was tugged upward, his body lifting three feet off the ground, an invisible force squeezing his middle, the echoes of laughter filling his ears.

He felt Carter grab his leg, pulling hard. His skin burned as if it was being torn apart. He looked down, his eyes vague. "Let me go. I … can't … take … it." He was going to be ripped in half.

Carter's hoarse voice filled the room. "Take me. Leave my kid." He held on, Wyatt's legs clamped against his chest.

Wyatt dropped his hand to rest on Carter's head. He was losing consciousness; dots danced before his eyes.

"I just want … to … say thanks, Carter," he sighed.

"What?" Carter's voice was panicked. "No. Stop. Stay with me, Wyatt."

He heard Carter calling urgently for Raven to help, but it sounded far away.

Wyatt smiled. He thought about the first time he had met Carter. How much he disliked his mother's new boyfriend. He had bristled every time he saw his mom and Carter holding hands. Some small part of him wanted his mom to return to his father, even though he acknowledged it was a toxic relationship.

The images shifted, and his resentment dissipated. The memory of Carter selling his beloved Indian motorcycle so Wyatt could get a car, popped into his head. His car, *it was here somewhere in the Monsterland parking lot.* He should remind Carter, so they could get it, he thought hazily. The iron grip constricting his chest eased, allowing him to take great gulps of air.

Images filled his head again. The wind ruffled his hair, and he was back in the driver's seat, with the memory of Carter showing him how to make a three-point turn, taking him to Instaburger to celebrate passing his road test. He ate with his friends, leaving Carter alone with Manny. *Why'd I do that?* he wondered. *What was wrong with me? Why was I so rude to him?*

Laughter filled his brain, each negative thought making the invisible arms stronger, and Carter's hold weaker.

Wyatt shook his head. "Carter … Carter?" His voice sounded like he'd drank a bottle of vodka.

He looked down at his struggling stepfather, holding him tightly around the legs.

"Listen, Carter. Think happy thoughts … tell Raven to concentrate … on things that make him happy!"

Carter looked up, his face blank.

"Trust me. Remember something …" An invisible force rattled Wyatt, so he shook as if possessed. Well, he was, sort of. He laughed. The power weakened. "Remember something good."

"I … what?"

"You know what, Carter? I think you made my mom happy." Wyatt moved down; he hovered a few feet over the floor now.

"I loved her," Carter said. "I still do." Carter's eyes widened as he felt Wyatt's slow descent toward the floor.

Wyatt tilted his head dreamily; he pictured them all sitting at the table, his mother so desperately wanting them to be a family. Yet he and Sean had resisted. *Why? Stubborn pride? Stupidity? It was all a waste.* As the anger fanned inside of him, Wyatt began to rise higher again.

"Wyatt!" Carter called to him. "Don't go there. Think about whatever you were thinking when you descended."

Wyatt nodded weakly. Basketball, political discussions, talking about Jade. "Jade. Carter?" Wyatt said, his voice a whisper. "I need to speak with you about Lily."

"I'm here for you."

Wyatt landed flat on the floor; his head rolled sideways. A tear leaked from his eye. Carter sat next to him. "You are one smart kid."

"Did you get what you came for?" Wyatt touched his head, which felt like it wasn't attached to his body. The room spun a little bit.

Carter held a restraining hand on his shoulder. "Don't get up yet. Now we know why the hotel wasn't open for business. Raven, are you okay?"

Raven groaned loudly and sat up.

"This proves Vincent can't control everything," said Wyatt. "So, I'm asking you, Raven. Was that a good or an evil spirit?"

"Neither. They just don't want anyone here."

"Does that mean they don't want Vincent Konrad either? Will they help us?" Carter asked.

"They don't care what we do to our world," said Raven. "They want to be left in peace."

"Think you can get up?" Carter helped Wyatt stand. He half-carried Wyatt out of the hotel.

"Your arm." Wyatt glanced at Carter.

"Never mind. It's check-out time," Carter said.

Raven stood, raising his arms imploringly. Wyatt heard him whisper, "Ómakiya yo." Raven followed them out of the hotel.

"What did you just say to them?" Carter asked as they walked towards the exit.

"Help."

Wyatt peeked back to the shadowy room. The outline of a translucent figure gleamed in the darkness. It was a crooked old man holding a pickaxe. He wore a torn cowboy hat, dusty jeans held up by suspenders, and a rumpled plaid shirt. A scraggly gray beard covered most of his face.

Wyatt paused and repeated what Raven just said. "Help," he said softly.

The ghost glared malevolently at Wyatt, then turned, disappearing into the wall.

Chapter 32

Carter, Wyatt, and Raven found the group waiting for their arrival in the tunnel. It was plain to see that everyone was exhausted. Manny paced in his small area, muttering to anyone who would listen about his experience when the mummy touched his skin. Jade's father brooded menacingly, his feet dangling from a small outcrop while he watched Jade cuddle with Melvin in a cave-like space in the corner. Igor sat cross-legged on the floor, Gus glowering at him from behind. Lily and Keisha sat together whispering, while Howard dozed, his head propped on his hands.

Sebastian approached Carter and said, "What'd you find?"

"You wouldn't believe it if I told you. Igor was right," he said, pointing to the prisoner. "The only way in is through the tunnel."

Wyatt blurted out, "There were ghosts in there."

Howard perked up when he heard Wyatt's voice. "Ghosts? You saw ghosts?"

Raven told him to be quiet and then added sternly, "There is no time for this now."

Lily looked at her uncle with a question in her eyes; he refused to meet her gaze.

"The hotel was possessed by a spirit who wants us out of here," said Wyatt.

Igor chuckled. "I told you so."

Carter scrubbed his face. He glanced at Igor and said, "Gus, take him away and watch him. If he opens his mouth, muzzle him."

"Got it," Gus said, dragging Igor into the shadows.

"You guys good with those things?" Carter pointed to the bows and arrows. He looked up with narrowed eyes. He explored the upper walkway with the beam of his flashlight.

Raven laughed. "We've had a lot of practice. You think we should take the balcony?"

"You can use the height advantage. The objective will be to get Vincent."

"We'll handle his guards. The soda-dipped arrowheads will take care of the mummies," Raven assured him. "It's going to be a bloodbath."

"Wyatt, Keisha, Sean, Howard, Jade, Lily," Carter called quietly. "And Melvin, you head up to the … mezzanine with Raven and his men."

"What is this, a Broadway show?" Wyatt asked. "You're going to need us on the ground level with you. Lily's the only competent shot among us."

Carter looked at his stepson, his gray eyes intense. "We're going to need it to rain arrows. The more we have, the better chance it gives us to get in and out with Vincent."

"But," Wyatt began.

"Your stepfather is right," Raven told him. "We will make it rain."

"The pack, Melvin," Carter asked him. "They'll stay with me?"

Melvin nodded, his lips grim. "What do you want them to do?"

"Remember when they herded us in the tunnel?"

"You want them to round up the mummies?" Melvin confirmed.

"Can they do it? It's going to get hairy in there."

The coyotes surrounded Melvin, looking up at him slavishly. There had to be twenty of them, their bushy tails longer than Wyatt's arm, their chests the size of a lawnmower.

Melvin said something that sounded like a growl and a gurgle to the group of hounds. They panted back, their tails fanning the dry air so that it felt like a dust devil had invaded the enclosed space. "I have to go with you."

Carter shook his head. "I can't let you do it."

Melvin folded his arms over his chest. Wyatt wanted to ask when his narrow, bony body had become so jacked.

"If I don't go, they won't go," Melvin said with quiet determination.

"It's too dangerous," Carter said.

"Not for me," Melvin retorted. "If you want them, Carter, you don't have a choice."

"Me too." Jade moved closer to Melvin's side.

"Over my dead body," her father growled.

Melvin turned to the older man. "She'll be safer with me than anyone else."

Carter spoke to Jade's father. "He's probably right, Ernie." He turned to give out orders. "Gus, bring Igor with us."

"Why?" Wyatt asked.

"Carter may need Igor to give him directions once they get into the laboratory," Raven said. "Follow me."

Raven and his group started the ascent up the small outcropping of rocks. Wyatt took one last look at Carter.

"Watch out for your brother," Carter mouthed the words, then winked. "You did good today. I'm proud of you." He turned to the other cluster of men and coyotes surrounding him. Wyatt heard his whispered commands fading as he climbed higher into the tunnel.

Chapter 33

The upper level opened up to reveal a vast laboratory complex. As they climbed, Raven motioned to Keisha to walk beside him. They moved slowly. With his head bent down, Wyatt couldn't make out the soft murmur of their voices. Wyatt turned back to look at the other group resentfully. *I'd rather be with them,* he thought.

"What's that about?" he asked Howard, cocking his head toward Keisha.

Howard pushed his glasses up. "She's fascinated with shapeshifting. She asked Lily about it back there." He jerked his thumb toward the area they had come from.

Wyatt looked around, confirming they were alone.

"You think he really turned himself into a raven?"

Howard shrugged. "I saw a bird. Lily didn't deny or confirm it was her uncle. If they could shapeshift, why didn't her father shapeshift out of Monsterland during the massacre?"

"Maybe he never learned," Wyatt said with a raised eyebrow.

"Doubtful." Howard considered for a moment. "I read an article about it once. They say you have to get really, really relaxed and concentrate on that one animal. There should be the steady beat of a drum in the background or a similar noise."

"Why?"

"It creates a hypnotic state, opening the doorway to your

subconscious mind, where the real power is located. Then they have to imagine what it feels to be that animal, what would it be like to taste, or see, or even smell, what that animal would sense," said Howard.

"A year ago, I would have thought you were nuts," said Wyatt.

Howard cleared his throat. Lily was looking right at them. "It's making me think, just because I've never seen something, doesn't make it nonexistent. Like aliens …"

"Or ghosts," Wyatt said.

"Or God," Lily added.

Wyatt watched Raven, looking for any proof that he could be able to change his form. He stared at the muscles of his back, bunched under his shirt. There was no evidence of anything strange, like … wings, or something. But then, Melvin wasn't walking around with hair sprouting out all over his body either.

They reached the summit. He noticed a faint but regular sound coming from the Native American men. They were rhythmically tapping their fingers on the wood of their bows. It was very slight, but it was unmistakable.

A chill ran up Wyatt's back. Raven shushed his band of men, gesturing for them to lie down on their stomachs where they could peek at the lip of the edge.

Wyatt found a ratty blanket, a change of clothes, candy bars, and some cans of Whisp stuffed under the eaves of a rock. *Igor's belongings.* He kicked the clothes away, taking the soda and passing the cans to his friends.

"Extra ammo," he whispered.

Lily was on her belly, strangely subdued. Twice Wyatt tried to say something to her, but she appeared distant, not responding. Her eyes were focused, and her lips were moving in a silent chant; he could only guess what she was saying.

Keisha lay on the other side of Raven, with the same blank expression. Wyatt touched Howard's shoulder, directing him to Keisha's face. Howard observed her for a few minutes, then said in a low voice. "She's in a trance. Interesting."

Wyatt thought it was a whole lot more than interesting. Raven looked at him, then pointed down over the edge of the mezzanine.

Below them was a bustling laboratory filled with white lab-coated personnel. There was a large wheel with a backdrop of glass tubes bubbling with the alien fuel. He searched the room, wondering where Vincent Konrad was. Igor had told him he was attached to the wheel, but there was no sign of him.

There was a commotion. A tall, gray-haired man entered the room, followed by a gurney. He was directing the soldiers with a gold-headed cane. He wore a light blue gown over his suit. He looked like a doctor. The room grew quiet, all motion stopped.

Wyatt's breath stilled in his chest. On the wheeled table was a tall and muscular body that appeared to be over seven feet tall. It was held down by thick black straps. The body was covered with a white cloth, but Wyatt could see that the outline under the sheet was well-developed, with long legs and arms. The neck had a row of stitching, not unlike a baseball, with thick red thread. The skin on the face looked like a death mask; it was purple-tinged, eyes closed. Two thimble-like devices jutted out from either side of the neck.

Wyatt couldn't prevent the gasp that escaped his mouth. He'd recognize that face anywhere.

Vincent Konrad!

Raven threw him a look of warning.

Wyatt pointed to the body, mouthing the dreaded name.

Vincent Konrad's head was sewn onto a muscular corpse.

"He's just like Frankenstein's monster!" Howard said in awe. "The creature … he's become the behemoth!"

"Ladies and gentlemen, we are about to make history!" the man with the cane announced.

A crew carefully moved the body from the gurney to an operating table in the center of the room. The gray-haired doctor screamed directions. Nests of wires and dangling electrodes hung suspended from the ceiling. The crew worked with well-practiced movements. There were shouted orders, confirmations. The room hummed and crackled with excitement.

Lab technicians placed connections on the neck, arms, and legs of the body. Other assistants hurried with urgent efficiency, rechecking each electrode, then recording their findings on tablets.

"Hurry!" the gray-headed man urged, looking at a massive ticking clock on the wall. "We are behind schedule."

"It's too soon," a lab-coated man yelled back. "The fuel has to be drained …"

"I don't care!" the doctor cried out, laying his cane on a console, and threatening the tech with his bare fist. "The brain will die if we don't reanimate soon!" He stomped to the front of the main control panel; the room seemed to hush.

"Behold, I am about to change the world as you know it!" He flipped a switch, and the cave-like interior darkened for a moment. The air crackled with electricity; transformers buzzed. The chamber was filled with the stench of burning flesh. The body lay there, motionless.

"Again!"

All eyes were glued to the corpse on the operating table. The room hummed with the buzz of machinery. A circuit blew; sparks flew from a console. A female tech screamed, her lab coat smoking where the sparks hit it.

The body jerked; the eyes twitched but remained shut.

"It's not working!" he yelled. "Give me more power!"

"Dr. Frasier, you'll kill him," a white-coated assistant responded.

"Throw the switches, I said!" His face was flecked with spittle.

This time, when they engaged the machinery, sparks leaped from the electrodes, and the cadaver jiggled as if it was dancing. The eyes opened, blood-red and furious. Its mouth parted and let loose a fiendish roar. It struggled against the straps, the hands uncoordinated. The body pulled at the restraints, ripping the leather as if it were paper, then rolled off the operating table, wobbling toward the doctor. The others backed away, watching the monster warily, one tech fainted.

"It's alive!" Frasier screamed, triumphantly, his fists in the air. "Now I know what it feels like to be …"

"Oh, shut up and stop being so dramatic." Vincent held a hand to his head. His voice was rusty, as if it hadn't been used for a while.

The room erupted into cheers and clapping. The burst of

MICHAEL OKON

applause turned thunderous. Dr. Frasier beamed proudly, then bowed.

Vincent slid off the gurney, the white sheet pooling around his feet. He duckwalked around the room, twice having to be righted when he almost fell head over heels. He straightened and gingerly examined his new body. He then lifted his hands, marveling at the size of his new fingers. He flexed them once or twice, turning them into a fist, then lashed out and grabbed a tech who hovered nearby.

Vincent pulled at the man as if he was testing his strength. His huge hand wrapped around the victim's neck. He pulled him off the floor, letting him dangle. His head tilted as he observed the helpless tech gasp for air in a detached manner.

"Vincent," Frasier yelled. "You're hurting him!"

Vincent released the tech, who fell to his knees with a groan.

"Not bad, Hugh. Not bad at all." He coughed, spitting out purple fluid on the floor. "Get me a drink. I'm very dry."

Another lab-coated assistant arrived with a glass of liquid, handing it to Vincent, who took a healthy swig of the beverage, smacking his lips at the refreshing feel.

He grabbed his throat as if in pain. "What is this stuff?" He threw the glass at the assistant, who crouched cowering on the floor.

"It was Whisp, Dr. Konrad," the lab tech replied.

"You idiot!" Vincent screeched. "It has red dye 47! That stuff peels paint off cars."

"Didn't I tell you morons to keep the soda from mixing with W1457?" Frasier bellowed.

Wyatt heard Carter yell, "Now!" as his stepfather and his companions burst into the entrance of the cavernous structure. Coyotes barked, adding to the pandemonium, latching onto people, dragging them kicking and screaming into the center of the room.

Wyatt's eyes bulged from his head as an auburn-haired beast, larger than the others, followed closely by a petite wolf that seemed glued to his flank, charged into the room. the smaller creature sported a werewolf's head necklace with emerald eyes.

Howard whispered, "Melvin…and Jade." His voice filled with awe. Howard successfully lobbed arrows into the mob.

Raven's men stood up, bows ready, shooting arrows into the stunned crowd. They heard the thuds as the arrows slammed into the soft flesh below.

"Sound the alarm!" Vincent yelled, then grabbed his throat as if in agony. Sparks flew from his mouth; smoke seeped from the line of stitching around his neck. He stood, groping, unnoticed, as the room transformed into a melee.

Wyatt aimed, stretching the bowstring as far as he dared; his palms dripped with sweat. He loosed the cord; the arrow slipped from his wet fingers to fall uselessly to the floor.

All hell broke loose in the laboratory.

Mummies entered from four different doorways that opened with a *swish*.

Carter removed his soda-tipped knife, slashing at the linen-wrapped monsters coming at them.

Volleys of arrows rained down on them. Wyatt pulled the string; the arrow again slipped from his clumsy hands. *I'm wasting ammo*, he thought frantically, marveling at Howard's easy movements. He pulled another, watching in despair as it landed in the cracks of the rocks below him.

"Like this." Lily showed him how to draw the bowstring, the taut cord next to his cheek. This time the arrow flew further, although not as far as the rest of his friends.

The soda-tipped arrows caught on the mummies' cloth, igniting the purple-tinged linen.

Carter slashed, his knife leaving a trail of fire where it touched the wrapped bodies. Manny was being cornered by two colossal mummies; one had its hands wrapped around his neck. His face turned a bright shade of violet; his eyes lost their focus and looked blank.

Wyatt shouted, "Manny!" and shot an arrow that got lost in the confusion. He saw Gus stab the mummy attacking Manny, freeing him as the monster turned into a torch. It bumped into another one, the contact engulfing both monsters in flames.

Coyotes leaped around the room, their howling adding to the confusion. They herded the mummies into tight circles, making them easier targets.

Wyatt heard Sean screaming, "Carter!" He looked wildly around, but couldn't locate his stepfather in the smoke and confusion. He did see Igor crawling through the chaos toward Vincent, who appeared to be choking on the floor, in a pool of purple vomit.

Carter was in the center, cornered by a trio of flaming mummies. Wyatt grabbed for an arrow, but his hand felt only empty space. Had he used them all up? "Howard, shoot over there!"

Howard held up his empty hands. "I'm out."

Wyatt shook the soda can in his hand, knowing he was too far away to help. He looked for a way down, but the sheer drop would kill him. A hideous howl rent the air, pulling him from his racing thoughts. The reddish werewolf was looking straight up at him. It jumped, barking to get his attention.

"Melvin!" he yelled. He saw Melvin's golden eyes look at the can of soda in his hand. He barked loudly. Winding up, Wyatt pitched it directly at the werewolf, who caught it between his teeth. Melvin shook his head violently, aerating the soda, then crushed the can in his massive jaws, creating a deadly geyser that washed over the mummies attacking Carter.

They ignited instantaneously. Wyatt cheered. After a high five with Howard, he turned to say something to Lily, but she was gone, so were Raven and Keisha.

Wyatt searched for them, his eyes going wide when he saw a raven and a small falcon he recognized as a kestrel swooping down to unwind linen from the attacking mummies. They pecked, their beaks catching on the gauze cloth, then flying in the opposite direction as the mummies' coverings unwound.

One by one, the monsters that were not burning unraveled, separating the flesh from contact with the fuel-soaked cloth. Once the linen was removed, the zombies fell into a dead heap, until the floor resembled a charnel house of blood and bone.

Under a thick layer of smoke, Wyatt saw Igor with one arm under Vincent's slack form and the gray-haired doctor dragging the other as they hurried toward a door.

"He's getting away!" Wyatt yelled, but the fighting was too loud for anyone to notice. "Let's go." He pulled Howard by the arm, his useless bow on his shoulder. He didn't even stop to throw it down.

They ran down the tunnel. "Where are we going?" Sean followed, close on his heels.

"Go back," Wyatt ordered.

"No way," Sean said. "Where are you going?"

"We've got to get into the park," Wyatt said.

"It's too far to walk back through the tunnel. Let's go through the lab." Sean pointed to where the battle raged.

"No, we don't have time. I know of a better way in from here."

"The Copper Valley Inn?" Sean said.

Wyatt nodded.

Sean retrieved the lantern Wyatt had put down earlier.

"What are you doing?" Wyatt asked.

Sean held up the lantern and said, "It's dark in there, right? We're gonna need this."

They raced down the small corridor leading to the portal of the Copper Valley Inn. Wyatt grabbed the handle of the door and pulled with all of his might. The entrance was stuck fast.

Wyatt jammed his fingers inside the seam, pulling at the heavy metal, ripping and tearing his nails in the narrow space. His fingers couldn't find purchase in the small opening to budge the door. His face grew red with frustration; he was loath to admit tears smarted behind his eyes.

Vincent is getting away! he thought furiously. "It's no use." He was on his knees, trying to pry open the door.

"Gimme your bow," Howard ordered. Wyatt handed him the weapon that was slung over his back. Howard jumped on the bow, cracking the wood. Taking the two halves, he gave one to Wyatt.

"Shimmy it into the space ..."

"Got it." Wyatt understood.

Using the slivered wood, he and Howard pushed it into the narrow opening, levering the door. The solid metal groaned loudly. "Harder!" Wyatt cried. "It's working."

Sean needed no instruction; he squeezed his fingers into the gap, catching the door just before the bow disintegrated from the pressure. He yanked it open.

They raced through the first dark corridor. The second door

was just as tightly jammed. Howard shrugged; the bow was too broken to use.

Wyatt pounded the metal, tears streaming down his face. Behind him, he could hear the cries of the battle. "Please," he begged. "Please let us into your hotel. We don't want Vincent here, either! You'll have your mountain back. Help us."

It felt like time stopped. The three boys' gasping breaths filled the corridor. "It's no use. Let's go through the lab!" Sean urged, pulling Wyatt's arm. There was a moment when the air thickened and it was hard to breathe. The handle glowed as if it had an internal fire.

"What's happening?" Sean yelled.

Then the doorknob rotated ever so slightly. The door's creaking filled their tiny space, and it opened into the ghost's territory.

"Come on," Wyatt said, greatly relieved.

The boys raced in the darkness toward the front door. Wyatt spun, looking at the balcony. The old prospector stood there, a smile on his face.

"Thank you," said Wyatt.

The ghost tipped his hat, then disappeared.

They leaped outside. It was pitch black, except for the pool of light from Sean's lantern; a cream-colored three-quarter moon hung big in the night sky. They sprinted through the maze of construction vehicles in front of the hotel to exit by the wrought iron gate.

They raced toward the center of Monsterland, where all the avenues converged.

"Where are they?" Wyatt glanced around.

They were in the heart of Monsterland, or what was left of it. It was quiet, the battle raging beneath them silenced by its distance underground. Tents flapped where Vincent's army had unburied the dead to mummify them. All the soldiers Wyatt had seen earlier must have joined the fray in the laboratory.

Huge vats dotted the landscape, steam still rising from the liquid inside. Garbage was strewn all over the floor, tufts of linen hanging like tinsel decorations for the holidays instead of a bit of sparkle. It added a ghostly atmosphere.

They heard running feet and the sound of muffled orders, someone's shrill, tension-filled voice.

There was a chase. The boys spread out, trying to find their quarry.

"Igor," Wyatt called down the empty streets. "You can't get away. Bring him back."

They heard a scuffle, grunts, and a yelp, followed by a growl that could only belong to Vincent.

"There they are!" Sean shouted, pointing toward Plague Path and the shadow of the three figures running clumsily down the broken cobbles.

Vincent's new massive body was being supported by Igor's bent one. The gray-haired doctor pushed rather than pulled him, and they could hear his breathless commands. They were headed toward the haunted hotel.

The kestrel's cries bounced off the mountains behind them. Wyatt looked up, but couldn't find the flying bird. He realized Vincent was being pursued. His eyes widened at the sight.

"Holy crap," Wyatt said.

"Keisha?" Howard said, his voice cracking.

Wyatt looked at the moonlit path. Keisha was walking slowly, but deliberately. The kestrel flew above her; the three boys only had eyes for the strange sight. Keisha's hair was gone, and in its place was a snarled mass on her head. Keisha's braids had transformed into a nest of wildly wiggling snakes. Her eyes glowed like phosphorescent orbs.

"Don't look at her," Howard commanded, grabbing Wyatt and Sean from behind and twisting them away.

"She's shapeshifted," Wyatt said in awe.

"Yeah, into Medusa. Don't look into her eyes, or she'll turn you into stone," Howard said.

"Shapeshifting is only supposed to be cute forest animals. What the hell is she doing?" Wyatt demanded.

"Mythology is mythology. This is her interpretation. She loves the Greek myths. This is her vision, not yours. Medusa!" Howard called out, then added more to himself, "Intriguing choice. I find it quite arousing."

"Shut up, Howard Drucker," Wyatt and Sean said in unison.

Keisha neared them. They couldn't look at her, but they

could hear the hissing serpents as she passed. Howard held out a hand, pointing down a dark path leading away from the main area to the gates of the entrance to the haunted hotel, his eyes averted. "They went that way."

The kestrel screamed. The wings brushed Wyatt's face as it whispered past him. He touched his cheek, without opening his eyes, knowing it was a deliberate caress. They heard the shouts of Vincent's group dragging his oversized body and the pounding of Keisha's march as she followed through the twisted gates of the Copper Valley Inn.

He heard the falcon's cry again, followed by horrified shouts.

Pieces of masonry and rocks were pitched into the air, narrowly missing Lily as she navigated the barrage.

Igor yelled, "Lower! Aim lower!"

Lily dove and one projectile hit her squarely in the chest.

Wyatt screamed, "No!" He snatched the lantern from Sean's hands and took off in the direction where Lily plummeted. He raced back, vaulting over the fence to the haunted property.

Wyatt's search took him near the front bay window of the hotel. He combed the old wooden porch, frantically looking for Lily's small body. Nothing, he could find nothing.

A light glowed from behind the glass. The prospector appeared again. He pointed to a dark corner under a swing. Wyatt approached and found a handful of loose black feathers. "No," he whispered. He picked up a single feather, and with a shuddering breath placed it in his chest pocket. Wyatt looked up to see the prospector shake his head and motioned for him to go around the back of the property.

Wyatt jumped from the steps screaming to Howard and Sean, "This way!" His heart was heavy in his chest.

He rounded the corner of the hotel to see the vast maze of hedges he had noticed earlier. Up close, the shrubberies dwarfed him. His eyes rolled up to see a giant wall of greenery at least twelve feet tall.

"Come on!" Howard said and ran into the first opening.

Wyatt stared at the multiple entrances and gasped, "I don't know which way to go!"

"I've read about this," Howard said. "Sean, grab a handful of rocks."

"What are the pebbles for?" Wyatt asked.

"Trémaux's Algorithm. We're going to leave a pile of pebbles at each intersection, so we won't walk down the same corridor twice."

They scooped up a handful of white stones under the trees. "Whatever you do," Howard continued, "don't move your hand off the right side of the wall. You will always find your way out."

Wyatt added, "Don't let go of the wall, Sean."

"Keisha!" Howard yelled. "Keisha!"

It was pitch black between the tall columns of trees, the only light from their fading lantern. "Wyatt, this thing is running on empty." Sean held up the dimming light.

"What do you want me to do about it now?" Wyatt asked.

They moved deep into the maze, leaving small pyramids of rocks at the end of each lane.

They walked down a path. Muffled footsteps were coming from the next aisle. Wyatt pushed Howard forward, and they came to an intersection. "Which way?"

The sound appeared to be coming from the left.

"Stay to the right, Wyatt." Howard closed his mouth, his eyes going wide, when a high-pitched shriek split the night, followed by a long groan.

Wyatt watched as Howard ran past Sean, his feet flying awkwardly down the path through the towering bushes. "Keisha! Are you all right? Tell me where you are!"

"No, Howard!" Wyatt tried to stop him. "Close your eyes! Keep your hand on the right wall!"

Wyatt heard the smack of two bodies colliding, and the sound of retreating footsteps in the next section of the maze. He peered through an opening in the bushes and saw the combined shadows of Igor and Vincent running away.

Wyatt shoved the lantern at Sean, and said, "Don't move!"

He squeezed through a small gap in the hedge, entering a new leafy corridor. He then saw the outline of Vincent and Igor at the end.

Wyatt took off like a running back, his head lowered, his feet racing down the narrow pathway. He collided with Vincent, separating him from Igor. Wyatt and Vincent fell in a tangle of limbs.

The bushes behind them cushioned their fall. He saw Igor stumble away, and strong hands gripped his neck, lifting him four feet off the floor.

"It's Baldwin, right?" Vincent said in the dark. "Brave young Wyatt Baldwin. No relation to Alec, of course. Let me see your hand." Vincent's eyes gleamed in the night. Smoke seeped from his neck, circling their heads. Wyatt could smell burnt sugar.

Wyatt felt the surprisingly gentle touch of Vincent's fingers as he brought Wyatt's wrist up to his face. "Naughty boy. You didn't get your hand stamped to re-enter the park. You know what this means?"

Wyatt gasped for breath. "You monster. Why?" Wyatt was struggling to breathe and felt the sting of tears as they leaked from the corners of his eyes.

Vincent dropped Wyatt's hand and cocked his head, staring at the twin streaks of tears. "I should kill you. I can kill you, here and now. But dear Wyatt, this was not about killing people. Make no mistake; I am right about what I am doing. The rest of the world has to catch up with me."

Vincent touched the wetness on Wyatt's cheek with almost tender regard. "Are you crying for me, or for your shattered illusions? Your little American fantasies have been destroyed by the harsh realities of real life. Life isn't a theme park, my dear boy. It's about hard choices, and being man enough to do what needs to be done. Time you grew up and realized this."

Igor screamed, "Vincent, now!"

Vincent sighed loudly and said, "Much as I'd like to continue this chat, I really do have places to go and people to see. Thanks for the free burger, by the way. I'll never forget that act of kindness. Consider us even."

Vincent spun and tossed him like a rag doll over the high hedge.

Wyatt closed his eyes as he flew, landing with a thud, the wind knocked out of him. He lay in stunned disbelief, then rolled over to find himself staring at tangled feet. The cluster of legs was sprawled across the lane, completely still. A sob welled in his throat. He realized he was staring at Keisha and Howard's limbs.

He reached out to touch Howard's dirty sneaker. "Howard," he said.

"Ow, ow, ow. I think one of your snakes bit me," Howard whined.

"What the hell are you talking about?" Keisha said. "That's the barrette holding the end of my braid. Give it back."

Wyatt scrambled closer. Keisha was leaning against Howard, her braids caught in his glasses.

Wyatt moved forward, gently separating them. "What happened?"

"I thought Keisha was hurt. I barreled into her. I think I stunned my gorgon back to gorgeous." Howard looked at her dopily. He had a bump the size of an egg on his forehead.

"He pushed me into this statue," Keisha said. She had a hand to her temple.

All three teens sucked in their breaths.

The moon reflected on a white marble statue. Frozen in stone was the gray-headed doctor who had been trying to help Vincent escape.

The kestrel's cry made them all look up. Wyatt smiled broadly, relief flooding through him. "Lily!" he said triumphantly. She fluttered around them, lifted her tail feathers and dropped a huge poop on the statue's forehead. Wyatt laughed. The falcon wheeled upwards, circling around.

"Lily!" he called again. The bird disappeared, leaving them alone, and Wyatt strangely bereft.

Sean arrived breathlessly, shining the light on everyone. "You guys okay? Is it safe to look at Keisha?"

"I don't know what you're talking about," she answered.

"Forget about it." Howard smiled, brushing off the back of her pants, as he helped her rise. "She was having a bad hair day."

Sean shined the light around the small clearing. "Where's Vincent and Igor?"

Lily walked from between the bushes and into Wyatt's open arms. He kissed the top of her head. "Are you hurt?"

She shook her head.

Wyatt pulled a feather from her hair and added it to the other one in his pocket.

Lily's smile turned into a frown. "They're gone. I can't find them anywhere."

Words choked Wyatt's throat, and he couldn't even reveal his last conversation. He said simply, "Let's head to the center of the maze. We have to stop them."

The lantern went out, leaving them in total darkness.

"What now?" Sean asked.

"Find the right side of the wall," Wyatt said. "Put your hand on it."

They groped in the gloom. Wyatt started to lead them through the dense foliage of the maze, when the unmistakable sound of helicopter rotors filled the air.

"The army arrived?" Howard's voice came out of the darkness. The air whipped around them, buffeting them with leaves and other debris.

"No," Lily screamed. "Get down; it's Vincent."

"Dive!" Wyatt ordered.

The helicopter wheeled toward them, spraying the area with bullets. "Squeeze in between the bushes!" he shouted. He pulled Lily with one hand and his brother with the other, into a wall of branches, feeling them poke his skin. "Is everyone all right?" he asked them all.

"Fine," Howard responded from the other side. "I have Keisha."

Bullets hit the hard-packed dirt with dull thuds, and the explosive charges lit the night sky.

The helicopter banked low. The lights from its underbelly bathed them in a red glow. Wyatt looked up through the leafy canopy to see Vincent's face floating in the cockpit, his smile wide. Smoke still escaped from the seam around Vincent's neck. His skin had turned a permanent shade of lilac.

Their eyes met.

Vincent pointed his forefinger at Wyatt as though he were aiming a gun. Wyatt could see him mouth the words, "Bang, bang," as he cocked his thumb back twice.

"This isn't over, Vincent," Wyatt said as he emerged from the bushes.

Vincent altered his hand into a salute and then took off west, toward the Pacific Ocean.

"I can't believe he got away," Sean said.

"The smoke from his neck … the tech must have given him

soda," he heard Howard's voice say from another clump of bushes. "The orderly, when Vincent asked for a drink."

"He gave him Whisp. It interacted with the residue of The Glob that was still inside him," Keisha added.

"It wasn't enough to kill him," Wyatt said bitterly.

"Perhaps," Howard said, "being a behemoth has changed his DNA into something impervious to reacting with the soda."

"This is bad." Wyatt shook his head. "This makes him stronger, and more dangerous."

"He could have killed us," Lily said in a puzzled voice. "It felt like he was toying with us."

"Doesn't matter now, he's gone," Sean added.

Wyatt held out his hand to help Lily. Sean followed.

"We better get back and see what we can do to help."

Chapter 34

Wyatt led the race back to the lab. They leaped over bodies and debris which littered the crumbling paths of the theme park.

They could see people, their lab coats flapping, as they ran to escape the carnage. Vincent's soldiers were abandoning their posts.

Wyatt pointed to the escaping criminals and screamed, "Don't let them get away!" Sean and Howard peeled off to tackle the cowards.

A cry to Wyatt's right made him turn. Two soldiers froze in their flight, their movements stilled forever as their skin hardened to stone. He heard Lily yell, "Don't look at Keisha, Wyatt! Keep going!"

Wyatt pushed through the fleeing horde. It was chaos inside the lab. Flaming torches of mummies stumbled around.

Eyes smarting from the smoke, he doubled over, coughing violently. Strong hands gripped his shoulders and spun him around. A sharp jab to his midsection caused Wyatt to double over again, this time in agony. A vicious chop to the back of his neck made stars fill his vision. His eyes focused on a pair of combat boots, and he thought his life was about to end.

With sudden clarity, Wyatt realized it didn't matter whether it was werewolves, vampires, or zombies, The Glob, mummies—or even Vincent Konrad—who was the strongest monster. Monsters came in all varieties, more than he ever realized.

As long as humanity was stronger, that was all that mattered.

Instinctively he balled his fists, surging upwards, screaming as he delivered a killer uppercut to his aggressor.

Adrenaline coursed through his body. He parted the fighting mass, brushing away the hands that tried to stop him.

A mummy grazed him, his skin freezing from the contact. He stared at his empty hands. He had nothing to stop the encroaching lassitude from the monster's touch.

Wyatt heard the falcon screech, felt the brush of her wings once again, as her sharp beak tore into the linen, unraveling it and exposing the zombie to the deadly air.

He searched the room for Carter. His stepfather was backed into a corner, surrounded by six mummies. Wyatt darted through the crowd, their eyes locked as if Carter was saying goodbye.

Wyatt looked frantically for a weapon. Frasier's cane lay abandoned on a console.

Wyatt screamed, "Melvin!" His friend's ears perked up. He pointed to the cane and yelled, "Fetch!"

Melvin leaped over the console, grabbing the staff in his iron jaws, and raced back to Wyatt, who gripped it and sprinted toward Carter.

Carter was turning a pale purple, a mummy's hands wrapped around his neck. His eyes rolled upward.

Wyatt tapped the wooden end of the cane on a burning mummy, watching the tip ignite. He then used his makeshift torch to set fire to the monster attacking Carter.

Jade leaped between the mummy and Carter, catching him on her narrow canine back as Carter fell toward the floor in a dazed stupor.

Wyatt smiled with gratitude as he hopped in a circle, lighting up the remaining mummies surrounding them.

Carter got unsteadily to his feet as Wyatt reached him. He grabbed Carter by the arm and told him, "I know what we have to do."

Carter stared back, his eyes unfocused.

Wyatt pointed to the alien fuel bubbling furiously in the glass wall. "We have to destroy the source of Vincent's power. We have to destroy The Glob."

Carter and Wyatt searched the room, looking for a weapon. Wyatt spied the hospital gurney that Vincent had used earlier. It lay abandoned on its side. They plowed through a cluster of Vincent's soldiers, punching and kicking to get to the hospital bed.

Wyatt righted it and then pushed, his feet sliding on blood. He knew that in order for it to impact, he had to have speed. Carter must have had the same idea, because he looked back and started rolling the gurney to the edge of the room until they were back up against the furthest wall.

Carter's eyes locked on him.

"This is it, Carter," Wyatt said.

"We're gonna have to push this thing as fast as we can."

"Let's shut this theme park down."

They took off, gathering speed as they sliced through the vast room. They both ran as fast as their feet could fly.

Wyatt didn't know what they hit—it was a blur—but he heard thumps and grunts, and in one case, the crack of bones snapping. He concentrated only on his destination, pushing harder and faster than he ever had in his life, feeling Carter next to him pouring every ounce of energy into their thrust.

With a loud cry, they gave a final shove, propelling the huge gurney into the protective glass wall. It shattered on impact, and the rolling bed slid into the glass tubing with a crash, smashing it into a million pieces. The sound silenced the fight as purple fluid leaked into a sluggish pool on the wheel below it. The once-dominant fuel became nothing more than a puddle of useless liquid.

All the mummies simultaneously dropped where they stood.

The battle for Monsterland was over.

Chapter 35

Bodies littered the grounds. Technicians in white lab coats were sprawled next to piles of decomposing zombies, their linen gone, which exposed them to the elements and their eternal rest.

"This place stinks." Sean put his shirt over his nose. Monsterland smelled like a garbage heap, the dead bodies giving off an odor so intense, the air was thicker.

Carter was sitting on the floor, propped by a doorway. His wound stained his shirt with fresh blood. His face was so white, he looked like a corpse himself.

"Vincent …" Carter started, his eyes desolate.

"Vincent escaped," Wyatt said.

"I heard. With Igor. It doesn't matter."

Wyatt merely shook his head. "This isn't finished." He kneeled down. "You all right?"

"I popped the stitches. Raven went to the reservation for help. He should be back soon." He looked at Lily. "They're actually okay there and offered us living space until we rebuild."

Keisha was ripping linen to place on Carter's bloody wound. "No hard feelings, honey, but I'd rather bleed to death than have that material touch me."

She looked down at the gauze indignantly. "This is clean." She held it up, her face impatient.

"I wouldn't make her angry if I were you, Pop," Wyatt told him.

"Pop?"

He shrugged and exchanged a glance with Sean, who shrugged as well.

"It feels … right."

"Works for me," Carter said with a smile.

"Me too," Wyatt returned.

Wyatt glanced around at the battlefield. "Where's Melvin, and … Jade?"

"They took off with the rest of their pack." Carter's head rested against a pole wearily. "I think he didn't want to deal with … you know." He jerked his thumb at Jade's father, who was drinking a can of soda with a bunch of other survivors. "His future father-in-law."

"I don't blame him," Howard said. He held out his hand to Keisha, who looked up at him expectantly. "I'm heading out."

"Where?" she asked, her voice a mere whisper.

"I've got to find my parents."

"You're going to your dad's base out west?" Wyatt asked, then looked at Carter.

Carter looked up at both of them. "There'll be plenty to do here."

"Vincent's out there," Wyatt said. "That's where I have to go. It's not finished between us."

Wyatt watched Carter sizing him up. His stepfather nodded once, and said quietly, "A man's gotta do what a man's gotta do."

Sean's face was eager. "I'm going too."

Both Carter and Wyatt said, "No!" at the same time.

Keisha walked with Howard, shaking her head. "Lily told me I could stay with her. I have to, I mean, I want to find out what happened to me."

They paused, their arms entwined, their faces close together. She hugged Howard fiercely. "You'll come back?"

"As soon as I locate my parents." Howard kissed her deeply.

Wyatt pulled Lily from the group. "You could come with us," he told her. He was holding the quills of two black feathers in his fingertips.

Lily leaned close, her forehead touching his in an intimate

way. She kissed him then. His arms wrapped around her, dragging her against him. He heard a throat clear behind him.

Raven stood, his hands behind his back, watching them.

"I'll come back to you," Wyatt said.

"When your journey ends," Lily said, her voice choked, "come home to me."

He placed the feathers back in his pocket, knowing that Lily was a part of him.

They left later that day. Raven managed to put together backpacks for their trip. The sun dipped behind the hills, making the air cool.

Wyatt and Howard hiked toward the west, thinking of Vincent and Igor, and their escape.

A chill skittered down Wyatt's back. He searched the desolate landscape, his hand tightening around the shotgun in his right hand.

"I wish Melvin was with us," Howard said, pushing his glasses up his nose.

"I miss him too," Wyatt was surprised to admit.

Every so often, they glanced at the mountains surrounding them. "Do you feel like we're being followed?" Howard asked in a hushed whisper.

Wyatt turned as he walked, marveling at the fuchsia and lilac sky. And then he heard it. The first howl, which set off another and then another, until the entire valley was singing with a wolf's song. It grew quiet.

Howard said, "We don't even know if that's him."

Wyatt smiled. His green eyes searched the rugged mountains, his ears straining for the cry of one lone wolf. He glanced at the darkening sky, knowing the night was near. He knew that Melvin was close. Cocking his head, he listened. It was faint at first, almost a whisper on the wind, then the keening wail picked up the volume.

The lone wolf howled, letting Wyatt know Melvin was alive and well, and happy.

Acknowledgments

Life to me is a hero's journey. From the first movie I saw to the earliest books that were read to me, every story has revolved around self-discovery. I have been around storytellers my whole life, each one of them a product of the storyteller that influenced them. I am so honored to be a part of the widening circle. Who knows where the hero's journey will take the reader, as well as myself?

In order to go on a journey, one needs to be prepared to meet challenges along the way. Without the vast network of people who worked beside me, and stepped in time with my vision, I couldn't have gotten to this point.

I'd like to thank Susan Grode, Nick Mullendore, and Kim Yau for lighting my path and making sure my steps didn't falter.

Kevin J. Anderson and the wonderful crew at WordFire Press. You're the best Sherpas in the literary world.

To Sharon, Alexander, and Cayla
To Eric, Jennifer, Hallie, and Zachary,
To Mom:
You are the light at the end of the tunnel.

And lastly to my father, who got the ball rolling despite getting knocked down time and time again. He was the bravest man I had ever met, and his will and determination are his greatest gifts to me. I will always miss you dad.

To my readers, thank you for continuing this journey with me. And yes, I heard you, there will be more Melvin in Monsterland 3.

About the Author

Michael Okon is the award-winning, best-selling author of 15 books, including *Witches Protection Program*, *Pokergeist*, *Stillwell*, and The Battle for Darracia series, all of which were written under his *nom de plume* Michael Phillip Cash. Michael writes full time and lives on the North Shore of Long Island with his wife and children.